Vanessa fled from the parlor...

Curious, Hugh opened the dining room door in time to see her slip out the French doors. He rounded the long table and stopped, peering out on the heavily shadowed gallery. Dimly he could make out her slender figure slumped against a column, her shoulders heaving.

Silently, he slid out the partially open door and glided to her side. His heart pounded as he stared down at her. "It's all right, love," he murmured, turning her to face him, in agony that she should be in such pain.

She turned easily, and in the pale moonlight he searched her face. His jaw slackened. She wasn't crying, she was laughing!

"I-I'm sorry," she finally managed. "In some ways, I feel I should be crying; however, the humor of all your actions in the parlor did not escape me, and belatedly I recalled your expression when you realized you had been beaten at your own noble game!" She laughed freely again, her eyes shining up at him.

"You think it funny, do you," Hugh growled deep in his throat. He looked down at her, the moonlight softening her features to true beauty. His hands were shaking as he pulled her against him. Then he lowered his head and claimed her lips...

Also by Holly Newman

Honor's Players

Published by
WARNER BOOKS

ATTENTION: SCHOOLS AND CORPORATIONS

WARNER books are available at quantity discounts with bulk purchase for educational, business, or sales promotional use For information, please write to SPECIAL SALES DEPARTMENT, WARNER BOOKS, 666 FIFTH AVENUE, NEW YORK, N Y 10103

ARE THERE WARNER BOOKS
YOU WANT BUT CANNOT FIND IN YOUR LOCAL STORES?

You can get any WARNER BOOKS title in print Simply send title and retail price, plus 50c per order and 50c per copy to cover mailing and handling costs for each book desired New York State and California residents add applicable sales tax. Enclose check or money order only, no cash please, to: WARNER BOOKS, P O BOX 690, NEW YORK, N.Y. 10019

Gentleman's Trade

HOLLY NEWMAN

WARNER BOOKS

A Warner Communications Company

WARNER BOOKS EDITION

Copyright © 1988 by Holly Newman
All rights reserved.

This Warner Books Edition is published by arrangement with Wildstar
Books, a division of the Adele Leone Agency, Inc.

Warner Books, Inc.
666 Fifth Avenue
New York, N.Y. 10103

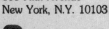A Warner Communications Company

Printed in the United States of America

First Printing: March, 1988

10 9 8 7 6 5 4 3 2 1

I heard it on
WBAP

45¢

I heard it on WBAP

Bitty Bobs

AUTHOR'S NOTE

The contredanse Hull's Victory was an actual American dance of the period. The remainder of the dances mentioned are the work of Mr. John Hertz, Dancing Master for the *Friends of the English Regency*. Mr. Hertz's choreography is based upon his extensive research of the period. The problems with re-creating dances of the period are we don't know what music was used, and little documentation exists on the dance steps.

I once asked John to tell me how faithful to the period his dances were. He likened them to a Renoir painting, bearing the beauty and the spirit of the subject rather than its actuality. I like his description, for it explains better than I ever could my attitude toward writing Regency novels.

Thank you, John Hertz.

Holly Newman

885-5506
@ TRiMbLE
Ellen Rose

CHAPTER
ONE

♥

"And what are your expectations for the year, Mr. Danielson? Shall we ladies once again be able to find exquisite French laces and Chinese silks in our local shops?" Vanessa Mannion asked with teasing lightness before guiding a silver spoon full of fresh strawberries to her lips.

"Oh, *oui!*" And what of those *merveilleux plumes de l'autruche* from Australia?" Paulette Chaumonde added excitedly, her spoon clattering into her fragile bone china dessert dish.

"Only English, please, Paulette," Amanda Mannion, Vanessa's mother, gently remonstrated their young guest. Mrs. Mannion was beginning to believe they'd never turn Paulette into the American young lady her father wished her to be, for she clung tenaciously to her Creole roots.

"*Pardon*, madame," she returned meekly, bobbing her sleek dark head in her hostess's direction before turning shining eyes back toward Mr. Danielson. Mrs. Mannion shook her head, amusement pulling at the corners of her mouth.

Vanessa laughed. "Paulette's enthusiasm runs away with

1

her, but I too confess a certain weakness for hats adorned with those magnificent feathers," she said, airily tracing an ostrich feather curving around her face from an imaginary hat on her head.

"And may I say how charmingly those plumes would frame your visage, Miss Mannion." Mr. Danielson made an elegant show of bowing while seated.

"Why, thank you, sir." An irrepressible twinkle danced in her eyes as she acknowledged his gallantry with a little tilt of her head.

Russell Wilmot, seated on the other side of the elegantly appointed dining table, grunted, and from the corner of her eye Vanessa saw him glare at Trevor Danielson from under lowered black brows. His reaction pleased her, though she continued to ignore him while smiling engagingly at Mr. Danielson. Mr. Wilmot was a determined suitor for her hand. Though she was flattered by his attention and intrigued by his person, she did chafe at his possessiveness. Vanessa feared he had the mistaken notion—from her father, no doubt—that she was a pliant, mindless female. This was an idea she wished to suppress before their courtship progressed any further.

A faint inquiring lift to her brow served as a gentle reminder to Mr. Danielson of her original question. She took a small sip of lemonade, her gaze sliding from him to her father seated at the head of the table. Her smile slipped when she caught his condemning eye and viewed the slight downturn of his lips. Plainly, he was annoyed at her presumption to ask any question that might be construed to be of a business nature. Her father possessed lamentably outmoded notions on subjects suitable for discussion before ladies—and talk of commerce was not of their number. Fashion, the arts, home management and social engagements were the only subjects he considered fitting for his genteelly reared daughters to discuss, Vanessa acknowledged to herself with wry disgust. It was no wonder Mr. Wilmot had mistaken perceptions of her.

Belatedly she realized Mr. Danielson was answering her question. Her smile brightened and she cocked her head in an attitude of intense concentration and interest.

"To return to your original question—without digressing into the mechanics of trade—" Mr. Danielson was saying easily, with a brief nod and smile in Richard Mannion's direction admitting his awareness of his host's strictures.

"I should trust not." Richard Mannion's baleful glare directed at his daughter bespoke a wealth of meaning. To her chagrin, Vanessa felt a faint blush warm her cheeks.

Her father, a prominent cotton factor and commission merchant, was a proponent of mixing business habits with eating habits, claiming volumes could be learned about a man at the table, from the cut of his manners to the cut of his meat. Nonetheless, at the business dinners he hosted in his home, he expected his daughters to display elegant manners and a gift for social repartee, not business acumen or political interest. Still, for Vanessa, his select dinner parties were an opportunity to feed her voracious appetite for information. Knowing her father's sentiments, however, she tried to couch her questions with feminine interests and thereby mitigate any accusation of trespassing on male preserves. Judging by his expression, this time her ruse had failed; soon he would be passing to her mother that little secret signal they shared that said he deemed it time the ladies withdrew from the dining room and left the men to their port, cigars, and business discussions.

She glanced again at her father, a small, rueful sigh escaping her lips. She chafed at his restrictions for she held a lively curiosity and interest in trade and politics—and for goodness' sake, this was 1816! Had not the women of the city aided their countrymen in the Battle of New Orleans by sewing warm clothes for the Kentucky militiamen who came to fight the British with scarcely more than rags on their backs? And afterward, of course, there were the long hours spent greeting the returning soldiers, bandaging wounds and bathing fevered brows. Such efforts were not done without knowledge of war or the politics involved.

Some of these same thoughts must have occurred to Trevor Danielson for he paused before continuing, an amused smile twisting his lips. "As you say, Richard," he murmured, nodding. He turned back to Vanessa, appearing to choose his words carefully. "I believe New Orleans shops will soon be overflowing with the latest feminine fripperies from all over the world."

"Without recourse to smuggled goods from that pirate, Jean Laffite, and his band?" Vanessa asked with wide-eyed innocence. She did not have to look at her father to feel him glowering.

"I must protest, Miss Mannion," Russell Wilmot interjected, his heavy, raspy voice commanding her attention. A slow smile claimed his broadly planed face, pulling at a long, thin white scar running up his neck and alongside his face that lent him a rakish appearance. Vanessa heard tell it was the reason for his unusual voice.

"Laffite proved himself a loyal citizen in the Battle of New Orleans and was commended for his efforts by Jackson himself." His harsh voice managed to convey a silky warning.

"Temper your praise, Mr. Wilmot," growled Richard Mannion, tossing his napkin on the table and slamming his chair backward several inches. "That pirate was always one to go for the main chance. The man has no conception of loyalty—unless it is to himself."

Russell Wilmot's eyebrows twitched and his color darkened. He leaned toward his host.

"Truthfully," Mr. Danielson interceded quickly, "with all trade doors open once again, I doubt in the long run his kind can compete with legitimate commerce."

"Why is that?" Russell Wilmot demanded aggressively, glaring at him.

"Volume, sir," Trevor Danielson assured him. "The sheer volume of goods entering our city will bring prices down to a level where it will not be economical for pirates to operate off our coast."

"Indeed?" Vanessa murmured, faintly encouraging him to continue, her smoky blue eyes carefully hooded to disguise their gleam of excitement.

"Now that the war is over I expect our profits to easily double this year." He raised his napkin to dab at the ends of his sable brown mustache, glancing around to the rest of the company at the table. "And not just for the Danielson and Halley Company. This will be a record year for all business in New Orleans."

"Perhaps I should consider acquiring more warehouses."

Wilmot's sarcastic, heavy humor intrigued Vanessa. He was a curious man, this suitor of hers, and even after three years in New Orleans, his antecedents remained a mystery. He operated the largest warehousing operation on the Mississippi. It was located in the city's worst area, and he employed men others deemed undesirable; yet he'd managed to acquire money and position in society—an unusual feat in so short a time, especially for an American within the Creole-dominated social hierarchy.

Richard Mannion harrumphed and scratched the side of his nose. "Acquiring more warehouses may not be an idea to dismiss out of hand, Wilmot."

Trevor Danielson paused, a faintly quizzical expression on his face as he glanced at his host. Then he leaned back in his chair and nodded. "This is the beginning of a new era for New Orleans," he said slowly. "The city has always been a major trade center, but I think its importance is just beginning to be realized."

"On what do you base your comments?" Vanessa asked, ignoring how her father's grizzled gray brows had descended to form a thick iron bar above his eyes. Mr. Danielson was in an expansive mood, and she was going to reap what she could. Out of the corner of her eye she noted her father signaling to her mother and her heart plummeted; nevertheless, she kept her attention centered on Mr. Danielson.

That gentleman failed to note his host's increasing dissatisfaction with the tenor of the conversation and responded heartily to Vanessa's question. "Why, on the number of Englishmen present in our city, Miss Mannion! There are also scores more on their way, I understand."

Adeline Mannion gasped and clutched a napkin to her chest, her clear gray eyes staring wide out of her delicate, heart-shaped face. "What? But I thought you said . . . Surely you don't mean—" she babbled in confusion.

"No, he don't," tossed out her father, impatiently.

Amanda Mannion leaned toward her youngest daughter and patted her hand reassuringly. "Finish your dessert, Adeline," she instructed calmly.

Vanessa closed her eyes briefly at her sister's naïveté. Hers was such a quite nature, she was often thrown into confusion.

Mr. Danielson, however, smiled gently at Adeline and responded in kind: "Have no fear, Miss Mannion. The war is, as I stated, truly over, and I doubt we shall see another for the English are here to trade with us. They badly need our goods, particularly our cotton for their mills."

Russell Wilmot laughed shortly. "And they'll pay a pretty price, too," he rasped, his dark voice like gravel grating against itself, sending an odd ripple of feeling through Vanessa.

"Oo-o-o," Paulette Chaumonde breathed as she also reacted instinctively to the dangerous menace in his tone. Then, mercurially, she cocked her head to one side and directed her attention to Mr. Danielson, suppressed excitement evident in her eyes. "These Englishmen, are they aristocrats? I would adore meeting a real English duke or earl!''

"I'm afraid I don't know of any dukes or earls in New Orleans, Miss Chaumonde,'' he said kindly.

Her pretty bow-shaped lips formed a little pout of dissatisfaction.

"But, Miss Chaumonde, surely you don't expect the aristocracy to dirty their hands in trade?'' Mr. Wilmot mocked lightly.

Paulette tilted her chin up at him, her brown eyes flashing. "And why not? There are many here in New Orleans who still bear the titles of their families in France and Spain, and they are among the most successful in the city. They made this city long before you *Américains* arrived!''

"Paulette!'' warned Richard Mannion.

"Pardon, Monsieur Mannion, mais il fait un affront—"

"English, *please*, Paulette!''

"He insults the English aristocrats only!'' Adeline put in quickly, her voice breathy and anxious, for she hated altercations.

"Actually,'' Trevor Danielson drawled, drawing attention back to himself, "Mr. Wilmot's comment no longer holds steadfast among the ranks of the younger peers. As a matter of fact, a friend of mine recently arrived in the city on business, and he's the son of a viscount.''

Paulette shrugged philosophically. "I suppose a viscount is better than a mister.''

Vanessa shook her head wryly at her friend. "You are incorrigible, Paulette!''

"I'm sorry to disappoint you, Miss Chaumonde, but Hugh Talverton is only a mister.''

"But heir to a title—''

"That goes to his brother and his brother's sons.''

"Phtt!'' Paulette muttered dismissively. "Accidents may happen.''

Russell Wilmot gave a shout of laughter. "I hadn't realized what a bloodthirsty wench you are."

She shrugged and addressed Mr. Danielson again: "Nevertheless, this *Mister* Talverton," she said, rolling the word mister around in her mouth as if it were a distasteful bite of food, "he was raised to the manner born, *non*?"

"Well, yes—"

"*Bon*. Is he married?"

A slight smile appeared, despite Mr. Danielson's efforts to contain his humor. "No, Miss Chaumonde," he replied gravely, "he is not."

Paulette nodded. "Ah-h-h," was all she said, but her eyes were contemplative as she reached for her lemonade.

Vanessa delicately hid a smile behind her hand, while her esteem for Mr. Danielson rose at his handling of Paulette's enthusiasm without snubbing her for obvious infatuation with aristocrats. For herself, Vanessa had no respect for what she considered a parasitic society claiming veneration for an empty title versus a man's deeds. She did not share her young friend's awe of aristocrats. Though in fairness, she admitted Paulette probably came by her attitude fairly, for it was true that remnants of French and Spanish aristocratic families still lived in New Orleans, hanging on to their tattered emblems of glory.

Vanessa had long considered the Creole population of New Orleans to be frivolous, and had often found herself condemning those she did not understand. With her older sister Louisa's marriage to Charles Chaumonde, however, and now with Charles's sister, Paulette's, stay with them while her father was away in Washington, she had been forced to revise her thinking. She had begun to develop a more sympathetic attitude toward Creole ways. Still, their preoccupation with social position and frivolity was daunting.

Amanda Mannion moved to rise from her seat at the table. "I think, ladies—"

Paulette interrupted her. "You will, of course, bring this Mr. Talverton to the Langley ball tomorrow evening."

"Miss Chaumonde, he is in town to do business. I hardly think—"

"Mr. Danielson, if a gentleman wishes to do business in New Orleans, he must socialize in New Orleans," Paulette chided gently with a calm assurance and regal manner far beyond her eighteen years that drew reluctant smiles from the rest of the company.

Richard Mannion cleared his throat. "As much as it goes against the grain, I admit the child's right, Trevor. Damn nuisance, but true. But let's allow these ladies to withdraw. We've pounded their poor pretty heads with enough business for one evening."

Vanessa raised her eyebrows in supercilious disbelief when her father glanced over in her direction, but took his cue with good grace, rising smoothly to her feet.

"Over a glass you can tell us about this Talverton fellow's business," he went on, turing his head briefly to smile benignly at her.

She smiled sweetly in return and followed her mother, sister, and Paulette Chaumonde to the parlor.

"You were clever this evening, Vanessa." Amanda Mannion straightened her russet silk skirts and settled herself next to Adeline at their quilting frame. "But I'm afraid your father is now so sensitive to your machinations that nothing gets by him."

"Why does he wish to keep us wrapped in lamb's wool? It is not as if I wish to enter his business. I just want to know." Vanessa paced in front of the quilting frame, her hands gesturing emphatically before her. "He never used to be this way when we were younger, but in the last three or four years he's positively become a bear at the idea of our possessing any thoughts of our own."

Her mother sighed. "I know, dear. I believe his attitude

comes from growing up on a plantation." She looked over at Paulette seated on a cream-colored jacquard sofa, painstakingly embroidering an initial on a small, lace-edged handkerchief. "Do you have enough light, Paulette?"

"*Oui*, madame."

Amanda closed her eyes for a moment to deal with her exasperation. "English, speak in English."

A mutinous expression passed briefly over Paulette's face. "Yes, ma'am."

Vanessa halted her pacing, her head tilted as she contemplated her mother's last comment to her. "Mama, that doesn't make any sense. He hated the plantation and couldn't wait to leave."

"Your stitches are a little large, Adeline. Look at mine." She watched Adeline for a moment, nodded approval at her new efforts, then turned back to Vanessa. "I know that, but it was how *he* was raised that he disliked, not how his sisters were raised."

"Can't you talk to him, Mama, convince him his attitude just doesn't make sense?"

Amanda smiled ruefully. "I can try, but I don't foresee success. Something drastic would have to occur before your father would allow his thinking to be modified."

"Me, I think you are complaining unnecessarily," proposed Paulette. "Here I have much more freedom than other Creole girls. Most all are convent bred, and oh-so-strictly chaperoned."

Vanessa crossed the room and sat down next to her. "Strictly chaperoned until they are at a ball, play, or some other social event," she said ironically.

Paulette's shrug was typically French. "One must still find a husband."

The Mannion women laughed.

"Is that why you are so interested in Mr. Talverton? Is he a possible husband?" Vanessa absently picked up a tangled strand of embroidery silk, working it free of its knots.

"*Certainement*. One may not discount his eligibility. He has birth, we know from Mr. Danielson—"

"But no title," reminded Vanessa.

"Ah, this is true; however, he has been raised to the manner."

"And that is enough?"

"*Non*. Of a certainty, he must also possess wealth."

"Consider, if he was raised so, and possesses wealth, he is also probably possessed of a high degree of arrogance," Vanessa said dryly, laying the untangled silk next to Paulette.

"*Merci*. I mean, thank you," Paulette corrected herself, casting a smile in Mrs. Mannion's direction.

"Oh, surely he cannot be so arrogant if he is a friend of Mr. Danielson, for he is the most considerate gentleman of our acquaintance," Adeline gently protested.

Paulette handed Vanessa more tangled strands. Vanessa raised her eyebrows in wry acknowledgment of the way Paulette was putting her to use; nonetheless, her slender fingers began sorting the strands as she turned to answer her sister.

"Remember, Mr. Danielson lived in England for several years and only returned to the United States eight years ago, after he married Julia. I doubt he has seen his friend since then, and memories have a way of changing with the passage of time. Witness our father," Vanessa finished dryly.

"That is beneath you, Vanessa."

She bit her lip in consternation and tried to look contritely at her mother. "I'm sorry, Mama," she murmured.

Mrs. Mannion's lips quirked, but she kept her gaze serious as she accepted the apology with a little nod before she turned her attention to Paulette. "My dear, if you are looking for birth and wealth, I am surprised you have not cast out lures to Mr. Danielson. After all, his mother was part of the English aristocracy and after his parents' death he went to live with his mother's people. Wouldn't that make him *raised to the manner born*?'' Her needle flickered swiftly in and out of the fabric of the quilt as she spoke.

"Oh, Mrs. Mannion, me, I am not *stupide*. He has, I think, a–a– tendre for Vanessa. *Non*, if he is suitable I shall—how do you say it?—set my cap for Mr. Talverton. Vanessa!'' she said, excitedly turning in her seat and shaking her finger rapidly back and forth between the two of them. "We two are friends, *n'est ce pas*? It would be *très convenable* for us to marry friends, *oui*?''

"Paulette!'' Mrs. Mannion's tone was a cross between exasperation and good humor.

"I know, I know, Mrs. Mannion, English only. I am sorry. When I am excited, however, I forget. And it would be truly wonderful, wouldn't it, Vanessa?''

Vanessa roused herself from the stunned state she'd fallen into at Paulette's breezy assurance that Mr. Danielson was a suitor for her hand. She had known him anytime the past five years, her family had even taken his two small children into their household when his wife, Julia, was ill with yellow fever. Then, for a long while after Julia died, their invitations to dinner were the only social invitations he would accept. She had come to think of him as a friend of the family, someone she could talk easily with, without artifice. Had their relationship been changing, becoming something deeper? She did not think it had for her, but what of him? How could she talk to him now with the easy friendship they'd shared in the past? No. Paulette had to be wrong—or did she? Suddenly, Vanessa felt confronted with a variety of confusing feelings, and she had no idea if she wanted Trevor Danielson as a suitor or just a friend.

"I don't know, Paulette,'' she said slowly, gathering her scattered thoughts. "I have never thought of Mr. Danielson as a possible husband before.''

A tinkling little laugh escaped from Adeline. "Oh, Vanessa, why do you think Papa invites him here so often?''

"Business, I assumed.''

"And you, with your professed interest in business, have not wondered just how much business a cotton factor and trading merchant might have together? Particularly a trading merchant who deals primarily in finished goods and luxuries, such as the ones you asked about at dinner?" Adeline teased, shaking her head woefully at her older sister.

Amanda Mannion studied her daughter, Adeline, a moment, then smiled, her lips faintly twitching. When she turned to look at Vanessa, her expression was carefully neutral.

Vanessa's mouth dropped open slightly, while her eyes glazed over in thought. Then she blinked and snapped her jaw shut. A blush rose to stain her cheeks, though her lips curved upward to a wide grin. "You're right, I have been ludicrously blind. I knew Mr. Wilmot considered himself a suitor, but I had no idea Mr. Danielson did as well."

"Be careful, my dear, that you do not play one off the other," her mother warned.

"And do not think to add Mr. Talverton to your list," warned Paulette, "for he is mine!"

"But you don't even know what he looks like, or if he possesses wealth," protested Adeline good-naturedly.

Paulette shrugged. "The looks, *n'important pas*. If he fails to possess wealth, however, then I say Vanessa, you may have him, too."

At that, the three Mannion ladies fell to inelegant whoops of laughter, followed reluctantly by Paulette.

Finally, Mrs. Mannion wiped her streaming eyes with a handkerchief, swallowing another chuckle. "Hush, girls, hush. I think I hear the gentlemen approaching," she managed in a choked voice. She tucked her handkerchief away and sat straighter before her quilting frame.

Quickly Vanessa, Adeline, and Paulette composed their features and resumed their tasks, not daring to look at one another lest they resume their laughter as well.

"Ring for tea, please, Vanessa," Mrs. Mannion serenely

requested as the double doors to the parlor opened and the gentlemen entered.

Through the mirror above her vanity table, Vanessa absently watched Leila's long dark fingers wind some of her hair in curling paper and secure it in place. The tedium of the procedure vexed Vanessa, though she was glad it was only done to the strands in front of her ears. The rest of her glossy brown hair was long and plaited in a thick braid for the night.

Leila was so slow. Vanessa inwardly moaned, but she suffered her efforts with forbearance, for truly the woman was a wizard with hair. Her mind wandered as Leila picked up another lock of hair, combing it out. Vanessa thought of Trevor Danielson. She liked the man. He was congenial company, and his two children were darlings. Unfortunately, search her mind and heart as she would, she could find no hint of deeper stirring within her. She did not love him, or at least, not as she intellectually understood love. It seemed to be a state characterized by strong feelings, feelings that were alien to her in all ways save for her temper.

Still, Mr. Danielson did possess other attributes she felt important in a marriage. He was a friendly, likable person, and her father approved of him. Unfortunately, she had yet to find anything beyond those attributes that would augur well for wedlock. Particularly, she was looking for a certain zing, or exhilaration, that her elder sister Louisa mysteriously mentioned but refused to describe.

When the gentlemen rejoined them in the parlor, she made a push to cultivate Mr. Danielson's company, searching for those feelings. He remained as charming as always. Ultimately, all she felt was the extent of Mr. Wilmot's jealousy, for he glowered darkly—almost menacingly—and seemed to be forever interrupting their discussion. The emotions Mr. Wilmot managed to arouse this evening were far stronger than any engendered by Mr. Danielson; lamentably, the only warmth they received was the warmth of her ire.

Vanessa considered Mr. Wilmot a handsome man in a large and swarthy manner, his dark eyes and brows lending him an almost saturnine appearance. His everyday clothes were sober, even to the point of plainness, his single affectation a large diamond stickpin in the folds of his snowy white cravat. His austerity of dress, swarthy complexion, and raspy voice, along with the mysterious white scar, gave him an aura of power, danger, and excitement that sent many a New Orleans maiden's heart fluttering.

Were those fluttery feelings akin to love? Did some men inspire love easier than others? Vanessa acknowledged she was no more immune to Mr. Wilmot's dark charm than other women, and she accounted herself fortunate to have drawn his attentions. During the evening, though, she saw his social elegance slip, revealing a rough-hewn core. It made her wonder about his background. Now she was not as confident as she had been earlier that she was flattered by his attentions. In all fairness, however, he'd never previously witnessed her devoting such considerable attention to Mr. Danielson, so perhaps she shouldn't judge his actions too hastily or harshly. The same forbearance in judgment should also be extended toward Mr. Danielson. She would give both gentlemen another chance; after all, it was nearly past time she was married and she had no other suitors waiting in the wings. Since at twenty she chafed terribly at her father's restrictions, remaining in her parents' home all her life did not bear imagining.

Leila carefully positioned her nightcap on her head, rousing Vanessa to the exigencies of her nightly toilet. She thanked the older woman for her help and tied the ribbon under her chin. She leaned toward the mirror, searching for the telltale evidence of her encroaching years. She knew herself to have a pleasant enough countenance, though lacking in true beauty such as her younger sister Adeline possessed—not that Adeline saw any benefit from her appearance, as shy as she was. Any gentleman attracted to Adeline for her looks soon wandered away for her silence.

"What are you looking for there, Miss Vanessa?" Leila asked, her wide grin revealing large white teeth.

Vanessa pulled back, laughing ruefully at herself. "My youth, Leila."

The woman snorted, shaking her bandanna-covered head at Vanessa's folly.

CHAPTER
TWO

♥

Hugh Talverton cradled a glass of port between long, tanned fingers and leaned back in his chair, joining Trevor Danielson in the contemplation of his cravat in the mirror above the mahogany bureau. His amused smile under sleepy, tawny-colored eyes gave mute eloquence to his thoughts on Danielson's efforts at sartorial elegance.

He yawned. "It appears you've become a curst dandy, my friend. Is all this—" he waved his hand in Danielson's direction "—necessary? One would infer by your fastidious primping that you're about to attend a court function or embark on a nuptial engagement." His tone held both the hint of a question and the aura of amused derision.

Trevor's shoulders shook with silent laughter at the reflection of Talverton seated leisurely behind him, faintly swinging one impeccably attired leg in controlled patience. Still grinning, he gave a fold in his cravat one more sharp crease before turning to face his guest.

"And you've become a hard-bitten military man shunning the social graces. If I appear to be fastidiously *primping*, as you call it, it is because society demands it."

17

"Here? What semblance of society could there be in this swamp? No offense, Trevor, but I believe you've been poached in this sultry climate," he drawled.

Hugh's attitude amused Trevor and he laughed good-naturedly. "I assure you, we take our social life seriously." He leaned back against the bureau and crossed his arms on his chest. "Parties, balls, the theater—they're all prominent parts of life here."

"I believe you." Hugh Talverton's voice filled with dry skepticism. "Nonetheless, as important as this town—"

"City," corrected Trevor.

Hugh inclined his head, his lips twitching with humor. "All right. As important as this *city* is to trade, I'm amazed people take time for socializing. There are fortunes to be made here!"

"How well I know. But it was bored into me just last evening that it is important to participate socially if one desires lucrative business contacts *and* contracts."

"And the ball this evening that you're so determined I attend will supply such contacts?" Hugh asked dubiously.

Trevor uncrossed his arms and pushed himself away from the bureau, laughing at his friend's faintly sneering doubt. "Miss Chaumonde was right, you were *raised to the manner born*."

"Raised to what?"

"To the manner born," Trevor returned patiently, though a smile threatened to twist his lips upward.

"What is that supposed to mean?" Hugh demanded, his sandy brows drawn in toward his hawklike nose.

"It means that though you are not titled, you were bred like a titled aristocrat." Trevor grasped his port glass from the top of the bureau and took a sip while he watched Hugh grimace, then laugh.

"You make me sound like a racehorse bred for Newmarket." He raised his glass to his lips. "Who is this Miss Chaumonde?"

"Paulette Chaumonde, and she is determined that you shall meet her tonight, for she is enamored of aristocrats."

Hugh Talverton groaned.

"Miss Chaumonde's father is a lawyer on a mission with the state legislature in Washington. While he is away she is staying with the Mannions, a thoroughly American family. And—" he said, leaning forward—"Richard Mannion is a cotton factor. One of the most important."

His guest stilled the gentle swing of his leg and raised an eyebrow.

Trevor straightened and looked smug, for he knew Mannion was the type of business contact his friend was anxious to make. "Yes," he drawled, "he, too, will be at the ball. Listen, Hugh, if you wish to deal successfully in this country, you will have to learn a new set of rules. Those people ridiculed as the bourgeoisie in London are the leaders of society here, while aristocrats and aristocratic arrogance suffer ridicule."

An arrested expression settled on Talverton's surprisingly rugged aquiline features. He drained his glass, placing it next to the port decanter resting on a small table at his elbow.

"Do you consider me arrogant?" he asked neutrally.

"I? No, no more than most men of your standing. You English have the habit of looking down on the rest of the world. I'd venture to say that is what lost you the original colonies," he answered humorously.

Hugh Talverton frowned. "That is a nonsensical statement coming from you. You were practically raised in England."

Trevor considered Hugh carefully a moment. "And I was never allowed to forget I wasn't English. Even though you're my friend, you can be damned daunting at times."

An expression of irritation hardened his friend's features into a cold mask.

"If you desire lucrative cotton contracts for that mill

you've invested in, then I strongly suggest you don't dismiss my words out of hand," Trevor hastened to continue. "Remember, to the people here who lived through the Battle of New Orleans, *you* lost the war; a little humility would not be unwarranted."

His friend's brow cleared and he spread his arms penitently. "You see before you a properly chastised citizen of England." He hung his head with mock shame. "I shall endeavor a humbler aspect."

Trevor laughed and shook his head wryly. One of the characteristics Hugh possessed that had drawn Trevor to him when he was a shy young man in a strange land had been Hugh's ability to laugh at himself. "Enough of this. Come. It's getting late, and we should be off," he said, setting his glass beside Hugh's.

Talverton rose to his feet with leonine grace and unconsciously twitched the set of his jacket across his broad shoulders to a more accommodating fit.

"Why is it," he asked languidly, as he followed Trevor out of his room, "that I get the feeling I'm about to be thrown to the wolves?"

Trevor laughed heartily and turned to clap Hugh good-naturedly on the back. "That's because I suppose, in a way, you are. But when have you been known to shirk from danger, eh?"

"Never," he admitted. "I have learned, however," he murmured as he accepted his hat and cane from Trevor's man, "that sometimes caution is the better part of valor."

Vanessa descended the stairs slowly, a slight frown marring the image of an elegant young woman about to embark on an evening of dancing and good company. She knew Paulette and the rest of her family were gathered in the parlor for the typically New Orleans leave-taking ceremony of admiring each other's gowns and toilette. It was not a practice she anticipated with pleasure. To get completely dressed for a ball, stand and twirl around before the rest of one's company, only to remove one's shoes and stockings to don sturdy boots for the short trek across muddy New Orleans streets, seemed ridiculous.

She crossed the tiled hall, pausing a moment by the parlor door to compose her features.

"Vanessa! Finally you come," cried Paulette, running forward to grasp her hand and pull her into the room. "We have been waiting and waiting. Stand here, please." She prodded her into position under the parlor's ornate chandelier.

Richard Mannion, seated by the fire, lowered the newspaper he was perusing to look at Vanessa. "Very pretty, my dear," he said perfunctorily and resumed his reading.

Vanessa shared an amused look with her mother, for it was her father's stock answer. He considered it his dutiful response. Sometimes Vanessa thought he'd make the same comment if she were wearing a sackcloth and ashes.

Amanda Mannion motioned her to turn in a circle. "That is an exquisite gown, and you wear it beautifully."

Vanessa spread her arms to pirouette gracefully, but when she stopped, her shoulders drooped slightly. "I know it is a lovely gown, but somehow I don't feel I show to advantage in it. I think it's the color," she said, looking down at the ivory zephyr skirt edged with a reseda-colored rouleau and surmounted by similarly colored rows of Spanish puffs. The same light gray-green color accented the bodice and sleeves.

Her mother looked doubtful. "I am not persuaded there is a problem with the gown. But perhaps it does lack something."

"What problem?" Paulette demanded.

"This color," Vanessa explained, fingering a slash of green satin material on her sleeve.

"But the color is—what do you call it?—the high kick of fashion, *non*? And the dress, it is *magnifique*!"

"But on me, it is just a dress."

"*Pourquoi?*"

Vanessa shrugged impatiently.

Paulette frowned, one of her quick storms of temper brewing in her eyes. Adeline laid a gentle hand on her arm. "As Vanessa said, it is not a color in which she thinks she shows to advantage." She turned to study the gown objectively. "Still you will be readily admired, for it is obvious that this dress is one of the newest Paris styles."

Unconvinced, Vanessa glared down at the gown. "How could I have chosen so poorly?"

"Vanessa, Vanessa, you are being a silly goose," teased her mother. "That is hardly like you. As Paulette said, that reseda color is all the fashion this year. I anticipate seeing several parlors and drawing rooms in the city redone in just such a color. You might account yourself a fashion leader."

"Please, Mama," her daughter protested, closing her eyes briefly.

Adeline chuckled. "It is not as bad as you despair. You will still turn heads." She turned to ring the bell sitting on a table by her quilting frame. It was answered almost immediately by their *gens de couleur libres* butler, a freeman colored servant. "Jonas, have Leila fetch my pearl choker, please." She turned back to her daughter, straightening and fluffing one short puffed sleeve on Vanessa's dress. "Your problem, my dear, is you have discovered how well you look in your French blue gown, so now, though you desire to wear other colors, you are forever making comparisons."

"I suppose you are correct. This is perhaps why I despise the ritual of displaying my attire before leaving for some social function. It gives me time for second thoughts."

"Bah! You think too much," offered Paulette derisively.

"Falling to vanity, love?" her mother humorously queried.

Vanessa grinned. "My sins appear to be increasing with my age."

"Then for a certainty you must marry lest they become worse!" Paulette declared.

Adeline and her mother laughed.

"Paulette!" Vanessa admonished indignantly, though she laughed, too.

"I say, what's this?" Richard Mannion laid his newspaper aside and rose from his chair. "Such a cackle's hardly proper for a ball."

"Pardon, Father, yes, of course," Vanessa managed, clamping her lips tight to stifle another laugh. She glanced at her mother, amazed at how quickly she regained her serene demeanor. Her mother caught her eye and slowly winked, nearly sending Vanessa into another paroxysm of laughter.

Richard Mannion crossed the room and opened the door just as Jonas arrived with the pearl necklace. He stood impatiently while his wife fastened the necklace around Vanessa's neck and the others stood back to admire the effect. "Well, let's be off then. We're wasting a good portion of the evening and I've promised to talk with McKnight. I'd like to meet this Talverton fellow, too."

"So should I!" cooed Paulette.

Mr. Mannion frowned, but Mrs. Mannion and her daughters bubbled with quiet laughter.

"But not for the same reasons as Father," said Adeline with a giggle.

"You were right last night, Paulette," Mrs. Mannion said ruefully as she ushered them out of the room. "Social engagements *are* bound to business. I fear I shall be lucky to have him stand up with me for even one dance this evening."

Behind her, Mr. Mannion harrumphed.

The night was dark, but in the deeply rutted muddy streets, silver pools of water glistened in the light cast from lanterns held by the Mannion servants. The family picked their way carefully along the wood plank banquette made from old keelboats, patches of mud on the wood making slippery footing. Though fashion now decreed ladies' dresses be above their ankles, the women still held their dresses a little higher to avoid marring their gowns. Their dancing slippers and stockings were carried wrapped in shawls, ready to be donned at their destination; on their feet, the sturdy boots they wore added an odd counterpoint to the elegant attire.

Vanessa followed behind her father, her eyes trained on the wood planks before her, though her mind was distracted. Last night her dreams had been fraught with confusion, and the first rays of dawn brought no welcoming resolution for those feelings. Before the dinner party, she had accepted Mr. Wilmot as her only suitor, their courtship proceeding at a steady if lackluster pace. She had accepted the situation, her experience with men being severely limited by the restrictions placed upon her by her father.

Until her sister Louisa contrived to meet Charles Chaumonde, the family had rarely socialized. They might as well have been living on the most remote bayou than in New Orleans. Thankfully, her elder sibling had been successful in prodding their father into entering the social milieu. Unfortunately, her whirlwind courtship and marriage left little time for the gregarious Louisa to educate her younger sisters on the niceties of society and the New Orleans matrimonial mart.

Vanessa smiled to herself as she carefully skirted a large clump of mud on the walkway. Mr. Danielson spoke of the year as being prosperous for trade. In truth, it augured well to being prosperous for society as a whole. The city was growing, its entertainment delights increasing, and a new excitement was in the air. Just look at the type of people New Orleans was attracting—English aristocrats! She couldn't help but wonder about this friend of Mr. Danielson. Her image of an English aristocrat was of a florid-faced, paunchy, arrogant gentleman whose pastimes consisted of innumerable parties, gaming, and riding to the hounds, she thought with a smile.

She had met some Englishmen after the Battle of New Orleans: young soldiers whose wounds she bound and who were for a time prisoners of war. But they were not aristocrats. The one aristocrat she met, a young officer with the veriest scratch upon his arm, had been an overfed, obnoxious boor.

Vanessa looked up briefly when they reached the first of two streets they needed to cross. Her father extended his hand to help her and the others down the slick, wooden steps, while Jonas hurried forward with his lantern to cast more light across their path. Vanessa perfunctorily thanked them both, and carefully picked her way through the muddy morass, her mind preoccupied with thoughts of Englishmen.

What would this Hugh Talverton be like? She owned she could not imagine a friend of Mr. Danielson being other than gentlemanly, but it had been a long while since they'd last spent time together. Wasn't it something like eight years, when they were both still callow young men? A lot happens between the cotton seed being planted and the cloth coming off the loom, and so it is with people when time, an ocean, and a different way of life separate them, she mused.

She studied a particularly wet and sloppy section of the street, cautiously choosing her steps.

"Richard!" Trevor Danielson's voice halted them at close range.

Startled, Vanessa looked up just before her foot hit the muddy street. As the fates would have it, her foot failed to find the mark she'd chosen and squelched sickeningly in the cold mud up past the top of her low boots.

"Ah-h-h!" Vanessa shrieked. She pulled her skirts up around her knees, teetering precariously.

A babble of voices crescendoed around Vanessa, echoed by the flutter of hands too far away to help. Jonas held his lantern higher, its light shining on her slender white legs liberally splattered with mud. Firmly clasping her skirts, she regally straightened. "I'm all right. No, Mama, don't try to help. Father, please see that the others make the sidewalk first." She nodded toward her mother, sister, and Paulette, forestalling his coming to her aid.

The sound of deep-throated laughter drew her attention to the sidewalk. Belatedly she remembered Mr. Danielson's presence and his role in her current dilemma. But he wasn't laughing. Embarrassed, with harried glances in Vanessa's direction, he was trying to halt the amusement of a tall, exquisitely attired gentleman standing next to him.

"But, Trevor," the gentleman protested with patently false meekness, "you said society here was different from England and I, in my arrogance, failed to appreciate your meaning. Such long-legged delights are certainly not what I had envisioned."

Vanessa dropped her skirt indignantly while everyone, including her humorless father, laughed.

"Oh, no, Vanessa, now you've muddied your gown, too," Adeline said.

"*Ma pauvre!* Your beautiful gown!" wailed Paulette.

Vanessa looked down to see the hem trailing in the deep muck. Her shoulders stiffened and a hiss of annoyance escaped her lips.

"Jonas, your arm, please," she said tightly, looking up to glare at the large, dark silhouette of her tormentor.

The old butler shuffled awkwardly to her side, sending small droplets of mud splashing up her skirt. Vanessa ground her teeth in frustration as she again raised her skirts a few inches and firmly clasped Jonas's arm.

"I–I be very sorry, Miss Vanessa."

The stricken tone of the old man drew her attention to him. The lines in his kindly dark face looked deeper and his eyes fairly bulged, their whites showing clearly in the lantern light.

Vanessa's expression softened and she squeezed the old man's arm reassuringly. "Do not concern yourself, Jonas, they balance out the design," she said wryly, leaning heavily on him as she struggled to extricate her foot from the mud.

Suddenly she felt strong arms around her back and legs lifting her free, and she found herself cradled in the arms of the stranger. "Wh–what?" she stammered, whipping her head around to look up at him. Her breath went out of her in a hiss, and a deep red stained her cheeks.

The lantern light caught the tawny gaze that gleamed down at her from slightly hooded, wide-set eyes. A heretofore unknown piquant feeling swept through her, sending her pulse racing. Astounded and embarrassed by the feelings he evoked, she writhed in his arms.

"Put me down! How dare you! Put me down, I say!" The words came without strength as Vanessa found herself gasping for breath.

His deep laugh rang out in the rain-washed night air. "Impossible. You are clearly a damsel in distress, and I could no more fail to come to your aid than I could fail to draw a breath."

His light tone did little to calm Vanessa's tumultuous pulse, for his voice was like silk over drawn steel. "It is you who are impossible! Father!" she cried, kicking her feet and pushing on the stranger's broad chest as he strode, unperturbed, to the wooden sidewalk and set her gently down.

Once on her feet, she whirled around, glaring at him. A thoroughly masculine, self-satisfied smile curved his aristocratic thin lips, capping her rage. How dare he make a May-game of her! Her right hand came up swiftly, inflicting a resounding slap to his smiling countenance.

A collective gasp was heard in the wake of her action, but the man's eyes never left hers. Slowly he raised a hand to nurse his cheek. Then he cocked a sandy brow in mute inquiry, and she knew a fleeting moment of regret.

"Vanessa!" roared Richard Mannion.

Guiltily she tore her gaze away from the man and turned toward her father.

"Such behavior is highly unbecoming," he said coldly. "You will apologize immediately."

Her father had placed her in an untenable position, and all eyes were upon her. She clenched her fists, her arms rigid at her sides. Tears of frustration glistened in her eyes. "I apologize," she said tightly.

The man nodded curtly and stepped up on the weathered boards to stand beside her. "It is I who should apologize," he murmured.

Vanessa found herself tilting her head back to look up at him. She was not a petite woman, yet the man seemed to dwarf her. A renewed flush of irritation rekindled her boldness.

"And well you might! Though I recognize the value of your assistance, your method was scandalous. And it would have been so even if we were acquainted, which—I may thankfully say—we are not."

"Enough, I say!" boomed Mr. Mannion.

The man turned toward Mr. Mannion and held up his hand halting further reproof. "No, sir, your daughter has the right of it. It was badly done." His conciliatory tone grated on Vanessa's raw nerves. "I may only say, in my defense, that since my great friend, Trevor Danielson, is of your acquaintance, I borrowed upon his favors."

Paulette pranced forward, her hands clasped childlike before her chest. "You are Monsieur *Talverton*, *non*?"

"The same. And you must be Miss Chaumonde."

Paulette cocked her head coquettishly, her dark lashes descending slowly to brush her pale cheeks, then opening wide as she stared invitingly up at him. "I am flattered you know of me."

"Excuse me, I have been frightfully remiss," broke in Mr. Danielson. "I should have introduced Hugh straight off.

I'd like you to meet Mr. Hugh Talverton of Bedfordshire, England. Hugh, this is—''

Vanessa only half heard the rest of the formal introductions he made and was barely aware of her own mechanical response, for her mind was in a turmoil. Hugh Talverton! How could she have failed to discern his identity? Easily, she thought with chagrin, remembering her image of an aristocrat. This gentleman almost entirely defied her mental description. The only aspect she appeared to have correct was his arrogance. She glanced over at Trevor Danielson, a stricken expression in her eyes. Could he forgive her rudeness to his friend?

She glanced back to where Mr. Talverton was talking easily with her mother, and her heart hardened. The man was arrogant and conceited. No true gentleman would dare to laugh at a lady's distress. He was obviously trading upon his aristocratic birth for absolution for his sins. Well, this was the United States, not England, and he'd learn soon enough his birth was not worth a tinker's pot in this country! The faint trace of a smile curled her lips as she contemplated his probable downfall.

An errant cool breeze suddenly reminded Vanessa of her bedraggled state and she knew she had other, more immediate concerns than the looked-for just deserts of one arrogant Englishman. She glanced down at her mud-streaked gown. With a sigh she realized it was ruined. She could not possibly account herself a leader of fashion in such attire, she thought wryly.

When Paulette, talking animatedly, again captured Talverton's attentions, Vanessa drew her mother aside.

''Mama, I must return home to change, but I do not wish to delay the others' enjoyment of the ball. May I take Jonas to escort me?''

''Oh, my love, I did not think— Here, let me look at you. Yes, you are right, it will never do,'' she said, squeezing Vanessa's hand understandingly. "But I do not know— Let me think a moment."

"But—"

"Shush," her mother said offhandedly while tapping her chin in thought.

"You two are as close as inkle-weavers. What are you nattering on about?" Mr. Mannion was in bluff good humor for he had discovered, while in brief conversation with Hugh Talverton, the magnitude of cotton he was authorized to purchase should the quality of this year's harvest prove satisfactory. He felt he had stolen a march on the other cotton factors in the city and was extremely satisfied with himself and his new potential client. Financially, it couldn't have come at a better time.

"Vanessa must change her gown, for this one is utterly ruined," explained Mrs. Mannion.

"Nonsense, dirt and mud are facts of life in this city."

Vanessa opened her mouth to protest, but her mother forestalled her. "Mr. Mannion, though you are correct," she said patiently, "we must consider your prestige. It would hardly stand in your favor for one of your daughters to appear at a ball as dirty as a street waif."

"I suppose not," he said reluctantly.

"Vanessa wishes to return home to change, but I don't believe that will be necessary. If this were one of the subscription balls, that might be our only recourse, but as we are going to the Langleys', I propose we send Jonas to fetch another gown and also bring Leila back to help dress her. Mary Langley is such an understanding soul, I'm confident she will provide Vanessa with a place to clean up and change."

Mr. Mannion nodded. "Sounds like a capital idea. Jonas!"

"Yes, sir?"

"Mrs. Mannion has an errand for you. Now Vanessa," he said, drawing her aside while her mother gave instructions to their butler. "I want you to be polite to Mr. Talverton and make amends for your inconsiderate behavior."

"What? But Father—"

He turned away from her, approaching the rest of the company with his arms outstretched as if to encompass them all. "Let's not stand on this damp street corner all evening. Mr. Talverton, would you be good enough to give my daughter Vanessa your arm? We don't need any more accidents."

"I would be delighted," he returned smoothly, his mouth kicking up in an amused smile as he noted Vanessa's open-mouthed shock at her father's audacity.

"And may I take your other, Mr. Talverton?" Paulette asked, tucking her hand in the fold of his arm. "Me, I am certain that a man of your—ah—" She paused, her eyes ranging over his broad frame. "—substance, could easily support two women."

Vanessa blushed hotly at Paulette's blatant perusal of Mr. Talverton's form. He—naturally—merely laughed and gave his assent. Mr. Danielson offered Adeline his arm, and in short order the company was off again.

Vanessa walked stiffly, silently seething at her father's machinations, for it was obvious he was blind to all matters save business ones. Mr. Talverton's business must be substantial in order to elicit such cheerfulness from her father. She glanced up at Mr. Danielson's friend, a pensive gleam in her eyes. He sensed her gaze and turned to look down into her face, and for a moment their gazes locked. Vanessa felt a flash of that same tingling she'd experienced earlier. He must have seen something of it in her face for a faint, quizzical look crossed his features. She abruptly looked away, training her eyes to the ground as if she were studiously watching her steps. She was relieved when Paulette, fairly hanging on to his other arm, reclaimed his attention and he turned those unfathomable leonine eyes away from her direction.

CHAPTER
THREE

♥

"This is our destination?" Hugh Talverton asked incredulously.

Vanessa stiffened at his arrogant tone and was forming a properly cutting return when Paulette answered.

"*Oui!* It is a most handsome *maison, n'est ce pas? Naturellement*, it was built by a Frenchman."

"Really," was his dry reply. He stepped back slightly to view the house.

"Speak English, Paulette!" Vanessa snapped, venting her annoyance with Talverton on her friend. He slid her an amused glance, then returned to his silent observation of the Langley home. To her chagrin, she discovered herself also studying the building. In truth it was a plain, unprepossessing edifice of peach-colored stucco, a house one might miss if unaware of its exact location. The only exterior hint of the family's wealth and prestige lay in the ornate iron grillwork of the wide front gates.

Vanessa looked back at Mr. Talverton. He possessed a strong silhouette, softened only by a wavy mane of dark blond hair. His jutting, hawklike nose stamped the description "arrogant" on his features, as did his studied languid manners and sleepy-eyed gaze. She was certain he was silently making comparisons of the Langley house to London homes. If he was passing judgments on first impressions, the gentleman was about to suffer the first of what she privately considered to be many disillusionments. The thought brought an anticipatory smile to her lips and lit her eyes.

Hugh Talverton glanced down at her as they passed the lanterns flanking the gated entrance. For a moment her face was brilliantly lit before they stepped into the dark carriageway. Her expression fascinated him. It was the first time he saw her in bright light, and he was caught by the vibrancy of her features. They were not, individually, beautiful. Her nose was not classically straight and her gray-blue eyes, the color of the ocean's horizon on a misty morning, were too wide-set; nonetheless, cast together and overlaid with emotion they were stunning. She was beyond a doubt endowed with a curious allure. In the dim and heavily shadowed passage, he found himself straining to see her and calling to mind aspects of her person that he remembered from when he held her in his arms.

He knew her hair to be brown; now he wondered what other colors would gleam in its dark depths when she stood in the light of a chandelier. Her skin was like ivory, but he recalled a delicate rose blush flaring across her creamy complexion when he picked her up in the street and stared down into her affronted features. In his arms, while she writhed and spat like an angry kitten, he felt the sweet curves of her figure through her voluminous short cloak. With wry self-abasement, he knew his grip on her had tightened as much to feel her form as to still her struggles. She had been within her rights to deliver a resounding slap. Any delicately reared woman of London would have done the same, if she didn't first succumb to a fit of vapors or faint dead away. Strange. He couldn't imagine this little American doing either, for she was an enticing combination of propriety, pride, and passion. Assuredly, Vanessa Mannion would make a bewitching wife for some fortunate gentleman. Dispassionately, he wondered why the thought disturbed him.

Playful tugs on his arm reminded him of the coquettish young miss at his other side. Miss Chaumonde pulled her hand out of the crook of his arm and gestured wildly in front of her as she skipped ahead. He looked up, following her lead, and was astonished at the courtyard they were entering. Festooned with lanterns, it reminded him of Vauxhall Gardens; however, the gardens in England never sported such exotic and perfumed flowers as filled every corner here. Camellias, oleanders, roses, and violets grew riotously amid meticulously sculpted bushes and small benches. At one side, elegantly gowned ladies, attended by Negro servants, were washing mud off their bare feet. Bemused by the view, he realized they had shunned even the low boots the women of the Mannion party wore. Though initially shocked, his mind adjusted quickly to the sight and, admiringly, admitted a certain practicality to their actions.

He felt Miss Mannion gracefully slide her arm away from him. He looked back to meet her amused countenance. The little minx knew the courtyard tableau would amaze him! Suddenly he felt as naive as a schoolboy seeing the wonders of London for the first time. It grated that she should so anticipate his reaction. He needed to recover and suppress her pretensions to success.

His eyelids drooped until he looked at her through narrow slits. "Interesting," he murmured, one corner of his mouth turning up in a condescending smile. "I am at a loss to know how I shall describe this scene in letters home. Perhaps barbaric—"

"Barbaric!" Vanessa's eyes flashed, and Hugh was suddenly reminded of an afternoon storm at sea.

"Too strong a word?" he asked innocently.

His tone did not deceive her, and she knew he was being deliberately provoking. Her mouth opened and closed as she fought against the urge to give him a blistering setdown, sure her words would only fuel his humor. He was the most infuriating gentleman she had ever met. She could not believe he and Mr. Danielson could be close friends, for Mr. Danielson was the soul of gentlemanly conduct. From now on, she would be certain to remain out of Mr. Hugh Talverton's orbit. He would not receive any encouragement from her to continue their acquaintance!

The quizzical expression arching his brow as he politely waited for her opinion suddenly gave way to a charming smile as he looked beyond her. Startled, Vanessa turned just as her mother appeared along with Mrs. Langley.

"Mary, I'd like you to meet Mr. Hugh Talverton, Mr. Danielson's friend from England," said Amanda Mannion, smiling warmly at Hugh. "Mr. Talverton, this is our hostess, Mary Langley."

"It is a pleasure," he said smoothly. "I hope you will forgive my presence at your home uninvited, but Trevor insisted."

Vanessa thought his voice sounded oily and his smile looked contrived. She rolled her eyes and pursed her lips slightly to keep from commenting.

"Oh, nonsense, nonsense, Mr. Talverton," Mary Langley enthused, patting his arm gently. "Mr. Danielson did just right. Why, if he had not brought you along and I'd discovered your presence and availability later, I can promise you Mr. Danielson would not be in my good graces. No, not at all." She shook her head emphatically, silver-gray curls dancing around her face.

"Vanessa, Amanda told me of your accident," she continued, scarcely drawing another breath. She glanced down at Vanessa's dress and clucked condolingly. "Such a beautiful gown, too. It is a shame, these streets are so miserable. Why, did you know, just last week Madame Simone caught her heel on a warped board as she was starting to cross the Rue de Chartres. I hear she landed very inelegantly in the mud. I know she wrenched her ankle dreadfully, poor dear, and suffered the embarrassment of being carried home by two young men just leaving Maspero's Exchange.''

Vanessa flushed to the roots of her hair at Mrs. Langley's mention of being carried, but their hostess didn't notice and she rattled on.

"She says she is still suffering mortification from the incident and refuses to go out. Says her nerves are exhausted. Can you imagine? Anyway, Vanessa, why don't you use Susan's old room. You remember, I'm sure—at the top of the stairs and to the right.''

"I'll accompany you, Vanessa,'' Amanda said.

"Oh, wonderful, simply perfect. And I'll just take Mr. Talverton around and make a few introductions. This way, Mr. Talverton,'' she directed, grabbing his arm and pulling him forward. "Now, you must tell me, what brings you to New Orleans and what do you think of our city—''

Vanessa laughed at the sight of the flighty Mary Langley taking the arrogant Mr. Talverton in hand. "I wager he'll be lucky to say two words,'' she told her mother.

Amanda merely smiled. She hooked her arm in her daughter's, and they walked toward the grand stairway leading to the gallery overlooking the courtyard, and to the bedchambers beyond.

"That man is impossible. If all Englishmen are of his breed, it is no surprise this country broke from England!'' Vanessa continued as they mounted the stairs.

"Remember, we are of English stock ourselves.''

"True, but Great-Grandfather Mannion at least had the sense to emigrate.''

"Don't you think you might be too hard on Mr. Talverton?'' Amanda asked.

"Hard! Mama, don't tell me you, too, have been taken in by his thin veneer of charm. The man does nothing but look down that beak of a nose at us. He finds us uncivilized and contemptible.''

"Indeed," Amanda murmured as she led Vanessa into a pretty pink and white bedroom. "Ah, good, the hot water is here already," she said glancing at a steaming copper bath set on the floor near the vanity. "Mary's servants are extremely efficient. Here, let me help you with those fastenings." She made short work of the gown's closures and deftly pulled the garment over her daughter's head without disturbing her coiffure. She laughed suddenly. "It is hard to warrant, but that petticoat does not have a speck of mud on it."

Vanessa sat on a low chair in front of the vanity, removed her boots, then plunged her feet into the copper bath. "Oh, this is bliss," she said, leaning back for a moment and enjoying the warm water.

Amanda picked up the soiled gown, examining its condition. "Your father wants you to be nice to Mr. Talverton," she said noncommittally.

"Why?"

"He is in New Orleans to buy cotton contracts for some new, modern mill in England. It could be a substantial amount of business for your father."

"Ah! I understand," Vanessa said, leaning over to wash her feet. "I am to make amends for my breech of etiquette." A disgusted smile twisted her lips. "Naturally, Mr. Talverton is not likewise expected to make amends for his behavior."

Amanda pursed her lips to keep from smiling. "Of course not," she returned lightly.

Vanessa shook her head at this hypocrisy, then she sighed. "All right, I promise to be sweetly pleasant should we chance to meet; however, I reserve the right to avoid him at all costs."

"I'm afraid that won't be possible."

"What?"

Amanda laid the dress on the bed and picked up a towel,

holding it out to Vanessa. "Your father is proposing a theater venture for Monday evening."

"He doesn't even like the theater! And what has this to do with Mr. Talverton?"

"He is to be invited, as is Mr. Danielson. Mr. Wilmot will be included, for his warehouses may be necessary for storage and as a staging area for the cotton bales."

"Surely he would not expect us to accompany them. Look how he gets now if any whiff of a business discussion is in the air."

Amanda held up her hand. "I know. I'm only telling you what was told to me."

A soft knock on the door interrupted her. It was Leila with Vanessa's gown of French blue thrown over her arm.

"I'm sorry, ma'am, that I weren't here sooner, only after we set out, I remembered I didn't have any of the geegaws that went with this, particularly Miss Vanessa's blue fan, so we had to go back. I hope I remembered everything."

"That's all right, Leila," soothed Mrs. Mannion. "Vanessa has just now finished cleaning her feet. Your arrival was perfectly timed."

"Thank you ma'am," the dark woman said, sketching a curtsy before taking the new clothing over to the bed.

"I shall leave you two alone. You will both proceed faster without me. Vanessa, remember what I said about Mr. Talverton," Mrs. Mannion adjured as she opened the door of the bedroom and slipped out.

"Well, Miss Vanessa, let's get you in prime tweak. They've struck up the music and I tell you, even this old soul's having difficulty keeping her feet still."

Vanessa laughed, and walked forward to put herself into the woman's capable hands.

Hugh Talverton stifled a yawn of boredom as he looked out across the room. The charming smile he'd adopted upon entering the Langley home faded as his mind wandered.

Mrs. Langley had perforce dragged him throughout her house, introducing him to all they passed, yet not allowing him time for more than a perfunctory "How do you do." Names and faces blurred in memory. Finally she'd led him to the ballroom, only to seat him on a small settee by her side while she entered into a voluble conversation with a substantially endowed matron. The woman, whose name he didn't remember, made Mrs. Langley appear a quiet and retiring speaker.

It struck him, as he looked at the ballroom's polished cypress floor, that continued comparisons of New Orleans to London were meaningless. He noted, during his twisted meandering in the Langley home, that there was a sense of austere elegance in the house's decoration. No seraphs or nymphs in varying degrees of dishabille adorned the ceilings. No intricate carvings of heavy wood, no gilt accent on furniture or walls, and most curiously, no heavy damask draperies cluttered the rooms. Odd. He'd never considered English decor as cluttered; however, seeing the Langley home somehow made him think of the fashion in England as suffocating. If he had to typify the Langley home with any style, he supposed it came closest to some of the estates he'd seen during the peninsular campaigns.

Yet for all of New Orleans's differences, there were commonplaces as well, like the social consciousness of the people. He thought he would be escaping that nuisance when he left England, but Trevor was correct, the people here took their society as seriously as most in England.

He looked across the dance floor to where a contredanse was forming. Trevor led out a shy Adeline Mannion, while the outgoing Paulette Chaumonde was partnered with a spindly gentleman in a bottle-green coat over a lavender striped waistcoat. Hugh raised a quizzical eyebrow at the lace handkerchief the gentleman clutched in one slender hand. Just then, Paulette and her partner cast down the line and as she passed Hugh, Paulette noted his expression and

saucily winked at him, her eyes glinting merrily. When she
met her partner at the end of the line and they joined hands
for a four-hand-around movement, she was the picture of
demure elegance. Hugh laughed silently, his big shoulders
heaving with contained mirth. Quickly he excused himself
from Mrs. Langley's side. Fortunately she heard him over
the loud diatribe of the matron, and she waved him an
acknowledgment, her quick eyes never leaving the woman's
face.

Hugh lounged against a pillar as he waited for the dance
to end, determined to solicit Miss Chaumonde's hand for
the next set. He caught many a speculative young woman's
eye on him, but coolly disdained to notice their regard. It
was a useful trick he'd learned after many years of being
considered a prime catch on the London marriage mart.

While he waited, he let his eyes casually roam the room,
only superficially heeding what he saw until *she* entered.
Vanessa Mannion was back, standing in the doorway under
a glittering chandelier, just as he had imagined her. And she
was glorious. Oddly mesmerized, he studied her.

In the bright light, her hair gleamed the rich brown of
earth, and her skin took on a warm creamy glow. Her neck
was long and slender leading to delicately sloping shoulders
his hands itched to touch; he flexed his fingers.

Out of the corner of his eye he spotted a swarthy gentleman in severe evening dress approaching her. Without
analyzing his actions, Hugh moved swiftly to her side and
raised her hand to brush a feather-light kiss across her
fingertips.

"Miss Mannion, I have caused you undue discomfort this
evening. Kindly allow me to make amends and grant me the
honor of the next dance." Hugh kept his gaze trained on
Vanessa's face though he was aware of a dark scowl
possessing the features of the swarthy gentleman he'd
outmaneuvered.

Surprised, a panoply of emotions crossed Vanessa's face.

A part of her wanted to reject him cruelly, while another remembered her mother's request. Then there was a third part, a small but insidious part, that felt a tingling rush at the touch of his hand and a certain weakness in her legs when he looked at her. She rudely shoved that part aside; however, with a modicum of relief, she adopted the mein her parents desired. Her face cleared and a slow, genuine smile lit her face.

"It would be unkind not to allow you to make amends," she replied, a faint teasing lilt coloring her tone. Suddenly she felt a heady, womanly power suffuse her. Her breath quickened, color blooming on her cheeks. "No, more than unkind," she said slowly, her eyes glowing like jewels, "it would be *barbaric*."

Hugh threw back his head and laughed, drawing many a curious eye in their direction. "Hoisted on my own petard. Miss Mannion, I salute you." He executed a courtly bow, then straightened and extended his arm. "A new set is forming. Shall we join?" As they stepped through the opening figures of A Trip to Paris, he asked politely, "Do you waltz, Miss Mannion?"

"Waltz?" She had no notion of what the word meant, and there was no time to question him further for they separated to circle the couple below them in the line.

"Yes," he said as he passed her on the far side.

She shook her head and waited patiently while they danced the figures with the couple next to them, then cast down the line to begin the series of steps again.

"What dances are done here?" Hugh asked.

"The minuet—"

He groaned comically, but there was no time to question him for again they parted.

"What else shall I have to suffer through?" he asked moments later.

She raised her eyebrows. Then, before the figures separated

them, her answer came out in a rush. "The cotillion and allemande."

He nodded noncommittally, which mysteriously infuriated her. "Will you dance Hull's Victory?" she asked archly when they came together again.

A brief frown furrowed his brow. "You have the advantage of me there, Miss Mannion. I am not familiar with it."

She nodded sagely before their steps took them apart. A smile played upon her lips for she now held him off balance, as he had held her.

He looked at her quizzically, but "Later" was her only reply, for Miss Chaumonde and the swarthy gentleman were now their partners in the line and he watched, with black annoyance, a wide smile spread across Vanessa's face as she greeted the gentleman with pleasure.

When the dance ended, Hugh led Vanessa to the refreshment table, procuring for her a glass of cool punch, then guided her into a nearby chair. "Now tell me, for I've always accounted myself conversant with all manner of fashionable dances, what is Hull's Victory?" He sat down next to her.

Vanessa laughed, nearly spilling her drink. "It is a contredanse that originated in this country. It commemorates the defeat of your *Guerrière* warship by Isaac Hull's *Constitution* frigate in the last war." She was impressed when he merely nodded at the information and took a sip of his punch. She had expected him to turn arrogant again.

"Battles and birthdays have spawned the creation of many dances. But the waltz—now that is something special." His deep voice held a warm affection that sent shivers down her back.

"Yes," sneered a dark gravelly voice, "a dance fit only for the Quadroon Balls."

Vanessa swung sharply around at the sound of Mr. Wilmot's voice. He, too, sent shivers down her back, but not the kind associated with pleasurable emotions. Even the ebullient Paulette on his arm looked a trifle subdued.

Hugh Talverton stood in deference to Paulette, though a cool, frighteningly blank mask descended over his features. He had heard of the Quadroon Balls while on board ship, for they were deemed a New Orleans attraction not to be missed by any gentleman of means. Like the Cyprian Balls in London, they were an open opportunity for cavorting with mistresses and other high-flyers. That the unknown gentleman should ally the waltz with lightskirts showed a gross stupidity on his part, or a desire to discredit him in the eyes of Miss Mannion. Hugh was inclined to believe the latter, though he thought it quite rag-mannered to mention the balls before ladies.

He studied the dark-complected visage before him. "I wouldn't know. I don't frequent such affairs," he said stiffly. "Concerning the waltz, however, I have heard it said that if *improperly* executed, it could descend into vulgarity."

Vanessa froze at the tangible tension existing between the two men, like wild animals warily circling before battle.

"Oooo— Then it is a dance I should like to see," Paulette said eagerly, gliding over to Mr. Talverton and placing her hand on his arm. She was oblivious to the crackling tension. "You will demonstrate to me one day, *oui*?"

"Paulette!" Vanessa interrupted. She did not know who to believe regarding the waltz, but she decided it would be safer to avoid further discussion, especially as it was a subject to arouse enmity between the gentlemen before they had even formally met. What would her father say if he knew they met in discord through her?

"Where are our manners? We have not even introduced these gentlemen!" she said in a rush, tittering a falsetto laugh. "Mr. Wilmot," she began again, a bright strained smile on her lips, "this is Mr. Hugh Talverton. He is the gentleman Mr. Danielson spoke of last evening." She clasped her hands tightly before her and chewed anxiously on her soft inner lip.

Hugh noted her perturbation and realized she was concerned that they should get along. Suddenly, the strange animosity ebbed, leaving only a feeling of disquiet. Even that he suppressed as he summoned one of his social smiles and stretched out a hand in greeting.

"Ah, you two have met!" Trevor Danielson congenially slapped Hugh on the back as he and a singularly glowing Adeline joined the group.

Vanessa thought she'd never seen her sister look quite so beautiful. She was shimmering with a gentle vibrancy that heightened her color. It appeared her shy sister was beginning to be comfortable in company. No doubt Mr. Danielson considerably helped to ease her discomfort by his kind attention. Vanessa was glad of that, for her sister needed attention in order to gain her own confidence.

Trevor Danielson leaned closer to his friend. "Eh, this is a dreadful crush, isn't it?"

"Is it? Come, Trevor, your memory can't have dimmed so with age," Hugh said caustically. Trevor looked at him blankly. "Surely you remember the gatherings in London."

Trevor's face relaxed and he waved a dismissing hand in Hugh's direction while Vanessa shot Talverton a tight glance. Would the man never stop with his blasted comparisons? It was obvious New Orleans always suffered, for his arrogance denied allowance and appreciation for the differences.

A wave of irritation swept through Vanessa. The man was conceited and toplofty. Worse was his chameleon coloring, his feigned social veneer. When he was smiling in his most superficially congenial manner, that was when she saw the secret laughter in his eyes. It was as if he viewed New Orleans as one would view Gaëtano's Circus!

Belatedly she realized Mr. Danielson was claiming her attention. She felt a swift stab of chagrin. She had been expending unconscionable time considering Mr. Talverton when her attention should have been directed toward her suitors. She turned her attention to Mr. Danielson and warmly smiled.

"They're forming sets for the Black Nag. Shall we join them?"

She took his outstretched hand and rose from her chair. "With pleasure. It is a favorite of mine for its exuberance." She shot a look at Mr. Talverton as they passed. "But most likely it is frowned upon by the highest English sticklers for that reason."

Mr. Wilmot watched them pass, scowling at Trevor's usurpation of Vanessa's attention. Abruptly he claimed a dance from Adeline and hurried to join the set with them.

Paulette looked up at Hugh, a puzzled expression on her face. "Do you truly disapprove?"

He laughed. "Hardly. It is an enjoyable dance, but I wouldn't want to spoil Miss Mannion's exit line by joining the set. I fear your friend does not approve of me."

"Oh, it is not you personally. I think it is all aristocrats that she dislikes. She is so-o *Américaine*, you know."

"No, I don't know. Please, won't you sit down. Here, what's this?" He picked up a fan from the chair.

Paulette took it from him and slowly unfurled it. "It is Vanessa's! She will be distraught to find it missing." She looked over to where Vanessa was dancing with Mr. Danielson. "I shall hold it for her," she said, sitting down in the chair and waving the fan lightly before her.

"You look hot, Miss Chaumonde. May I get you a drink?"

She smiled engagingly at him over the top of the fan and tipped her head in assent.

When he returned, she took the proffered glass from him, murmuring her thanks, then patted the seat next to her in invitation. Mr. Talverton bowed and sat down.

He was amused at her adept flirting with Miss Mannion's fan. It seemed that many social habits crossed the ocean with alacrity. He watched her and responded gallantly in kind until something about the colors of the fan she was so languidly waving captured his attention.

"Miss Chaumonde, may I see that fan a moment?"

"What? Yes, *naturellement*." She held it out to him, a puzzled expression on her pert features.

"This is New Orleans, isn't it?"

Her brow cleared. "*Oui*, from the wharf in late afternoon. See, the buildings, they catch the afternoon sun, while behind, *le ciel*, it is blue and red as evening comes."

"You say she is fond of this fan?"

"Oh, *oui*, monsieur," she said gaily. "Just as she is fond of her city. She is very loyal, you know, and very proud."

Casually Hugh looked in Vanessa's direction. She caught his eye and their gazes locked. He closed the fan with a snap and held it to his forehead in mock salute. She blushed and averted her eyes, nearly missing a dance step.

Hugh looked back at Paulette and returned the fan to her. "Are you familiar with the dance Hull's Victory?"

Her face brightened. "Certainly!"

"Regrettably, I am not. Will you tell me the steps?"

Enthusiastic to have so captured his attention, Paulette leaned toward him, her fingers tracing figures in the air as she talked. She was still talking animatedly when the Black Nag ended and the sets dispersed. Vanessa glanced over at them, a faint frown of annoyance crossing her brow at the sight of them comfortably sitting at the side of the room seemingly engrossed. As quickly as it came, her annoyance vanished, for she remembered her determination to ignore Mr. Talverton. She turned her head to smile up at Mr. Danielson, assenting to his suggestion to a turn about the courtyard for fresh air. Behind them followed Adeline and Mr. Wilmot.

CHAPTER

FOUR

♥

A faint breeze stirred the leaves of the trees in the small garden behind the Cathedral at the Place d'Armes. Vanessa, seated on a low bench, tilted her head back to capture the errant wind and cool her faintly heated face. She closed her eyes and inhaled the delicious mingled scents of the garden flowers. Ignoring the muted cacophony of sounds emanating from the busy square less than a block away, she let the peace of the small garden seep through her, concentrating instead on the sound of the birds conversing in neighboring trees.

"*Mon Dieu, mais mon pieds*, they are tired," sighed Paulette, resting her feet on the small pile of parcels that were the fruits of their labors amid the many shops in New Orleans.

Vanessa slitted one eye open to glance at her friend seated next to her. "You, tired? Then assuredly we must return home at once!" she declared, a teasing smile lifting the corners of her mouth.

"*Pourquoi?*"

47

"The only time I have known you to tire is when you're ill. You must be put to bed immediately."

Paulette's mouth formed a moue of dissatisfaction with Vanessa's humor. "And you, you tell me you are not tired?"

"Certainly I am, but I don't profess to your vigor." She sighed contentedly as dappled sunlight shifted across her face when a small gust toyed with the leaves above, sighing as it passed. "I will admit, however, that sitting here is doing much to restore my dreadfully flagging spirits."

"*Bon*," declared Paulette, "for you must be in the best of spirits for tonight."

Vanessa grimaced at the reminder of the theater party her father arranged. "I fear it will be awkward at best. I have two suitors accompanying us, while Adeline has none." She straightened, her eyes opening. "Worse yet, Father wishes me to be nice to Mr. Talverton, which would annoy you and *my* two erstwhile suitors—to say nothing of annoying me to be in proximity of the gentleman."

A bubbling laugh spilled from Paulette. "Rest assured, I shall take care of Mr. Talverton, and Mr. Mannion, he will not mind."

"And what of Adeline?" Vanessa's tone was full of exasperation, for she had been troubled by this problem since her father had issued the invitations on the night of the ball.

"You make of it too much a problem," Paulette said airily.

"So you say, but I am at a loss—"

Paulette shook her head tolerantly. "Vanessa, think! You will devote your attention to Mr. Wilmot, for that gentleman is becoming—how do you say it? *Jaloux?*"

"Jealous."

"*Oui, merci*. He followed you around the ball with a ferocious scowl, even when he was dancing with another!

Believe me, I know. And it was an insult I would bear for no one but you."

"That's preposterous—"

"*Non*, Vanessa, it is not. You, you must open your eyes and see! You spend too much time thinking and worrying, and little time seeing. You did not even consider Mr. Danielson a suitor until Adeline said he was one. Then your mind took over and you have been dissecting the man like an insect, weighing his suitability, judging your feelings. Bah! One day, my friend, you will awaken. I hope you do before you find yourself married to the wrong man or too old to capture one."

Vanessa laughed. "You're impossible, Paulette, and so ardent."

"Am I? Phtt, *n'important pas*. Let us return to tonight. You will give your attention to Mr. Wilmot, let Adeline succor Mr. Danielson. He is a good-natured gentleman, he will not slight her. Mr. Wilmot would overwhelm her into a silent doorstop," she said carelessly.

"A what?"

"A doorstop," Paulette averred. "She would be just there, a prop, no more."

"You're probably correct, and with Mr. Danielson, she's known him long enough to feel comfortable conversing—at least about his children if nothing else. He did put her in quite good spirits at the ball," Vanessa admitted consideringly.

"You see, it is *très convenable*."

Vanessa sighed. "You are probably correct." She straightened, distractedly fiddling with the ends of her shawl. Her older sister never had such a complicated courtship, she mused. Louisa knew immediately upon meeting Charles Chaumonde that he was the man she would marry, and his response to her was equally straightforward. It was uncommon for a Creole man to marry an American woman, yet from the instant they met, their differences melted like ice in warm water, then blended to create something infinitely greater than their separate identities. Love, she called it. A pang of envy stabbed Vanessa. She wished she understood that emotion Louisa sighed about whenever she talked of Charles. The next time she saw Louisa, she must make her explain.

Vanessa dropped the shawl's fringe and pulled the garment closer around her. "I wonder what Charles is doing," she said suddenly.

"Mon frère?" Paulette looked at Vanessa strangely, struggling to follow the train of her thoughts.

"Yes, I was just thinking of him and Louisa, and realized we haven't seen him in a while. Why don't we see if we can persuade him to invite us to lunch?"

Paulette scoffed, "Impossible, my brother's head is filled with laws and statues—"

"Statutes."

"He will be impossible to persuade," she said, waving her hand dismissively.

"Let me try. I'll say I'd like to discuss Louisa and the baby, little Celeste. That topic might be good for three hours." Vanessa rose to her feet, gathering her parcels.

"Mon Dieu, my head, already it is aching and you wish me to socialize? What is the phrase? *Do the pretty?"*

Vanessa laughed. "Nonsense, I know what has you concerned. You are afraid he will start into one of his brotherly lectures." She extended her hand to help her friend to stand. Groaning, Paulette accepted the aid.

Vanessa laughed. "Come on, you, the one who is never tired. Let's accost your brother before my stomach begins to grumble in a highly unladylike fashion."

"It would never dare," Paulette said stoutly as they made their way out of the park and headed for the Rue de Chartres.

The wide streets, muddy just two days before, were dry, and a dusty haze, kicked up from the passing swarm of people and carts, glowed in the air. Paulette and Vanessa threaded their way quickly through the traffic, almost sagging with relief when they reached Charles Chaumonde's snug little town house with its first-floor law offices facing the street.

"Mr. Danielson was correct," Vanessa said with a laugh as she reached forward to open the French doors leading to the office. "Trade has increased. I don't recall this many people about since the victory celebration for General Jackson!"

"Our city, she is important, *non*?"

"Very," Vanessa answered with pride.

A little bell tinkled as she opened the office door, commanding the attention of a young clerk seated by a high desk at the back of the room. He laid down his quill and slid off the stool. "Good morning, Miss Mannion, Miss Chaumonde."

His eyes only briefly touched Vanessa, his attention centered on Paulette. Vanessa compressed her lips tightly for a moment to conquer a threatening smile. She cleared her throat to remind the infatuated young man of her presence. "Mr. Pierot, is Mr. Chaumonde available?"

He looked toward Vanessa and blushed guiltily. "Uh–uh—Yes! Yes, he is. Just a moment and I'll–I'll inform him you're here." He scurried past them, his eyes darting toward Paulette, and disappeared down a short corridor.

"Paulette, for shame, teasing that young man so."

Her companion raised a faintly haughty eyebrow. "I? I do not. I cannot help it if the man admires me."

"But you do not discourage him either," Vanessa ruefully pointed out. She laid her packages on the floor and flexed her cramped fingers.

Paulette shrugged. "Such admiration is a woman's due."

"And you see to it that you receive more than your fair share!"

"Are we sniping at one another, Vanessa?"

"Oh, Paulette, I apologize, but you have an ease of

manners with the men that I admire and am jealous to possess. You amaze me, for you are so young to practice such wiles."

"It is not that I am so young, it is you who are too serious. Just as you wish to know and understand trade, you wish to understand all that surrounds you. You expend your energy thinking rather than feeling. A waste." Her cheeks dimpled. *"Et ce n'est pas très amusant."*

"Still speaking French, Paulette?"

Paulette started guiltily at the sound of her brother's voice, then twirled around to hurl herself into his arms. "Charles! *Mon frère*, it has been too long!"

Charles gave Vanessa a wry look. "And if I were to see her more often, she would accuse me of being a meddlesome big brother. I fear, I cannot win." He spread his hands deprecatingly, then gently set his sister away from him. "Would that I could believe your sincerity, little one."

"Oh, you are impossible! I cannot even greet you with affection without you doubting me. Vanessa, I can see it was a mistake to come. Let us go."

As Vanessa knew Paulette's demonstration of sisterly affection was lacking the depths of sincerity she professed, she was not inclined to humor her. The truth was, Paulette was glad she was not staying at her brother's country estate while her father was in Washington and her usual chaperone, her aunt, Madame Teresa Rouchardier, was aiding Louisa with the baby. Louisa and the infant were ensconced on their small plantation ten miles out of town for fear of yellow fever. Paulette knew that soon it would be summer, and they would all retire to the country to flee the contagion which swept through the city every late summer and early fall claiming untold lives. Until that time, she wanted to taste the fruits of society: to flirt, shop, and dance until she dropped.

Charles strolled over to Vanessa's side and claimed her hands in his. "And you, how are you today? You appear, I do not know, tense—drawn like a bowstring perhaps, before the arrow is released.''

''I? No. There is a great deal on my mind, that's all.''

Paulette strolled over to the French doors and watched the traffic in the street. ''Thoughts of all her suitors are occupying her mind,'' she said over her shoulder.

''Really?'' Charles said, grinning broadly.

Vanessa blushed. ''Paulette exaggerates, but it does seem both Mr. Danielson and Mr. Wilmot have been attentive.''

An indelicate snort came from the direction of the doors.

''Paulette!'' Charles admonished.

''You would laugh, too, if you had seen her maneuverings. I did better when I was fifteen!''

''Eighteen is not much beyond that,'' drawled Charles.

''It is compared to Vanessa,'' exclaimed Paulette matter-of-factly. ''Oh! Oh, look!'' she exclaimed from her post by the door. ''It is Mr. Talverton!'' She pointed eagerly to the tall, broad-shouldered figure coming down the street.

''Richard stopped by the other day and mentioned the gentleman. I should like to meet him.''

Paulette didn't need any further encouragement. She opened the door, setting the entrance bell tinkling again. ''Mr. Talverton!''

Hugh raised his head and turned to see Paulette Chaumonde exuberantly waving at him.

''Mr. Talverton, *à moi, s'il vous plaît!*'' She urgently motioned him toward her.

Charles laughed and joined her at the doorway. Vanessa sighed deeply and followed.

Hugh cocked an eyebrow in inquiry, though a smile curved his lips.

''Miss Chaumonde, what a pleasant surprise! What are you about today? I had not anticipated the pleasure of your company until this evening.'' He drew her hand to his lips for a feather-light salute across her fingertips, then straightened, noting Vanessa's presence.

"Miss Mannion, you also? This is a delight."

Vanessa compressed her lips tighter, striving for a neutral visage. A broader smile split his lips as he noted her endeavor. She was obviously not aware how her features were a canvas for her emotions. He liked watching her shifting moods and unguarded moments, endlessly fascinated by the beauty they created on a pleasing, but not otherwise noteworthy, visage. He bowed low before her, his lips lingering longer on her hand. She pulled it peremptorily away, whipping it behind her, eliciting a chuckle from Hugh.

"Mr. Talverton," she said primly, and Hugh immediately knew she was in her "propriety" mood. "I'd like you to meet someone. This is my brother-in-law, Charles Chaumonde. Charles, Mr. Hugh Talverton."

"Brother-in-law, you say?"

"I had the good fortune to marry Vanessa's older sister," Charles said amiably, shaking Hugh's hand. "Richard told me about you. He said you were here to buy cotton for a mill you have interest in in England."

"Yes, there have been some intriguing innovations developed in the past few years that a few of my friends and I decided to invest in. Most mills are archaic and depend upon long working hours and child labor to provide profits. We're hoping these new innovations, coupled with better working conditions, will lead to a revolution in the mill industry by increasing productivity from the machines and the workers."

"An aristocrat with a social conscience?" sneered Vanessa.

Instantly she regretted her ill-considered words, but it was too late to recall them. With dismay she noted shocked expressions on Charles's and Paulette's faces at her rudeness, while a dark scowl turned Mr. Talverton's face into a stony mask. She bit her lip, wishing she could be anywhere but standing before him. Her only recourse, she decided, was to brazen the situation out. She tossed her head up to look him straight in the eye, an eyebrow arching quizzically, and a determinedly neutral expression sliding over the rest of her features.

Hugh almost burst out laughing. He saw chagrin sweep over her swiftly, and recognized the moment the impudent wench decided to meet his ire boldly, though she knew herself to be impertinent. The woman was enchantingly transparent.

"What opinions you Americans have of us," he drawled. "They are almost as ludicrous as our opinion that all Americans are ill-mannered, uneducated, bumptious louts."

Vanessa blushed, and she swallowed the hot retort that rose in her throat.

Paulette laughed. "That is an opinion shared by numerous Creoles, Mr. Talverton. Before there were many *Américains* here, all were called *Kaintocks* and when children were naughty, our mothers and nurses would say: *Tois, tu n'es qu'un mauvais Kaintocks!*"

"*Kaintocks?* I'm afraid I'm unfamiliar with the word," admitted Hugh.

"Kentuckians," reluctantly explained Vanessa. "Many of the keelboats coming to New Orleans start in Kentucky, and those keelboat men lead a rough life, so perforce they're rough men."

"Now we are much more democratic in our prejudice," Charles said dryly. "There is a new song sung by children in the street. It goes:

> *'Méricain coquin,*
> *'Billé en nanquin,*
> *Voleur di pain*
> *Chez Miche D'Aquin!*

Of course, what these young songsters fail to remember is that they, too, are Americans!"

Hugh Talverton laughed. "I like that, I shall have to remember it. Let's see if I've got it right:

American rogue,
Dressed in nankeen,
Stealer of bread,
Mr. D'Aquin!''

Paulette and Charles laughed at his ready translation, and even a rueful smile and small laugh escaped from Vanessa.

"All right, I call craven!" she admitted. "My comment was uncalled for, and I apologize."

Hugh nodded once, acknowledging her words, while a warm smile transformed his features. With his blond and tawny coloring, Vanessa suddenly realized he reminded her of the sun and unaccountably, she basked in the sunlight warmth of his smile.

"I suggest we forget the matter," he said easily.

"Please," she said with relief. She felt the tension drain out of Charles, who was standing next to her.

"Vanessa and I, we came to steal Charles away for lunch. Would you care to join us?" Paulette asked.

"Lunch!" protested Charles.

"*Oui, mon frère*. Vanessa is determined to discover all the news regarding Louisa and *la petite bébé*, Celeste."

Charles looked at Hugh helplessly. "Our women, they are determined to rule our lives."

Hugh chuckled. "I believe that is a universal trait. I shall bear you company to lend what fortitude I may."

Paulette pouted prettily. "You gentlemen are unkind."

"And you are a conniving little manipulator," retorted her graceless brother.

Paulette shrugged and they all laughed.

"Excuse me a moment while I inform my clerk," Charles said, heading back into his office.

Hugh surveyed the traffic in the street as they waited for Charles. "This city astounds me."

"How so?" Vanessa asked politely, determined not to be provoked again.

"I don't know that I can explain it. It has a color and life like no other city I've ever seen. But I suppose what impresses me most is the sound."

"Sound?"

"Je ne comprende pas," Paulette said, shaking her head in confusion.

"Yes, the sound, or sounds actually. While walking through the city today, I heard no fewer than six different languages spoken, heard vendors hawking their wares in singsong fashion, bells have tolled from what seemed like every corner, drums have sounded, bugles have been blown, and I saw Gypsies singing and dancing in the streets. New Orleans has a music unlike any other city."

"Drums? You heard drums?" Paulette squealed, pulling on his arm.

Hugh raised an eyebrow at her strange enthusiasm. "Just this morning," he said, carefully studying her.

"Vanessa, did you hear?" Paulette asked breathlessly as she did a little hop.

"Heard what?" Charles asked, coming out the French doors and shutting them firmly behind him.

"Oysters! There are fresh oysters in the marketplace!"

A puzzled expression twisted Hugh's brow. "I thought we were discussing drums."

Vanessa laughed. "Drums are played when a ship docks with a fresh load of oysters."

"Ah— I take it, Miss Chaumonde, you like oysters."

"Like is too mild a word," grimaced her brother. "I need not ask what she would like for lunch, and have immediately reconciled myself to banishing the idea of a nice meal in a quiet café. I hope, Mr. Talverton, that your feet are not tired. Unless we are fortunate and find a vacant bench along the levee, we shall be standing as we eat."

Laughing, Vanessa hooked her arm in her brother-in-law's and prodded him toward the market. "We shall eat until past sated, then wander through the market and enjoy a pleasant hour."

"After which I shall have to return to the office and try to concentrate on my legal work while you two will no doubt return home to nap before some social engagement this evening. You have me at a disadvantage, Vanessa."

"Hmm," she replied mildly, "it is interesting how perceptions may vary. And here I thought you had *me* at a disadvantage. Father would have us all be frivolous creatures without a thought to call our own. I would gladly exchange places with you." She sighed ruefully. "Sometimes I have the wild desire to disguise myself as a boy and seek employment as a clerk in Father's offices."

"*Mon Dieu!* But I believe you are serious!"

"Speak English, Charles," intoned a saucy little voice behind them. Vanessa and Charles looked back to see Paulette and Hugh but a step or two behind them.

"Baggage," Charles said to his sister, who laughed delightedly.

Vanessa quickly turned forward, for she felt another hot blush climb her neck. She hadn't realized they had been walking quite so close to the other couple and hadn't considered the possibility of being overheard.

Behind her, Hugh Talverton grinned, then turned his attention once more to Paulette and her nonsensical chatter.

Only a few white clouds scudded across the blue empyrean, chased by the spring breeze. The sky looked open and empty and the yellow sun hung like a pendant in the clear ether. The loneliness of the sky was in marked contrast to the color-crowded streets. Vanessa studied the people and the things they passed with new eyes, imagining how Mr. Talverton viewed her familiar surroundings. Was there an exotic quality here, something unique?

People from all social levels swarmed the street, and Mr.

Talverton was right. The sounds were almost musical but more than that, there was a sense of living theater.

She had only faint memories of a life in a Virginia city before her family had come to New Orleans, but none of her memories held such vivid color or sound—it was more drab red brick and hushed scurrying. She was proud of New Orleans, proud because she loved it. It was like no other city on earth.

As they crossed the Place d'Armes toward the market-place, Vanessa became aware of knots of people, in all manner of dress, speaking volubly in different languages. Smiling Negresses milled through the crowds balancing baskets and cans on their heads, calling out the availability of gingerbread, milk, coffee, rice cakes, and flowers. Brilliantly bedecked quadroon women sauntered elegantly by with their parasols. Choctaw, Houma, and Natchez Indians sat squat-legged, wrapped in tattered blankets, trading for trinkets and strong spirits. Old cart wheels, improperly greased or not greased at all, groaned and squeaked as they rolled by while children darted and danced between them, harrying their drivers.

Vanessa smiled as she absorbed it all. This was her home. She glanced back toward Mr. Talverton to see if he was as entranced with the scene as she. His eyes were directed to some spot in the distance, following the direction of Paulette's pointing finger. Vanessa turned back to see what caught their attention. She laughed when she realized what held their interest and Charles looked down at her, a quizzical expression on his face.

"Paulette has spotted an oyster vendor," she explained as the other couple came abreast of them.

"Now, Vanessa, my stomach could rumble as inelegantly as yours!" exclaimed Paulette as she hurried Hugh forward.

Vanessa was mortified by Paulette's careless words. Without thought, she turned her shocked eyes in Mr. Talverton's direction to see him looking down at her with a faintly amused expression on his face. She blushed bright red, but her gaze stayed helplessly locked with his.

Suddenly her toe caught in a deep rut in the road and she lurched forward, falling. Charles and Hugh grabbed her, halting her headlong plunge.

"I know you like your city, but must you carry it with you everywhere?" Hugh Talverton teased as he stared down at the dust on the hem of her skirt.

A look of dismay crossed Vanessa's face when she noted the dirt streaks. "Only when you are about," she said grimly, grabbing her skirts to shake some of the dust off.

"Are you all right?" Charles asked solicitously.

Vanessa smiled at him, touched by his concern. Concern, that was a trait she should look for in a husband, she decided. It was probably a necessary prerequisite to any warmer emotions. It was also certainly lacking in anyone of Mr. Talverton's aristocratic breed. To him, her stumble had been an opportunity for continued condescension.

"*Vite! Vite!*" Paulette was saying, pulling at Mr. Talverton's arm.

Vanessa roused herself, summoning a polite smile to her lips. Determinedly, she clasped Charles's arm and followed in Paulette's and Mr. Talverton's wake.

Beside her, Charles studied her averted face with a curiously intent look. Then he smiled, his smile broadening into a grin, followed finally by laughter.

Astonished, Vanessa turned her head to stare at him, wondering what he could possibly be laughing at. He merely shook his head, his eyes twinkling, and led her forward to join Paulette and Mr. Talverton in purchasing oysters.

CHAPTER

FIVE

♥

"Why aren't you resting, my dear?" inquired Amanda Mannion when Vanessa entered the parlor late that afternoon.

"I don't know." She shrugged and smiled gently. "I guess I'm just not tired."

"It's fortunate I did not accompany you. From all the packages that nice clerk of Charles's delivered here this afternoon, I'd have thought you trudged the length and breadth of New Orleans. Such exertions would have me recumbent the entire afternoon."

"I find that difficult to believe," Vanessa said laughing. "I suppose we did indulge ourselves, though." She sat down on the small sofa across from her mother's quilting frame, tucking her feet up beside her. "Mr. Danielson was correct. The shops are bursting with new and quite exciting items. Mama, I tell you we saw some lace the like of which I have never seen before. It was exquisite!"

"Did you buy any?"

"It also commanded an exquisite price," Vanessa responded dryly.

Amanda chuckled warmly. "What about Paulette, did she purchase any of this exquisite lace?"

"She wanted to, but I diverted her attention."

Her mother shook her head and laughed again. "You are very like your father. You will not spend a penny unless you are assured of getting its value in return. Worse, you will not allow anyone else to spend theirs!"

Vanessa shrugged and gave her mother a wry smile. "I guess I'm a merchant at heart. Sometimes I think it was a pity that I was not born a boy," she finished softly.

"Vanessa, I'm shocked at you."

"I'm sorry, Mama." She rose and began to pace the room. "But there are so many things I'd like to know and understand. It's not like I'm terribly bookish or anything of that nature, for in truth I see no reason to read those dreadfully dry accounts of long-dead Greeks and Romans. I'm more interested in the world around me."

"So much so that you've persuaded Jonas to save your father's newspapers for you to read."

Shocked, Vanessa wheeled around to face her mother. "You know about that?"

"Of course, darling. There isn't much that goes on that I don't know." Mrs. Mannion tipped her head to one side as she contemplated her daughter, her needle still, poised above the fabric. "Though I'll admit, at the moment I have no idea what is troubling you."

Vanessa sighed and blindly stared at the ceiling for a moment. "Maybe that's because I don't know either."

She turned away from her mother, her skirts swishing behind her. Aimlessly she wandered over to the fireplace and picked up a porcelain statue from the mantel. It was a figurine attired in eighteenth-century court costume. She ran a delicate finger over the porcelain cast powdered wig and the masses of ruffles on the gown. "We ran into Mr. Talverton today. He had oysters with Paulette, Charles, and me down by the market-place," she said absently. She set the statue down again and stood studying it a moment. "I don't know why it is, but when I'm with the man I get irritated and end up saying or doing something to embarrass myself."

"Really?" Mrs. Mannion's needle resumed its course through the fabric.

"Yes, and he began talking to us about his business—which fascinated me and about which I'd love to know more. But what did I do?" she asked aggressively, whirling around to pace the room again. "I acted capriciously and insulted him by doubting his sincerity to better the lot of the mill workers."

"And to say the least, that ended the conversation swiftly," Mrs. Mannion ventured, looking up from her work and smiling slightly.

Vanessa nodded ruefully. "Just when it was getting interesting, too. I don't know what made me speak in such a rude manner."

"That does seem a pity," her mother responded noncommittally.

"It doesn't help that he teases me."

"Teases you?"

"Sometimes he says things merely to get me to react—and I do! In the next moment, however, he can be charming and gallant. He even purchased flowers for Paulette and me before we left the market."

"My goodness," murmured Mrs. Mannion, struggling to maintain her poise.

Vanessa stopped before the sofa, sighed, and sat down again. "I do want to be nice to him and like him for Paulette's and Mr. Danielson's sakes, you know. But he elicits such odd feelings in me. I feel out of balance."

"I see. That is a rather unusual circumstance for a gentleman you have seen on merely two occasions," her mother observed.

"I am aware of that. I think it is his aristocratic attitude I react to. I cannot tolerate that type of arrogance. It must be the Federalist within me," she mused.

"No doubt." Her mother smothered another smile, keeping her attention on her needlework.

Restlessly, Vanessa rose again and walked toward the tall French doors that let out onto the gallery overlooking the courtyard. She didn't want to talk about Mr. Hugh Talverton, nor think of him for that matter. Maddeningly, he kept invading her thoughts. What she needed to contemplate was how to handle her suitors; how to evaluate their feelings for her, and how to judge her own in return. Those concerns should carry far greater weight than any thoughts of Mr. Talverton. She particularly needed to understand her feelings for Mr. Wilmot. It was unfair that she did not possess her elder sister's confidence in dealing with emotions. She envied Louisa her fairytale courtship.

A deprecating smile hovered on her lips as she looked down into the courtyard. Adeline was there, gathering spring flowers as she seemed to do every day. Her favorite pastime was pressing flowers and afterward creating intricate floral designs under glass. Vanessa's smile warmed, some of the tension leaving her body as she watched her industrious sister. Once again the giant tomes in her father's study would become repositories for fragile blooms nestled between pieces of blotting paper. Father had never come to understand Adeline's hobby, but he had become resigned to the use of his library. Now if he took down a heavy book from a shelf to show some business associate and a pressed flower fell out, he would casually replace it among the pages and proceed.

Adeline's hobby had provided countless presents for relatives and friends. Sometimes virtual strangers, seeing examples of her work hung in the house, ventured to inquire where they might come by like works of art. Invariably Adeline made the picture a present to whomever inquired, leaving a bare spot on the wall that in time was replaced with a new creation.

Adeline was like the flowers she loved: fragile, floral scented, and beautiful. And perhaps also naive—fresh and unspoiled with the hint of dew still on her petals. Still, flowers often took a severe buffeting from man and nature and survived. Nonetheless, watching her sister, Vanessa knew Paulette was correct; she could not leave Adeline to Mr. Wilmot's less than tender mercies. While a man like him fascinated Vanessa for his financial success and aura of leashed power, he terrified Adeline. Vanessa wanted to understand the source of his power and magnetism. He aroused strange feelings within her, and she wondered if they might not be the precursors to love. If he would quit his possessive nature and strive to acquire an empathy and concern for others around him, he might make an ideal husband. She knew she could do worse.

Tonight she needed to spend time in his company. It would not do for him to lose patience with her and disappear out of her life. A young American woman's options for matrimony in New Orleans were slim, at best, within their social circle.

It was a pity Adeline did not have a suitor; she deserved her own happiness and, truthfully, was more ready for marriage than Vanessa herself. Vanessa decided that in the future she would have to account herself as matchmaker for Adeline. Tonight, however, she did need her to accompany Mr. Danielson. Luckily, they had for years maintained an easy friendship. In many instances, Adeline talked more with him than with anyone! Of course, it was his children— whom she adored—that drew them to such familiarity.

That was another matter. Children. Vanessa did not know how she felt about the possibility of becoming the stepmother of two rambunctious children. With Adeline they were like meek lambs, looking up at her with adoration. Adeline would definitely be a favored aunt should she marry Mr. Danielson.

Could the warm, friendly feelings she felt for Mr. Danielson evolve into love? He and Mr. Wilmot were so different, but truthfully, Vanessa didn't know which of the two she could love. To be quite blunt about it, Vanessa admitted she didn't even know what love was.

She fiddled restlessly with the fringe on the drapery swag hung on either side of the French doors. "Mama," she said over her shoulder, "how will I know when I'm in love?"

Behind her, Amanda Mannion jabbed her needle into her finger, quickly raising it to her lips to nurse the afflicted member. "I beg your pardon?"

Vanessa came back to the sofa and sat down, her face earnest. "How will I know when I'm in love? I guess what I really want to know is: *What is love*?"

Mrs. Mannion carefully slid her needle into the fabric so as not to lose it, then leaned back in her chair. "That is a difficult question to answer," she began slowly. "It means different things to different people for it is a very personal feeling." A dreamy reverie transfigured her face as she paused. She looked at Vanessa who was staring at her so intently, anxiously awaiting her answer, and a slow smile transfigured her face, setting her eyes glowing with memories and feelings. "When love comes, you will know."

Vanessa closed her eyes and heaved an audible sigh. "That is not an answer, Mama."

"I know, darling, but it's all I can tell you."

Her daughter opened her eyes and shook her head ruefully. "I once received much the same answer from Louisa. And her face wore the same vague expression as yours. As I cannot imagine myself in such an amorphous state, perhaps I am not destined to know love."

Mrs. Mannion laughed. "Give yourself time, my love. You may be closer to it than you think," she said enigmatically.

Vanessa slumped back into the chair and lightly massaged

her temples, feeling more confused and unbalanced. She needed to understand. It was one thing to know love intellectually, but it was another to understand it emotionally. She was beginning to realize the vast difference between the two types of comprehension, although that realization was no help in deciphering the puzzle. She would have to study other relationships carefully for clues, while maintaining awareness of her own reactions. At the moment, however, her mind was too muddled for further thought.

She gathered herself together and stood up, smiling wanly at her mother. "I cannot fathom it, but perhaps I am more tired than I thought. I believe I will lie down for a while."

Her mother pulled her needle loose from the fabric and again began plying it with quick, sure little stitches. "Perhaps that would be best," she agreed, while a stubborn little smile kept playing across her features, refusing to be dimmed.

Vanessa knocked on the door of the bedroom shared by Adeline and Paulette with a certain degree of trepidation. It was nearly time to leave for the theater; Mr. Wilmot was already below and Mr. Danielson and Mr. Talverton were expected momentarily. She hadn't known how to broach the subject of Mr. Danielson to Adeline, and she still needed to resolve that arrangement for the evening. She hoped her sister wouldn't mind, and go along with the plan. Though Adeline was a shy, quiet woman, she was noted for occasionally revealing a hidden iron determination and strength— like her beloved flowers, bending but not breaking in the wind. It was odd, Vanessa thought, though she and her sisters were very different (Louisa was the sociable one, she the serious one, and Adeline the kind one), they all possessed a stubborn strength. None of them would contemplate falling into a fit of vapors at shocking events, and they had all been among the leaders of the corps of women who aided the soldiers after the Battle of New Orleans.

Adeline opened the door, and so deep was Vanessa in her thoughts, she nearly jumped.

"Come in," Adeline invited, stepping aside. "Leila is still working with Paulette's hair, but we shouldn't be too long."

"I came to tell you Mr. Wilmot has arrived and Father desires we make our entrance."

"Has Mr. Talverton arrived?" Paulette asked, hardly daring to move while Leila coaxed an errant curl into place.

"Not yet."

"Well, I, for one, will not descend until he does. I shall make a grand entrance on the stairs, and he shall look up and admire me." She flung her arm out dramatically. "Ouch!" she yelped, feeling a sharp tug on a lock of hair.

Leila placidly waited for Paulette to settle down before continuing to pin her curls in place.

"And what are your plans for us?" Adeline inquired good-naturedly. "Are we to go down before you or are we to wait until after you've made your entrance?"

"In truth, that is a good question. I think you go before so that will heighten the anticipation for my appearance, *non*?"

"Oh, of course," Vanessa agreed dryly. She silently watched Leila arrange Paulette's hair for a moment more, then took her sister's arm and led her over to the bed. She sat down and urged Adeline to join her. Adeline looked at her inquiringly, but nonetheless she acceded and sat down beside her.

"I have a favor to ask of you. I know you believe Mr. Danielson to be my suitor as well as Mr. Wilmot," she said slowly, staring down at her tightly clasped hands. She failed to see the delicate pink blush begin to stain Adeline's cheeks. "Unfortunately, Father has placed me in an untenable situation by inviting both gentlemen to this theater party. I like and admire both gentlemen well enough, though honestly, I cannot say who I prefer as a suitor. I am thus left in the uncomfortable position of balancing my attentions to both.'' She looked up at Adeline to see if she understood. Adeline nodded briefly, her color strangely high.

"At the Langley Ball I virtually ignored Mr. Wilmot, and he is not a gentleman to take kindly to that. I fear he used you most abominably, dragging you along as he followed in my wake. It was highly flattering, but very poorly done on my part. I have decided I must make amends this evening. That, however, will leave Mr. Danielson bereft.''

Color flared brighter in Adeline's face and she was moved to interrupt. "Oh, no, Vanessa, I don't think—''

"Yes, it will.'' She clasped Adeline's hands in her own. "Calm down, please. I'm not asking you to do anything I wouldn't do for you. All I ask is that you pay attention to Mr. Danielson, talk to him, and allow him to be your escort. He is a very charming man.''

"Yes, yes he is,'' whispered Adeline miserably.

"I know you don't like to put yourself forward, but please, do this for me.''

Her sister smiled wanly and nodded. "I hope you know what you're doing, Vanessa.''

She patted Adeline's hand and stood up. "Everything will be fine.''

"And I hope I know what I'm doing,'' Adeline murmured softly, ruefully, but Vanessa didn't hear. She was already across the room, teasing Paulette on the length of time she was taking with her toilette.

Vanessa and Adeline paused at the head of the stairs, trading mute requests for courage. Each was preoccupied with uneasy feelings of trepidation, and both were annoyed that they agreed to Paulette's plan to precede her down the stairs.

Vanessa's glance swept the hall below. The gentlemen gathered there, under the light of the graceful crystal chandelier, presented an intriguing tableau. Mr. Wilmot, dark and swarthy, resplendent in black, exuded an aura of alertness and measured determination. Mr. Danielson, arrayed nattily in a coat of royal blue and tan pantaloons, displayed a boyish charm when he looked up and saw them on the stairs. Mr. Talverton, his broad shoulders filling a darker blue coat with a casual elegance seemingly at odds with his proportions, smiled lazily, his eyes so hooded he might have been asleep on his feet. Instinctively, Vanessa bristled at Mr. Talverton's inattention. Perhaps Adeline and she did not possess Paulette's young, vivacious beauty, but, they were ladies, more than passably attractive ladies, worthy of a gentleman's attention. A slight frown wrinkled her forehead and her lips set in a straight line as she descended the stairs with her sister. Most likely he was again making odious comparisons to the fashionable ladies of London, and in his arrogance he found them lacking. Paulette was welcome to this rude, insufferable Englishman. She wished her joy.

Her father's wishes to the contrary, her attentions this evening were going to be directed at Mr. Wilmot. Guiltily, she realized she had not yet returned that gentleman's steady regard. Her brow cleared, and she slid her gaze in his direction, smiling warmly just as they reached the point in the stairs where the chandelier's glow bathed them in a halo of bright light.

For all his sleepy-eyed appearance, Hugh Talverton had been aware of Vanessa's approach since she set her foot upon the first stair. He watched her slow, graceful descent with Adeline. As always, he found himself studying the play of emotions upon her features. He saw her coolly regarding him and watched as her expression changed from studied acknowledgment of the men gathered in the hall, to the tiny frown aimed at him that marred her expressive countenance. She had seen him and in some way found him lacking. He repressed an urge to look down at himself, or find a mirror to see what was so amiss with his appearance. He was relieved when her frown dissipated as quickly as it had come; however, an indefensible annoyance settled over him when he realized he was not the recipient of her dazzling smile. He looked over at Mr. Wilmot. The man's face bore a raffish, rakehell expression. He'd run into his type before and did not trust him. Men of his ilk attracted women likes bees to honey. He wondered at his interest in Vanessa Mannion, certain it stemmed from more than an appreciation for her womanly charms. Miss Mannion, though a feisty, intelligent morsel of womanhood, was not up to dealing with a man of Mr. Wilmot's weight, and could be heading for a nasty surprise.

He hung back a step when Trevor and Mr. Wilmot approached the women. He was a little surprised to see them both greet Vanessa first, though in truth, Trevor turned quickly enough to greet Adeline. Uncertain as to what was expected of him, he smiled a smile that failed to reach his eyes and gave them only polite, perfunctory greetings.

Inwardly, Vanessa fumed at Mr. Talverton's standoffish manner, but she raised her chin haughtily and spared him no more than a polite glance and acknowledgment of his presence. Mr. Wilmot was offering her his arm, and she really had no more time to consider the arrogant Englishman.

"Where's Paulette?" demanded Mr. Mannion, striding into the hall from the library.

Vanessa started at the sound of his voice and looked up to see him pinning her with one of his piercing stares from under his iron-bar eyebrows.

"*Ici*, Monsieur Mannion," came Paulette's clear tones from the top of the stairs. All eyes turned in her direction, and Vanessa was forced to admit she did make a grand entrance.

"It's about time, and confound it girl, speak English. Your father will be extremely displeased when he discovers you're still lapsing into French." He turned to address the gentlemen. "Paul Chaumonde's the only frog I know who knows what it means to be an American, but I certainly

can't say the same for his daughter. These Creoles have the
most ramshackle upbringing.''

Adeline blushed. "Father, please!" she implored. "Paulette
is our friend and guest.''

"Yes, and we're supposed to be teaching her American
ways.''

Paulette sniffed disdainfully in what Vanessa later remarked
to her mother was a very theatrical manner. Born into
another family she'd probably have trod the boards. Ignoring Mr. Mannion's comment, she held her head high and
gracefully descended the stairs, her attention and smile
directed toward Mr. Talverton. It was truly a magnificent
entrance. She regally glided down the stairs, exchanged
gracious words of courtesy with Mr. Danielson and Mr.
Wilmot, then turned the full force of her regard on Mr.
Talverton. Vanessa was nearly scandalized and hoped the
sudden warmth rising to her face was not visible to the
others.

"I've ordered two carriages to transport us to the theater," Mr. Mannion bluffly interrupted. "I'll leave you to
sort yourselves out and decide on the seating while I collect
Mrs. Mannion from her quilting frame. Seems every moment she has free she's in there with it. Says she wants to
get it done so she can begin something she calls a Double
Wedding Ring patterned quilt. Now I wonder who that one's
for." He smirked at his middle daughter, his iron brows
twitching.

Feeling all eyes upon her, Vanessa blushed anew.

CHAPTER

SIX

♥

When the carriage hit another rut in the road and swayed gently, Hugh Talverton repressed a smile. It was not the coach's sway that amused him, however. He was actually quite impressed by the vehicle, principally because it was of American rather than British craftsmanship. It was surprisingly well sprung, and only a modicum of effort was needed to maintain one's upright position despite the abominable condition of New Orleans roads. No, what aroused his humor was the use Miss Chaumonde made of each jolt and sway the carriage received. Every rut and curve in the road was an excuse to throw herself across his lap, then profess coquettish embarrassment and a breathy thank you for catching her.

As Miss Chaumonde offered her latest pleas for forgiveness, he looked at Trevor seated across from him. The man was openly smiling, no doubt enjoying the charade. He surmised, too, that the gloved hand shielding the lower half of Adeline Mannion's face was not to cover a cough.

Miss Chaumonde's blatant bid for his favors both amused

and exasperated him. She refreshingly lacked the poised artifice and scheming machinations of the London beauties who in the past had set their caps for him. But her schoolgirl transparency made him feel the aged roué. Needless to say, that was not a feeling that sat comfortably. He decided he much preferred Vanessa Mannion's reserve, though he perversely delighted in upsetting her equilibrium. Also, it was quite evident she did not consider him a potential husband. That knowledge did much to raise her credit in his eyes. He was not in the market for matrimonial leg-shackles, especially to any hoydenish American miss.

He was, however, strangely concerned that she should view Mr. Wilmot as a possible mate. She had certainly allowed herself to be kept close to his side, and made no demur at the carriage seating arrangements Miss Chaumonde took upon herself to dictate. If anything, she was amused, for he was quick to note the tiny tightening and curving of her lips at Paulette's suggestions. For all her seriousness, there was a streak of humor in Miss Mannion that he desired to see released. It was an adjunct of a hidden passion she possessed, bubbling just below the surface. Was Mr. Wilmot cognizant of that well-spring? Somehow, Hugh hoped he was not.

Miss Chaumonde clasped him tightly as the carriage drew up before the theater. "I shall have to speak to Monsieur Mannion about this coachman. *Mon Dieu*, but I swear I shall be black and blue come morning from this wild ride," she babbled earnestly, looking up at Hugh with soulful dark eyes. "And this last— One would think the man would know how to rein in his team in a less hectic fashion. I would have landed on the floor if it hadn't been for you, Mr. Talverton."

"Somehow I doubt that, Miss Chaumonde," he drawled. "But I thought you were to converse only in English."

"Bah—English is such a tiresome language." She paused

at Adeline's and Mr. Danielson's sudden burst of laughter, furrowing her brow in exasperation, for she detected nothing humorous in her words. She cast them a resentful little look and shrugged her dissatisfaction before turning her attention back to Mr. Talverton.

"But don't you consider my French lapses *charmante*?" she asked prettily.

"Truthfully, Miss Chaumonde, no," he said as he descended from the carriage and turned to extend his hand to her.

Momentarily subdued, she meekly accepted his aid. She sighed loudly as they stood to the side awaiting Trevor and Adeline, and for an instant, Hugh regretted his caustic words. Then he felt her hand tuck itself into his arm. He looked down to meet her twinkling eyes.

"I have it now, Monsieur Talverton. You are roasting me most unkindly." She edged shockingly closer to him as Trevor and Adeline joined them.

A chuckle welled up in his chest. Truly, Miss Chaumonde was irrepressible. Trevor shook his head in silent commiseration while Adeline frowned warningly at Paulette.

Ignoring Adeline, Paulette batted her lashes and preened. She was proud of herself for making Mr. Talverton laugh. Soon she would have him eating quite contentedly out of her hand. Giggling at her success, she skipped forward to meet the other Mannion carriage, pulling Mr. Talverton along in her wake.

"These streets, they are horrible, are they not, Vanessa?" Paulette inquired when the other party had descended.

Vanessa was nonplussed but smiling. "I'm sorry, have I missed something?"

Trevor laughed. "Only Miss Chaumonde's complaints." The group started toward the theater steps.

"Now it is you who are horrible," complained Paulette petulantly, while clinging to Hugh's arm.

Trevor professed astonishment and innocence.

"I know I shall be quite bruised tomorrow, and if I am not, it will be only because Mr. Talverton was kind enough to protect me from being completely tossed about like a child's ball."

"Yes," Adeline said, her soft gray eyes gleaming mischievously in the lantern light. "It was quite amazing how she was jostled about."

"I can well imagine," Vanessa said dryly, though she looked at her younger sister intently. There appeared a bloom in her fair cheeks and a rare gaiety in her spirit. It was unlike her quiet sibling to enter into conversation in company, much less to tease. It appeared Mr. Danielson was a fortuitous choice for an escort. Perhaps, now that she is comfortable with him, she will learn to be comfortable with other gentlemen.

Mr. Mannion did not let the party dally on the steps of the theater but quickly ushered them into the building. Hugh Talverton followed amiably along with the group, though his attention was diverted by the variety of people entering the theater. One aspect that particularly struck him was the preponderance of French being spoken.

"Trevor," he said sotto voce as the women were divested of their wraps and seated by the box railing, "where are we?"

"What?"

He waved his hand out before him to indicate their sumptuous surroundings and all the elegantly attired theater patrons. "Is this Paris?"

Trevor laughed softly, and sat down in his seat behind Adeline and Paulette. Hugh sat next to him, behind Paulette and Vanessa. He crossed his legs and leaned toward Trevor. "This mimicry is comical."

"It's not mimicry. Most of these people are of French or Spanish antecedents and are fiercely proud of their heritage. Actually, they don't care for us Americans much. The Chaumondes are among the few exceptions."

The hand Hugh had rested on his knee received a stinging little tap. He turned in surprise to see Vanessa frowning at him and waving her closed fan above his hand, prepared to deliver another tap.

"I beg your pardon?" he said with chilling politeness.

Paulette turned her head to look back at him. "*Chut!* The play, it is about to begin!"

Vanessa nodded and turned her attention toward the stage.

He leaned forward between them. "My humble pardon. And what is it we are to see?"

Paulette raised her eyebrow in disbelief. "A Molière play, of course. *L'Ecole des Femmes.*"

He groaned. "Don't tell me," he said heavily. "It's in the original French."

She looked perplexed, then shrugged. *"Mais naturellement."*

Vanessa kept her eyes directed toward the stage, though her shoulders shook with silent laughter.

Hugh nodded and leaned back in his chair. "Naturally," he muttered.

Trevor, seated on one side of him, smirked; Mr. Wilmot, seated on the other, looked at him with disdain. Hugh had the distinct impression he was in for a long night.

Later in the evening, after the requisite intermission to allow the patrons to saunter the halls, purchase refreshments, visit, exchange gossip, and—most important—be seen, the Mannion party settled back comfortably in their chairs to watch the second half of the play.

Vanessa sighed, her brow furrowing a moment with the effort of concentrating on translating the French dialogue. It was rumored the theater would soon begin producing plays in English as well as in French. She hoped the story was true. She would particularly enjoy seeing Shakespearean plays like *Romeo and Juliet* or *Twelfth Night*. She enjoyed the Molière comedy, but the undivided attention necessary to achieve enjoyment could also engender throbbing temples.

That was, perhaps, unfair. She was restless tonight, bound up by unknown feelings. She had toured the halls on Mr. Wilmot's arm during intermission and felt content, almost proud to be seen in his company, for she'd noted many a considering eye turned in their direction. By the numerous nods and little waves he bestowed upon the different people they passed, he appeared to know all of New Orleans, and not—judging by their attire—strictly the elite. He would not stop, however, to introduce her to anyone. Nor did he choose to stay near Adeline, Paulette, and their escorts to converse. He seemed to desire her to himself. She didn't know whether to be piqued or flattered by his possessive manner. Nonetheless, she admitted she did find satisfaction and a measure of delight in his company.

Vanessa stiffened when she felt a light touch on the top of her shoulder. She looked over, shocked to see it was Mr. Wilmot's hand resting there with a license she had never bestowed to him. And here she had just been thinking about how she liked him. His conceit was greater than Mr. Talverton's if he believed that by returning his attention she was granting him license.

Very slowly and precisely she raised her other arm to disengage his hand. He allowed his hand to be removed but clasped her fingers tightly in return. Stunned, she tugged, only to feel his grip tighten, though his thumb lazily caressed her knuckles. The blast of a cold, all-consuming fury shook her. Turning, she glared at him with frosted eyes—cold and glittering like icicles—and issued a silent, daring challenge.

In answer he smiled, his dark eyes gleaming with something predatory flickering in their depths. Her eyes widened, her delicate nostrils flaring. Panicked, she tugged again at her captured hand. Suddenly she felt startlingly alone and helpless although they were surrounded by many people.

Mr. Wilmot was a stranger, a man she didn't recognize, and he frightened her.

Hugh Talverton looked over in time to see Wilmot clasp her fingers and Vanessa turn toward him. Her expression was hidden from him by the deep shadows in the box, but by the rigid set of her body he knew she was not pleased with the gentleman.

The situation amused Hugh, for he'd earlier thought she was no match for Wilmot. He turned the other way to poke Trevor in the ribs to share his appreciation of the scene. He was startled to see him already watching the encounter with outrage evident in the tight clenching of his jaw and of his white-knuckled fists resting on his knees. He had never witnessed Trevor in a rage. He was always friendly, and likely to be an arbiter of disputes, not a participant. Instinctively, Hugh knew he couldn't trust his friend to act rationally. He'd heard duels were commonly fought in New Orleans over trifles, and this was no trifle. He had to diffuse the situation quickly. He saw Mr. Wilmot smile wolfishly at Vanessa while refusing to relinquish her hand. At any moment he expected Trevor to jump to his feet and mill Wilmot down, then demand satisfaction.

He uncrossed his legs and swung his other leg up to change sides, letting the momentum of the swing carry his foot into the side of Vanessa Mannion's chair with a resounding jolt.

"Oh, Miss Mannion, I'm terribly sorry. It's these confounded great long legs of mine. I didn't hurt you, did I?"

The jarring action took both Vanessa and Mr. Wilmot by surprise. The man's grip loosened, and Vanessa's fingers slid free.

She felt disoriented, like a top, spinning off and dancing away. The force of her fury melted rapidly, leaving her dazed and numb. She slowly turned to face Hugh Talverton, struggling to pull her scattered wits about her, realizing he was speaking to her.

"No—no— I'm quite all right, I–I—" she stumbled, then paused. She found herself staring up into Mr. Talverton's face and was astonished when he slowly winked at her. And there was no mistaking it for a wink, for at the moment he was not sleepy-eyed, and accompanying the wink was an audacious smile pulling up one corner of his lips.

He'd kicked her chair on purpose! The realization washed through her with an almost dizzying sense of relief, for he had saved her from an intently embarrassing situation. Immediately she recovered, a quick smile warming her features. Now it seemed every eye in the box was fixed upon her and she blushed.

"I understand, it was an accident," she said as solemnly as she could manage, though her breathing was rapid and shallow. "It is a wonder that more such incidents don't occur, as cramped as these boxes are," she tossed out lightly, her laugh barely escaping hysteria.

"No," he gravely protested, "you're just trying to make me feel better and I thank you, but Trevor here can tell you what a clumsy oaf I can be at times with this big frame, isn't that right, Trevor?"

With an effort, Trevor tore his hostile gaze from Mr. Wilmot, who appeared to be merely sitting at his leisure, his attention once again on the play.

"What? You, clumsy?" Instantly he felt Hugh's heavy hand descend upon his thigh and squeeze. "Oh, oh yes, very clumsy," he amended hastily and the pressure was relieved. He looked askance at Hugh and massaged his mistreated limb.

Vanessa smiled wanly at the byplay.

"*Chut!*" remonstrated Paulette, turning around and pouting prettily at them all for disturbing the play.

Hugh nodded his apology and leaned back in his chair, shifting around again so his long legs were angled in Mr. Wilmot's direction. It put him in immediate striking distance should the gentleman attempt to make another foray upon Miss Mannion's person.

Mr. Wilmot raised an eyebrow, but Hugh merely smiled congenially back at him. He decided he needed to have a long talk with Trevor. Tonight.

Still feeling agitated and unbalanced, Vanessa leaned forward in her chair, feigning an absorption in the play she did not possess. Her posture was at once a deterrent to further liberties, and an opportunity to cool her heated features. She could feel her cheeks still burning and she did not trust herself to look at any of the others in the box lest they see and question her high color.

What worried her was the knowledge it was not Mr. Wilmot's conduct that caused her blush—or caused the wave of light-headed giddiness that left a tingling awareness in its wake. She shivered slightly and wrapped her arms about her, though indeed, she was not chilled. It was strange, the tingling. She had experienced it the first time on the night of the ball when Hugh Talverton picked her up out of the mud. He had saved her from one embarrassing situation by creating another, as he had this evening. Part of her wanted to believe it was the embarrassment that spawned the tingling. She rubbed her hands along her upper arms as the tingling faded and her cheeks cooled.

The truth, illogical as it seemed, was she was attracted to Mr. Talverton. He roused her emotionally as no man had done before, and there was no comprehending the reasons. She began to realize emotions would neither be ruled nor understood by the mind. She knew herself to be an intelligent woman, but her intelligence left her foundering when emotions held sway. She was not confident she liked that fact. Maybe that was the reason her mother had merely smiled at her and Louisa looked so dreamy-eyed. Love, as the strongest of emotions, did not allow for intellectual definition. If that was the case, she was not altogether certain love could ever be hers.

What piqued her the most was the knowledge that it was Mr. Talverton who should cause her to think in this manner. He was certainly not a man to fall in love with, a man who was alternately arrogant and shamefully teasing. Nonetheless, it was interesting that he should have displayed a ready understanding of her predicament with Mr. Wilmot and chosen to remedy it by bringing embarrassment upon himself rather than upon her. He had never shied from embarrassing her in the past. Perhaps he did understand the depths of her discomfort in this situation. Whatever, his actions were not those of a man totally self-oriented and bereft of compassion. Perhaps she had been too quick in her judgments. She hoped she was intelligent enough to admit and profit by her errors. She determined she would look upon Mr. Talverton more kindly in the future. She owed him that debt.

A raucous burst of laughter from the gallery below drew her attention to the stage. The play was nearly over and the character Arnolphe was receiving the just recompense for his coxcombry. She tried to follow the rapid French. It was unusually difficult. Gnawing at the fringes of her mind was the knowledge she still had yet to deal with Mr. Wilmot. She shuddered. He also roused emotions within her, but they were not emotions she wanted to consider. Feeling cowardly, she shunted the problem aside. No doubt, she told herself, Mr. Wilmot was also thinking better of his behavior and would beg forgiveness later. Actually, she wanted it to be just a bad dream and best forgotten.

Though missing the comic meaning in yet another line, she joined in with the general laughter. Resolutely she turned her mind to the stage.

Hugh Talverton stared contemplatively at the cheroot he held in his hand. He rolled it between his fingers, then raised it to his nose, savoring its aroma, and smiled. He and Trevor were seated in the cozy parlor above the Danielson and Halley Company offices, drinking port and enjoying a smoke before retiring.

"Do you know," Hugh said, holding the cigar out before him, "these are still not popular in England." Shaking his head dolefully, he reached out to grab a lit taper from the table between them.

Trevor puffed on his, slowly releasing a blue cloud to wreath his head. "Mark my words, someday they will be, and snuff will be an anecdote of the past."

Hugh set the candle down and leaned back, the tip of his cigar glowing red. "Is that Trevor the smoking enthusiast, or Mr. Danielson, the importer/exporter, speaking?"

"Both," he answered, grinning.

Silent a moment, Hugh puffed on his cigar. Now, Trevor was relaxed and mellowed. No lingering signs of rage or animosity appeared. His friend's reaction to Wilmot's actions baffled Hugh. He had not thought Trevor possessed more than friendly feeling for Miss Mannion, preferring the gentleness of Miss Adeline. Could he have misconstrued the object of Trevor's affections? If he felt more than brother-to-be affection for Vanessa, Hugh realized he was again in trouble.

Years rolled back in his mind as he remembered when he and Trevor had both courted Julia Branholm. It nearly cost them their friendship. Julia, though choosing to wed Trevor, was quite demanding that they forget their differences. She'd possessed a rare grace and understanding; one could do no less than accede to her wishes. Hugh remembered how stalwart he'd stood as best man at their wedding, offering congratulations and support. Afterward, he purchased his commission and was off to war, claiming army life a proper occupation for a younger son. It was only much later, after enduring the heat of battle, the triumph of winning and the agony of defeat that he understood his feelings for Julia. He had not really loved her with the depth she deserved. She was a trophy he sought to win for winning's sake. She had recognized the shallowness of his affection while he could not.

Eight years later, it appeared he played the same games with himself. He was attracted to Vanessa Mannion because she was an object to win. He certainly was not in the market for an American wife, yet inexplicably, he wished she'd look favorably upon him. What particularly galled was the knowledge he would have gone on deceiving everyone as to his intentions, including himself. But with Trevor somewhere in the maze, as he'd been those many years ago, Hugh realized he could again be playing with mirrors. He had to determine Trevor's degree of emotional involvement. He also vowed, no matter what he learned, he would support Trevor in his quest. His friend was a damned fine gentleman, and Hugh was confident Julia would wish her husband to remarry, for he deserved happiness.

Hugh set his cigar down to reach for his port glass, his mind wandering to the events of the evening. He shook his head slightly at the memory of Trevor's expression when Wilmot refused to relinquish Vanessa's hand. That was when he'd first begun to feel as if he'd stumbled into a new, unknown maze, and he had vowed to tread carefully through the remainder of the evening with the Mannions. By virtue of some adept maneuvering—reminiscent of his peninsular days, he mused—he'd altered the seating arrangements for the return trip to the Mannions' home. He and Miss Chaumonde shared the carriage with Vanessa Mannion and Mr. Wilmot. And bless Miss Chaumonde's naïveté, she prattled incessantly with virtually a scene-by-scene review of the play. Fortunately, her chatter did not allow for response from anyone. It also precluded her falling across him on the pretext of a rough carriage ride, but under the circumstances Hugh would have even welcomed that, for certainly it would have created another form of diversion.

Upon her arrival at home, Vanessa retired immediately to her room, claiming a headache from the effort of understanding the rapid French dialogue throughout the play. After she left, there remained a curious tension in the air among the company that even Paulette's gaiety could not overcome. Mr. Wilmot quickly made his exit. He and Trevor soon followed.

Hugh picked up his cigar and looked over at his companion who sat quietly smoking, a faint smile on his face. He wondered what the man was thinking. No, more than that, he needed to know what Trevor was feeling, particularly toward one Miss Vanessa Mannion.

He flicked an ash off his cigar, and stared at its glowing tip. "This Wilmot fellow, where is he from?" Hugh casually asked.

"No one really knows, but speculators say he's from Kentucky, since he gets on with the keelboat men. Why?"

"Curiosity. I wondered how he became a favorite in society."

"So you feel it, too." Trevor shifted uneasily in his chair and took a sip of port.

Hugh raised a questioning eyebrow.

"That feeling of something criminal," Trevor explained, setting the glass on the table.

"I don't know that I'd go so far as to say criminal; however, the gentleman is a creature of both crude and polished airs. I do not trust that duality. I take it others do not see the split?"

"Oh, I think they do, but first they don't recognize it as anything sinister. It's more an indication of the man's worth, that he's been able to build a business and thereby raise himself above his birth. For many who come to this country, it is the American dream. Wilmot embodies that dream. He has looks, intelligence, and great strength—and that was almost all he had when he came to New Orleans three years ago. In that time he's been able to parlay himself into more deals and schemes than you can imagine. And they've paid off." Trevor paused and shook his head ruefully.

"Oh, there have been rumors about what his real business was. Most believe he was one of Laffite's legitimate fronts and might still be. Others connect him with the revolutionary filibustering that goes on over at Maspero's, though few agree on the subject of the revolution. I've heard the Texas territory, Mexico, and South American locations named."

"Egad!"

"Precisely," Trevor drawled.

"I'm surprised Richard Mannion countenances his presence around his daughters."

"He invites him. Look, Hugh," Trevor explained, "Wilmot is rich and powerful. He's slowly been taking over all the warehousing on the wharf. That's a key business in this city. New Orleans wouldn't be the rich city she is without trade, for, frankly, the products of this area alone cannot support her." He took another sip of port, then set down his glass and leaned forward.

"Right now, Mannion needs a new cotton press facility, but he has no place for it, nor the capital to purchase one for he's made substantial loans this year to cotton growers in order to insure a big crop. Because of this, he's hoping to strike a deal with Wilmot for warehouse leasing. Though if I know Wilmot, I suspect he's negotiating for a partnership deal, using Vanessa."

"And her father's agreeable to this?" Hugh inquired.

"Hardly. Richard Mannion's a wily old goat on his own—even if he does have a blind spot where his own daughters are concerned." Trevor picked up his cigar, frowned at the dead tip, and leaned forward to relight it in the candle flame. He drew in deeply before looking back toward Hugh. "Adeline tells me Richard's strongly encouraging Vanessa to be nice to you."

"To me!"

"Ostensibly to help cement his cotton deal with you. Personally, I think it's to throw off Wilmot."

Hugh's eyes narrowed as he considered this information. "But what about you, Trevor? Where do you fit in?"

Trevor sighed ruefully. "Now that is a good question. Less than a week ago, I would have confidently stated I was one of Vanessa Mannion's suitors. Now I'm not sure what I am." He ran his hand through his hair.

"I have never seen you possessed with rage to the extent you were at the theater," Hugh said slowly.

"Yes, I don't know what came over me. It was as if I was seeing her as some pawn in a big chess game. I cannot fathom any genteel woman being treated in such a fashion— or any gentleman so forgetting himself as to treat a lady like a lightskirt." He shook his head in bewilderment. "Miss Mannion is one of the most intelligent, entrancing women of my acquaintance, and to see her treated in that manner—"

"Easy, Trevor, easy. I'm sure this little mistake of his will turn Miss Mannion's attention elsewhere. Though the man is powerful, he is not so powerful that he can make a woman marry him. Perhaps if his background is as crude as you suggest, he is not at ease in society and is ignorant of proper behavior. This may well prove to be a salutary lesson for him. No, I doubt you will have to worry about socializing with Wilmot in the Mannions' company."

"Perhaps you're right. And truthfully, I, like Richard, cannot afford enmity with the man. Danielson and Halley Company is a frequent client of his. Our warehouses are just not sufficient to handle all our merchandise, and we're not intending to build more here. With the advent of the steamboat for hauling, we're building further upriver, land's already too dear around here, and, like I said, Wilmot's got a lock locally. It is hoped that our new warehouses will be completed in a few months."

"We need a battle plan," Hugh mused.

"What?"

"Tactics," he murmured. "The problem, as I see it, is to

divert Wilmot from his pursuit of Miss Mannion without ruffling his tail feathers.''

"That is, perhaps, a bit simplistic; however, I'll accept that.''

"Good. Then, to create our diversion, I propose we use me for cannon fodder.''

"What?''

"I believe that is what Richard Mannion is doing without my knowledge, so it's a small matter to become a willing participant. Safer, too.''

Trevor looked unconvinced but willing to listen. Hugh plowed on: "Look, I don't have to live here and work with the gentleman. In a few months I will merely be a memory.''

"So what do you propose to do?''

"Publicly, I shall continue to court Miss Chaumonde, for to do otherwise would cause comment.''

Trevor nodded his understanding and begged him to continue.

"Heretofore, Miss Mannion and I have maintained, at best, a guarded relationship. I shall continue to tease, slightly challenge, and otherwise upset the equanimity of Miss Mannion while playing upon Richard's juncture that she be friendly to me. Under these circumstances, I anticipate she will spend more time contemplating my comeuppance than she will be thinking of Mr. Wilmot and the trouble he might be planning.''

Trevor looked at him, stunned, then burst out laughing. "That is such a ridiculous idea that it might work. And if you really wish to divert her, talk business and politics with her; she has an unslaking thirst for knowledge in those subjects.''

Hugh pursed his lips. "Interesting,'' he murmured, his mind immediately formulating discussions bound to disrupt Vanessa.

"But seriously, Hugh, what of Miss Mannion? Is this fair to her?''

"Is letting her marry Wilmot fair to her?"

Trevor paused, exhaling sharply. "That is a point well taken, my friend. Very well taken."

Hugh nodded and took another sip of port. Truly, his motives were suspect. They were as convoluted as the twistiest maze, for now the problem was how to insure Trevor's place as suitor in Vanessa's mind and heart. Perhaps a few jealous words on his part, a seemingly unconscious praise of his accomplishments. Yes, it could be done. He would also draw Mr. Wilmot's fire; he only hoped the gentleman was a poor marksman.

CHAPTER
SEVEN

♥

Richard Mannion stood before the French windows, his
hands behind his back, tapping out a restless rhythm when
Vanessa peeped in around the open library door.

"Come in, Vanessa, and close the door," he said softly,
his back to her.

She started, for she didn't know he was aware of her
presence. When Jonas informed her she was wanted in the
library, a frisson of dread went through her. Her father never
asked anyone into the library unless it was for a private
upbraiding. She searched her mind for an explanation of the
summons, but none came—unless by chance he'd found out
about the newspapers. She approached the library quietly,
hoping to hear something that would give a clue to her
father's mood. Now she was baffled. Usually if called in for
some perceived fault, he would stand rigidly by his desk,
his face a stern study in disappointment and anger. Sometimes, if the error was great enough, he would pace the
room and mumble darkly to himself before turning to
address the miscreant. But he never stood staring out the
window, and he never, ever, spoke softly.

Quickly she stepped into the room, gently shutting the door behind her. She tipped her head to the side, studying her father. He looked old. Odd, she'd never noticed how he was aging, how worn he'd become. She took a few tentative steps toward him, uncertain what to say or do.

"Why didn't you tell me, Vanessa?" he sadly asked.

She blinked, her mind racing to understand. "I beg your pardon, sir?"

He turned toward her, dropping his hands to his sides. "Why didn't you inform me of Russell Wilmot's impropriety last night?"

"Who told you?" she gasped.

His fists clenched reflexively and his features shifted into anger for a moment, then relaxed. He laughed shortly and turned to walk over to his desk. "He did."

"Mr. Wilmot?!" She clutched the back of one of the chairs in front of the desk for her knees felt strangely weak.

Her father reached out to guide her gently into the chair. She murmured her thanks, her mind struggling with the information.

"Why did he tell you?" she finally managed, looking up at her father's deeply lined face.

A wry smile tilted up the corners of his lips and he snorted softly. "Why? Because the man is clever." He rounded the corner of the desk to sit across from her, his hands resting on the polished surface expanse between them. "He came to my office this morning, said he had offended you last night. He told me how he first took the liberty of putting his hand on your shoulder and then of clasping your hand, ignoring your attempts to pull free. Is that correct?"

"Y–yes." She felt like a mouse, caught in a corner and uncertain which way to run to avoid the cat.

"Why didn't you tell me? It's my duty as a father to protect my daughters." He surged out of his chair, pacing the room agitatedly. "Damn it, girl, I felt like a caper-witted fool this morning, not knowing what the man was talking about—and that's not a position to be in when dealing with a man like Wilmot."

"I'm sorry, Father, but after Mr. Talverton made him stop, I thought it best to forget the incident, and I didn't wish to worry you unnecessarily."

"Mr. Talverton? What has he to do with this?"

"You don't know? Mr. Wilmot didn't tell you?"

"Tell me what?"

"Last night, during the play, when Mr. Wilmot so insistently held my hand, Mr. Talverton crashed his foot into the side of my chair."

"I remember the accident—"

"It wasn't an accident, Father. He did it as a means to end the situation without embarrassing all of us."

An arrested expression captured Mr. Mannion's features. Slowly he sank back into his chair. "So, he did that on purpose." His eyes shifted and a tight smile curled one corner of his mouth. Vanessa watched, wary of his changing moods.

"Hmm— Tell me, Vanessa, what do you think of Mr. Talverton?"

"I'm not sure I understand the question," she hedged. She leaned forward in her chair, closely watching her father. He was not behaving in character. It was totally unlike him to solicit opinions from any of his daughters.

"Come, come, my dear, you're being too missish. Do you like the man? Do you like his company?"

Vanessa sat straighter in the chair, clasping her hands primly on her lap. "If you are thinking of wedding me to Mr. Talverton, I advise you to think again," she said austerely, twin flags of red blazing on her cheeks. "Aside from last evening's fiasco, he and I have been continually at crossed swords. He is entirely too toplofty for my tastes. And regardless of my sentiments, Paulette has staked her claim on him."

Impatiently, he waved her protest aside. "I wasn't thinking marriage. I've got plans for you, girl."

"Plans! What sort of plans?" An incipient panic threaded her voice. What was her father about? A sense of caution began seeping through her.

"Never you mind that now."

"Father!"

"No, and I'll not say another word on the subject. Now, tell me what you think of Mr. Danielson."

Bewildered, Vanessa sighed and shook her head. "Mr. Danielson has charm, manners, intelligence, and a manner of gallantry that is appealing," she enumerated patiently. "He is a true gentleman."

Her father grunted and scratched the side of his nose. "What about Mr. Wilmot?" he persisted.

Vanessa closed her eyes. Her father knew things he wasn't saying, and as always, he was setting traps for the unwary. It irritated her to consider her position. Was she to be the hunted or the bait? It wouldn't do any good to ask, for he wouldn't answer her. Whatever, she'd wager it was business related.

She opened her eyes to stare steadily at her father. "Earlier last night," she said crisply, "I considered myself fortunate to be in his company. He seems to be a popular gentleman, for he knows everyone. He is handsome in a devilish fashion, successful through his own efforts, intelligent, and gives a woman the feeling of being the center of his world by his attention and possessiveness. It is here, I hasten to add, that his possessiveness becomes suffocating and deadens his appeal. I believe that is what occurred last evening. He stopped thinking of me as a person and considered me as one would the purchase of a horse or new article of clothing, and treated me with the same carelessness as one would those objects."

Richard Mannion leaned back in his chair, folding his

hands across his chest, and nodded, a wry smile twisting his lips. "All right, I'll remember your words," he promised.

Vanessa's eyes narrowed as she studied his suddenly complacent, smiling demeanor. In the past three to four years, her father had rarely smiled, and never joked. If she had ever given the matter thought, she would have suggested that with the press of weighty business matters, he had forgotten how. Yet since the evening of the Langley Ball—nay, more precisely since the arrival of Mr. Talverton—she had on more than one occasion witnessed the upturn of the corners of his mouth and heard the deep rumble of rusty laughter. She was delighted to see humor restored to her parent, but fretted at its source.

"Now," he continued, sitting straighter in his chair and shifting his clasped hands to the desk surface, "I'm going to tell you what I want from you, and none of your mulishness."

"What?" she exclaimed indignantly, hastily dragging her errant thoughts back to the discussion at hand.

"First, you'll continue to be nice to Mr. Talverton, especially after last evening." He paused a moment, his thumbs circling each other. "Second, Mr. Wilmot will be coming to call this afternoon to apologize," he baldly announced.

Vanessa groaned and closed her eyes, her body sagging at the thought of again meeting the gentleman.

Her father ignored her and continued. "And if the rains hold off, you'll allow him to take you driving."

"Father, that's not fair!" she protested, gripping the arms of her chair until her knuckles whitened. "The man grossly insulted me. He treated me like a—a—a common trollop."

"You're exaggerating the matter," he said dismissively. "He only touched you without permission." He held up a hand to forestall her protests. "I know you feel he acted ungentlemanly, but, to use Paulette's words, he hasn't—as it were—been raised to the manner born. He claims he was swept away by your charm and beauty last evening and could not resist.''

"Swept away?'' She laughed hollowly. "I'm sorry, Father, but I doubt his veracity. Mr. Wilmot is a very determined, intelligent and deliberate man, oriented toward one thing: success. Everything else is merely a means to an end.''

"Don't be too hasty,'' he said, favoring her with another of his rare smiles, this one baring his teeth. "The more tender emotions rarely equate with the intellect.''

Vanessa blinked in surprise. That was what she had been discovering for herself. Could Mr. Wilmot be struggling with the same confusing notions as she? Impossible. He was a confident and forthright man. But what if— *No*, she thought, hardening her heart. Even if it was true, it was no excuse for his behavior last night, for she was certain he delighted in her discomfiture. She remembered that predatory look in the depths of his eyes and shivered slightly.

What was her father about? She didn't want to be the bait in some grandiose hunt. Was he going to exchange her for business dealings and concessions, settlement and dowry on both sides? But for whom?

"And do you have instructions for my dealings with Mr. Danielson, too?'' she ventured caustically.

He frowned at her tone, his brows descending in a thick iron bar shielding his eyes. "Yes.'' His voice was clipped, and instantly Vanessa regretted her tone to him. He stood up and proceeded to pace the room again, this time in a leisurely manner. "You shall be as friendly as always, yet remain somewhat distant, particularly around Mr. Wilmot. When Mr. Wilmot is not nearby, you may treat him with warmer affections—within the bounds of propriety, of course.''

Vanessa bit her lower lip and held her eyes downcast to hide the rage seething through her. It was a game, but the ultimate prize was unknown. Somehow, she was certain she was merely the pawn, not the prize.

* * *

Adeline, crouching down beside a thick patch of deep purple violets, looked up at the sound of Vanessa's footsteps. The expression on her sister's face made her quickly place the fragile blossom she held into her workbasket and rise to her feet. She wiped the dirt from her hands on the oversized apron she wore to protect her dress, and crossed to her side.

"Vanessa?" she said tentatively, disturbed by the degree of sadness and confusion evident in her face. "Are you all right? What did Father want?" She laid a gentle hand on her arm.

Vanessa looked at Adeline, slowly focusing on her presence. Her sister's wide-brimmed sunbonnet framed her face charmingly, despite her concerned frown. A genuine smile flickered briefly on Vanessa's lips before they twisted into a wry grimace. "I've always known Father holds our intellectual capacity in low regard; nonetheless, I am shocked to discover he has the nacky notion we are mere hubble-bubble creatures. I was quite ready to pull caps with him."

"Oh, no, Vanessa!"

"Rest assured, the opportunity did not present itself, and I also had the presence of mind, despite my increasing ire, to realize such action on my part would serve no purpose."

"Did he give you a trimming?"

"On the contrary, he was curiously soft-spoken. He even smiled."

"Vanessa, you have me on tenterhooks. What happened?"

"I'm sorry, Adeline. I must sound as obscure as Father did to me. Here, let's sit in the shade and I'll tell you all." She led her sister to a wooden bench at the edge of the courtyard. "By the way, where is Paulette?"

Adeline leaned down to place her basket under the bench. "She told Mama of some lace she saw that she wishes to purchase, for she's convinced that Mr. Talverton has only to see it on her to fall madly in love with her," she said, smoothing her skirt and sitting down.

Vanessa groaned. "I know what lace she was speaking of, and it is very dear. I thought I had distracted her sufficiently to forget its existence."

"Hardly. Anyway, that scapegrace child wheedled Mama into a shopping excursion to procure the lace and other materials necessary to make up a new gown."

"She is scarcely a child. Remember, you and she are of an age," Vanessa reminded her.

Her sister sighed heavily. "Sometimes I feel the aged anecdote."

"Oh, really, Adeline."

"No, truly. Take last evening. Do you know what that hoyden did on the way to the theater? At every bump and curve, she threw herself across Mr. Talverton, claiming that the faults of the road, the coachman, and the carriage forced her to fall."

Vanessa laughed. "She has always displayed a sad lack of sensibility."

"She displays none at all!" contradicted Adeline. "Occasionally I wonder at her familial relationship to Charles. She is so different from her brother in temperament."

Her sister shrugged, mimicking Paulette's expansive Gallic motion, and Adeline fell to laughing, clutching her sides.

"Oh, please, enough," she pleaded. She wiped her streaming eyes with the back of her hand and took deep, steadying breaths. "Sometimes, Vanessa, I don't know how you can claim you are serious minded. You are forever bringing me to whoops of laughter."

"Now and then I do seem to suffer a sad want of dignity—but never in company."

"It might be best if you did."

"I wonder if I could chase Mr. Wilmot away by becoming excessively silly," mused Vanessa.

"It would be too out of character; he'd know it for a

ruse," Adeline replied. "But I thought, after last night, you were not going to have anything more to do with him."

Vanessa sighed. "I don't have much choice."

"Why?"

"He visited Father this morning and made a full confession of his misdeeds. He claimed he was swept away by my charm and beauty."

"Gammon," scoffed Adeline.

"Why, don't you think I have charm and beauty?"

"Vanessa! Of course I do, now stop teasing."

"I'm sorry, I couldn't resist. You're right of course; he pitched quite a tale at Father."

"And Father believed him?"

"That's the strange thing. I don't believe he does; however, somehow it's to his advantage to accept and forgive Mr. Wilmot his actions."

"How odd," Adeline said.

"Yes, but it gets stranger still. He told me to accept Mr. Wilmot's apology and continue considering him a suitor, be friendly to Mr. Talverton, and ignore Mr. Danielson when Mr. Wilmot is around."

A tiny worried frown marred the perfection of Adeline's features, and her hands fluttered agitatedly in front of her. She looked away from her sister, then back. "W–w–why?" she stammered. "Does he think Mr. Wilmot might harm Mr. Danielson?"

"I cannot say," Vanessa replied distractedly, failing to notice the extent of her sister's dismay. "My summation is it has something to do with business. Perhaps the negotiations for a wedding settlement or dowry," Vanessa suggested sardonically. "I have the feeling Father is playing games within games and I resent my involvement."

"What are you going to do?"

"I'm not sure yet. I need to contemplate this further."

Adeline shivered slightly. "It terrifies me to even consider it."

The sisters sat silently for a few moments, each locked in her own thoughts of their father's strange behavior. Finally Adeline roused herself, shaking her head as if to shake out all troublesome thoughts.

"Oh, dear, I nearly forgot my flowers. I must get them between blotting paper and weighted before they wilt."

"I'll help you," offered Vanessa. "Perhaps I shall have an easier time solving my dilemma if I don't dwell on it constantly."

Adeline laughed softly. "I suppose at this juncture you could do no worse. Come, before Father returns and reclaims his library, let's see if we can get all these pressed."

"That's all of them, now what?" Vanessa asked as she slid the last blossom and leaf set between the pages of a heavy law book.

"Now we check on the progress of some I laid down earlier this spring. Let's see. I used the Greek books for those—" Adeline said, dragging a small stool over to one of the tall bookshelves and climbing up on it. Standing on tiptoe, she reached up to grab a thick volume of Greek plays and pull it off the shelf.

"Do you keep track of what you press by what type book it's in?"

"Yes. Well, actually that's how I record when I pressed it." She handed the book to Vanessa before turing to grab another. "For example, today we used all law books, so tonight in my journal I shall make note of what we pressed and where they are."

"How many Greek books are there?" Vanessa asked as Adeline passed her another heavy tome and she staggered under the weight.

"Four," Adeline replied distractedly, tugging at a particularly thick book of Greek essays.

"I hadn't realized the Mannion women were bluestockings," said a warm deep voice from the door.

Vanessa, her arms full of books, turned around to stare in surprise at Hugh Talverton standing in the doorway of the library. Adeline teetered precariously on her perch, another book bearing her precious blossoms clasped tight in her hand.

Hugh watched in stupefied horror as Adeline spun around, her arms flailing outward to restore her balance. "Vanessa! Look out!" he warned, ground-eating strides carrying him to her side as the heavy book in Adeline's hand swung in a wide arc and crashed into Vanessa's face.

He caught her as she fell sideways.

"Vanessa!" screamed Adeline. Jumping off the stool, she ran to her sister's side, the book she held falling heedlessly to the floor.

"Vanessa! I'm so sorry! Are you all right?"

She moaned, a hand fluttering up to her face as she sagged against Mr. Talverton.

With a grim expression marring his handsome features, he picked her up in his arms as if she were a featherweight. "Where can I lay her down?"

Adeline jumped at his harsh tone. "Wha— Oh, yes, of course. The–the parlor, I believe."

Carrying his precious burden, he turned on his heel, heading for the parlor. In his arms, Vanessa moaned and whimpered. Adeline ran behind him, her hands twisting together.

They passed Jonas in the hall.

"Jonas," called Adeline, "Vanessa's been hurt. Get some lavender water from Leila."

"No," contradicted Talverton harshly, "fetch a side of beef."

"A side of beef?" echoed Adeline faintly.

"Yes, a piece of raw beef," he ordered over his shoulder as he strode into the parlor, "else she'll have a wicked black eye."

Adeline jerkily nodded permission to Jonas, shooed him

on his way, then followed in Talverton's wake. She entered the parlor in time to see him settle her sister gently on the largest sofa in the room. Swiftly he turned to gather up pillows from other chairs and gently place them behind her head and shoulders.

Vanessa's eyes fluttered open as he smoothed her skirts down around her ankles, tucking them about her. "What—" she muttered, struggling to sit up.

"Hush," he quietly remonstrated, his voice sending odd, comforting ripples through her.

"Oh, Vanessa, I'm so sorry," wailed Adeline.

Vanessa furrowed her brow against an incipient pounding in her head and tried to concentrate. "What happened?"

"Your sister planted you a facer," explained Hugh as he smiled down at her. "Her form was questionable, but it was a nice flush hit."

"How can you jest about it?" complained Adeline, sinking to her knees beside Vanessa.

"It's all right, Adeline," assured Vanessa weakly. "Actually it was Mr. Talverton's fault," she declared, trying to glare at him but giving it up when it increased the pounding in her head.

"Somehow I knew you'd come round to blaming me."

"What are you doing here, anyway?" Vanessa demanded aggressively, then winced as a sharp pain pierced her cheek and eye.

"You'll probably feel better if you keep the eye closed," he counseled. "I was in the neighborhood and decided to pay an afternoon call. When your butler left me standing while he went to search out your location, I became restless. I heard female voices coming from the library, so I merely came to investigate."

"Excuse me, Miss Adeline, but I got the beef the gentleman requested," said Jonas from the doorway.

"Excellent," declared Talverton, striding over to the butler. He took it from Jonas, testing the weight and thickness in his hand before crossing back to the sofa where Vanessa lay.

"What's that for?" she asked in dismay as she saw him approach.

"For that black eye you're going to get if you don't put this on it."

"Black eye?"

"Yes, black eye," he said, pushing her back down among the pillows and laying the slab of beef over the left side of her face.

"This is ridiculous," Vanessa protested, reaching up to remove the meat.

He caught her hand, holding it firmly in his. "Leave it," he commanded, "unless you desire to resemble a pugilist who has lost a round."

"Perhaps you had best do as he says," Adeline said weakly, biting her lip in dismay.

"What's going on in here?" a harsh, gravelly voice demanded.

Vanessa looked toward the doorway and groaned. Mr. Wilmot had arrived, as promised.

Jonas pushed past him, scurrying to the sofa. "I tried to tell him you were indisposed, Miss Vanessa, but he wouldn't listen. Came right on in, he did, saying as how he was expected." He turned to glare resentfully at the man, his old face heavily lined, though his eyes stared out fiercely at the intruder.

"I understand, Jonas," she said. Suddenly she realized Mr. Wilmot's angry gaze was settled on her hand, which was still clasped in Mr. Talverton's. "You can let go of my hand now, Mr. Talverton," she said, pulling it free. "I promise I shall suffer the meat to stay in place for it is certainly not my desire to resemble any prizefighter."

Hugh allowed her hand to slide free and straightened to face Mr. Wilmot, though he maintained his position by the sofa.

"I apologize for not rising to meet you formally, Mr. Wilmot; however, I'm afraid I met with a slight accident."

"What did this man do to you?" Wilmot growled, striding forward to tower over her.

"Mr. Talverton? Do not be ridiculous, sir. If anything, he has been my savior."

Hugh's sandy brows rose at her comment. Just moments ago she had been blaming him. His lips tightened to suppress a smile.

Adeline rose from her knees to move away only to feel her sister's arm restraining her. Vanessa edged closer toward the back of the sofa, making a space for Adeline to perch beside her.

Casting a nervous glance in Mr. Wilmot's direction, Adeline settled herself next to her sister. "Oh, it was all my fault," whispered Adeline, folding her hands over Vanessa's. "I'm afraid I hit her with a volume of Greek essays."

"My classical studies professor at Oxford always said the Greek essays carried power," murmured Hugh, "but until now I failed to understand his precise meaning."

His wry sally was rewarded with a flickering smile from Vanessa and a hostile glare from Mr. Wilmot.

"What are you doing here?" the man demanded.

"I could ask you the same, with much more justification," replied Hugh calmly. He stood at his leisure, appearing totally unintimidated, a circumstance Mr. Wilmot was not accustomed to when he was angry. Men quaked and placated him; they did not stand nonchalantly. His eyes narrowed.

"I've come to take Miss Mannion driving," he said challengingly.

"Yes, beautiful day for a drive. I could wish for a rig of my own on a day like today. Pity she's no longer up for it," drawled Hugh.

"How did this happen?" Wilmot ground out, turning to fix Adeline with a malevolent stare.

She blinked and slouched a little, closer to Vanessa.

"You have no call to browbeat my sister, Mr. Wilmot!" Vanessa declared, pushing herself up on her elbows to address him. "And I'll thank you to mend your tone. I have a splitting headache that your insistent thundering is aggravating." She sank wearily back against the pillows.

He flushed and instinctively stepped back at her ferocious words, and Hugh Talverton smiled at his unconscious action. It was obvious the man was not used to people standing up to him.

"*Adeline!*" called Mr. Mannion from the hallway. "Adeline, what happened in my library?" He strode angrily into the room, stopping short when he saw the assembled tableau. "Egad, what's going on here? Wilmot, if you've harmed my daughter—"

"What?" demanded Mr. Wilmot.

"No, Father—" interrupted Vanessa exasperatedly.

"It was all my fault," chimed in Adeline.

"Quick assumptions can be quite amusing," said Mr. Talverton to no one in particular.

Vanessa tilted her head back and attempted to frown at him, only to burst out laughing at his insouciant expression. "Oh, please, don't make me laugh, it only hurts more." She looked back at her father. "I was helping Adeline retrieve some of her pressed flowers. They were in your Greek works, and she needed to stand on a stool to reach them," she explained patiently. "While on the stool she lost her balance and hit me in the face with the book she held. That's all. It was a silly accident and now I just wish everyone would go away. This grand assembly only increases my embarrassment."

"Your wish, fair damsel in distress, is my command," responded Hugh with alacrity, his voice almost whisper soft, subtly reminding her of the first time he'd played the gallant knight. He smiled at her and raised her hand to bestow a chaste salute. She looked so interestingly wan, laying back against the pillow, her brown hair sagging out of its formal coiffure, leaving wispy tendrils to wave across the pale skin of her brow and echo the tiny frown lines etched there, mute testimony to her battle with pain. A strange wave of tenderness surged over him. He paused, staring at her a moment as he rode out the wave of feeling.

"Just remember," he added with a wink, in quite his normal arrogant manner, "keep the beef in place. I shall return tomorrow with Trevor to see how you are faring, if that is permissible."

She nodded, sinking back limply into the pillows.

He turned to bid adieu to the others, his voice hushed. He was pleased to hear them respond in equally hushed tones.

CHAPTER
EIGHT

♥

Trevor Danielson closed the door to his office and joined Hugh on the banquette. "You say Wilmot acted as though he was expected?" he said as they strolled up the street in the bright afternoon sun.

Hugh nodded slowly. "Yes, and I was nonplussed by his appearance, I'll admit." They sidestepped a couple of ragamuffin street urchins laughing and chasing each other. Hugh turned to watch them a moment, an amused smile lighting his face. When he looked back at Trevor, his features sobered and he shook his head. "Yet, I'd hazard Vanessa was not surprised at his appearance," he continued dryly. "I believe she may have been expecting him. Regardless, I gathered she was grateful for the accident which prevented their outing."

"So I would think. I wonder why she even deigned to see him?"

"I cannot say. What was interesting was Richard's first assumption that Wilmot was responsible for her injury."

"Odd. It sounds as if he has found some way to ingratiate himself with them. I wonder if we are not too late, and he has succeeded in his negotiations for her hand and Richard's business."

"If so, it is not with Vanessa's agreement. We shall have to redouble our efforts to turn her attention and his," Hugh said grimly.

Trevor sighed. "At this point, that is the last I wish to do."

Hugh looked at him curiously, but Trevor didn't notice.

"Our appearance at the Mannion home this afternoon should help divert attention, or at least prevent anyone from making final plans for Vanessa's future."

"Perhaps," Trevor slowly conceded, "if she is up for visitors."

Hugh frowned briefly and shook his head. "I can't imagine her being so vain as to turn away callers. In fact, I would be more inclined to believe she would have me see her injury since, despite her words to the contrary, I believe she holds me partially responsible for the accident."

Trevor laughed. "You may be made to squirm, my friend."

"Indeed, I am aware of that possibility," Hugh conceded dryly.

"It may reassure you to know I have set about some investigations into Wilmot's background, but he is a hard man to investigate surreptitiously for he has many friends, particularly in the more seamy side of town. He is not a man I would openly antagonize."

"Why, do you fear he is the type to take physical means to assure his ends?" Hugh asked sharply.

"I don't know," Trevor answered slowly, "but I hope not. His compatriots are men of violence and generally not the sort to be drawn to loyalty by those not of their ilk."

"This is a bad business, Trevor," Hugh muttered darkly as they neared the Mannion home.

"I only hope we are wrong," his friend said with a sigh, tacitly acknowledging the truth of Hugh's statement. "It is ironic that what began as a gentle courtship should have the appearance of taking a particularly nasty turn."

"I begin to have the hope we are foolish dreamers, seeing demons at every corner."

"Aye, you have the right of it there," Trevor admitted, slowly lifting and dropping the knocker on the heavy carved wood door before the Mannion home. Hugh didn't comment further but bent to brush the dust off his normally gleaming Hessians, his lips pursed in thought.

It was but a few moments before Jonas admitted them and led them into the spacious foyer.

"One moment, gentlemen, while I inform the ladies of your presence," the old butler said.

"A moment, man, if you please. Tell us first, how does Miss Vanessa Mannion feel?" Hugh asked.

"Poorly, in truth, but it's not for me to be talking. I shall return directly. Please wait here."

Hugh scowled and would have said more had not the door to the library swung open and Richard Mannion appear.

"Ah, I thought I heard your voice, Mr. Talverton. A moment of your time, if you please."

Trevor and Hugh exchanged questioning glances, neither guessing Mr. Mannion's intent. Hugh shrugged slightly in Trevor's direction and walked toward the library.

Richard Mannion held the door wide and closed it tightly after his guest entered.

"Please, have a seat, sir," he said, gesturing to a comfortable corner of the room with two chairs placed providently for conversation. "Would you care for a smoke?" he asked, extending a box of cigars in Hugh's direction.

Hugh nodded and accepted one.

After lighting Hugh Talverton's and his own, Richard Mannion sat down.

"I wish to thank you for assisting my daughter, Vanessa. I understand from Adeline that you were very propitious in your actions yesterday when Vanessa's injury occurred."

"I must confess, Mr. Mannion—"

"Richard, please."

"Thank you. I must confess, Richard, I do account myself responsible for the accident. My presence startled Adeline and caused her to lose her balance."

"Be that as it may, you responded with alacrity—as I understand you did at the theater the other evening."

Hugh paused, an arrested expression narrowing his eyes as he stared at Richard Mannion. He puffed on his cigar again, a ring of blue smoke rising, blurring his features from Mr. Mannion's eyes. He tapped an ash loose. "You have me at a disadvantage, sir. I am at a loss for what to say."

"The truth, man," Mannion said sighing heavily, the lines in his face looking deeper. "I fear of necessity there is much hidden by all of us. In this matter I would wish a modicum of honesty to prevail."

"Why?"

Richard Mannion's mouth twisted at Hugh's bald question. "My daughter, Vanessa, is a remarkable woman. She has intellect, wit, charm, and grace. Most women with her qualities would be married by now." He puffed on his cigar, his expression one of sad irony.

Hugh straightened in his chair and set aside his cigar as he studied the older man.

"Though I am loath to admit it, Vanessa has always been my favored daughter. In her interest, I have done seemingly incomprehensible things. Heretofore, I have manipulated matters to keep her free from suitors. I have also endeavored to keep her innocent of business and political matters." He laughed mirthlessly, bitterly. "In this I have failed miserably. In all, however, what actions I have taken have been to protect her."

Hugh stirred restlessly in his chair, for a miasma of despair filled the room. He didn't want to hear Mannion's revelations, but he knew he must. Intuitively, he began to realize his flippant description of himself as cannon fodder could be truer than either he or Trevor realized.

"Four years ago," Mannion continued, "I arranged dowries for my daughters. I did this at the same time I drew up my will. At that time I did something unheard of; I drew up documents to give half of my business to Vanessa. She was my bright star, and I intended to train her in the business.''

He held up his hand to forestall an exclamation of shocked protest from Hugh. ''I know, I know,'' he said sadly, ''it was a foolish idea. Though she is capable of such intelligent endeavors, it would not be accepted in the realities of business. I was not, thankfully, so totally lost to all reason that I didn't make other provisions. First, I maintain control of her half of the business until her marriage. At that time control devolves on to her, not a husband. Of course, there are ways for an enterprising gentleman to get around this.''

''Sir, why are you telling me this?''

''Have patience, Mr. Talverton.'' Richard scratched the side of his nose thoughtfully for a moment. ''To my other daughters I have bestowed property and money. These were all investments I made four years ago. At that time, the Chaumondes were not my lawyers. Another gentleman, an American actually, was handling my papers. I soon discovered this gentleman was in the pay of Jean Laffite, and my careful, secret plans were a secret no more. That damned pirate,'' he said slowly, fairly spitting the words out. ''He found the situation humorous, but he kept those papers and showed me cleverly forged documents that implicated me in his piratical dealings. Me!''

Mannion exploded out of his chair to pace the room.

Hugh Talverton stroked his chin in thought. ''I gather he used those documents to prevent you from changing your settlements on your daughters?''

''Precisely.'' His agitated pacing slowed as he wearily continued his tale. ''Vanessa was barely sixteen at the time. I told Laffite I was planning for the future and did not intend to betroth her for at least two years. He agreed easily enough but told me the choice of a groom would be his, and if any gentleman not of his choosing came sniffing around, he would see to his removal.''

Hugh felt the skin at the back of his neck crawl and his muscles tighten at Mannion's bald words, but he remained silent. He would hear the man out—he had to.

Richard Mannion stopped by his chair, sighing heavily. He reached down for his port glass and tossed off its contents. ''It was then I began to deny my daughter any information on business and politics and carefully kept her immured in our household to the extent I was able. I did not want her to draw attention from either Laffite or some innocent worthy gentleman. She has chafed mightily at my restrictions, as well she might, but I was playing for time.

''Though Laffite is a favorite among many Creoles, public sentiment for him has been declining, and government action to end his business has increased. During the war he saw this was the case and, for expediency, offered to ally himself with the Americans.''

Hugh nodded his understanding. ''In England, it is now thought that Captain Lockyer's failure to win him over to the British cause back in September of '14 cost us our victory at the Battle of New Orleans.''

Mannion smiled sardonically. ''At the time, Laffite had more to fear from the United States than Britain. His headquarters, Grande Terre at the Bay of Barataria, was more defensible by sea than land, and there was a plan by the United States to attack and disperse his Baratarian organization. Also, his brother Pierre was in prison in New Orleans. When Commodore Patterson and Colonel Ross destroyed his headquarters, some eighty of his men were taken prisoner and all the goods and ships there taken as spoils of war. Because of prior knowledge of the planned attack through friends in influential positions, Laffite had already removed himself, all the stored ammunition, and the lion's share of his men to safety.''

"Yes, and with those circumstances, many in England wonder why he did not throw in his lot with us."

"First, he liked his autonomy, but aside from that, you British had too many strings attached to your offer. He would have faced losing his privateers, and it would have forced him into an alliance with Spain—a hated enemy of his family's for he held them responsible for his father's death. Though he is a shifty and untrustworthy character, no one can fault his intelligence. He offered General Jackson his cooperation in the defense of the city in the hopes of gaining a general pardon for himself and his men, along with restitution of property. His actions aided General Jackson greatly, though it galled many to be beholden to a pirate. All the Baratarians have received pardons, but that's all. Laffite's filed court cases for the restitution of his property, but so far that's been useless."

Mannion circled the room again. "I calculated that with his star on the wane, he'd have little time, if any, to chase the fortune of one American woman. Truthfully, it is a small pittance in comparison to his properties. To a great extent, I have been correct." He paused and turned to face Hugh Talverton.

Hugh sat forward in his chair, for he realized that his host was now approaching the heart of the matter.

"This spring I made several substantial loans to cotton growers. With the wars ended everywhere, trade is expected to increase dramatically. I wanted to be in on grabbing a lucrative part of this business, so I overextended myself. But in my eager calculations for success this year, I failed to take into account increased warehousing and cotton press demand. What I currently own will be lamentably inadequate. Earlier this year I began courting Mr. Wilmot for warehouse space. As is my wont, I brought him home for business dinners. Here he met Vanessa and seemed captivated by her. Later, he came to me and formally asked permission to pay her his address. Feeling Laffite to be powerless now and concerned with other matters, I agreed. Shortly thereafter it was subtly made known to me that he was aware of the terms of my will and bride dowry. Imagine my surprise, for I thought that threat ended.

"At first, Wilmot also seemed content to play his own game and legitimately woo Vanessa. I figured he would have to win her on his own merits, and therefore it was a safe agreement to enter into. After all, no mention was made of the forged documents that would have labeled me a traitor, and—now that we are at peace—they no longer have the threat they once bore. Knowing this, I really saw no harm in the man; in fact, Wilmot at times has a chilling formality and politeness. I certainly did not hold a grudge for him using his information in order to set himself up as a suitor. I even found it comical, for to me it displayed an uncertainty on his part of his acceptability in New Orleans society. I thought the man to be grossly underestimating himself. Though he has been in the city a relatively short time, he is popular."

Mannion stood by the window, staring blindly out. He sighed deeply, like a man wresting with some deep, unfathomable pain. "Then somehow, last Friday night, things started to fall apart. I don't know why, unless he finally saw Trevor Danielson as a rival for Vanessa's hand. I admit I've been encouraging Mr. Danielson merely to give Mr. Wilmot competition, though I certainly would not be adverse to welcoming Trevor as a son-in-law. I believe Wilmot's recognition of rivals for Vanessa's hand has spurred his activity to claim what he feels is his. Thus the possessive actions toward Vanessa. But I do feel he generally likes her; he just doesn't understand her. Damned if I don't at times, and I've lived with her these twenty odd years!"

He turned back to face Hugh. "Anyway, it seems Wilmot's got me over a damned whiskey barrel. I need his cooperation in business, but I don't want to force Vanessa into anything that will not work for her. I also get a might restive when someone tries to force my hand. I figure if I can keep my daughter unencumbered until the summer and we leave New Orleans for the country, I can start to see my way clear of my debts and obligations. After that, Vanessa can make her choice freely—even if she chooses Wilmot, which at this juncture I doubt. Whatever devil inspired him to try to force intimacy with her worked greatly to his disadvantage.''

"I'm afraid I don't understand. If the forged documents are no longer a threat, how can he coerce you or Vanessa?"

"I told you I've overextended myself to finance some planters. I've also had to take out some loans myself, with half my business as collateral."

Hugh's mind raced ahead of his host's words, and a chilling scenario occurred to him. "Wilmot has purchased your notes," he said softly, each word falling distinctly like pebbles into a still pond.

Richard Mannion's face looked gray and ravaged. He nodded.

Hugh whistled silently through his teeth. "And I take it the half of your business you used as collateral was your own, not Vanessa's? So, if you cannot meet your obligations, and Wilmot weds Vanessa, then he gets the entire business."

Mannion nodded again, then turned once more to stare out the window. He looked as if he'd aged twenty years since Hugh entered the room. Hugh pursed his lips, touching his fingertips together in steeple formation. He tried to think, to puzzle a way out of this new dimension to the maze; but his emotions kept rushing in. His rage at Wilmot's duplicity was at the man's callous use of Vanessa—merely a means to an end, for he did not believe, as Richard wanted to, that Wilmot truly cared for Vanessa. He had to will the violent emotions to ebb. They would serve no purpose and only cloud his reasoning.

The library door opened, and the figure of a woman in a white cotton gown printed with delicate floral trails backed stealthily into the room, her head still peeking out the door into the hall.

"Vanessa?" queried her father.

She jumped, her breath whooshing out of her chest, and turned toward him. Her hand clutched over her heart in recovering surprise.

"Shsh!" she hissed, swiftly closing the door, her back against it. "Mr. Wilmot's here!"

"Again?" asked her father.

"Yes," she whispered, "and I just heard him ask Jonas if he could see me. I had Jonas tell him earlier that I was not coming down to see anyone with this bruise." Her hand unconsciously rose to touch a spot below her left eye.

"It doesn't look too bad," observed Hugh.

Vanessa's eyes opened wide, and a bright red flush swept up her neck and face to burn her cheeks as she assimilated Mr. Talverton's presence in her father's library. Turning sideways, she presented him with her right side only, the bruise out of sight, her gaze directed at the wall.

"What are you doing here?" she squeaked, then nervously cleared her throat. "This is wonderful. If Mr. Wilmot finds me in here with you, my excuse for avoiding his company will be hollow, and I shall be forced to speak with him again."

"I told you before, Vanessa, you are being ridiculously missish. I want you to continue to socialize with Mr. Wilmot." The falseness of his words made his tone flat and harsh. Hugh's eyebrows rose in amused recognition of the lie.

"I understand that, Father," Vanessa responded distractedly, failing to catch the innuendos Hugh heard. She went on, exasperated: "I chose to do so from a position of strength, however, not an embarrassing weakness for a physical flaw." She stared resolutely at the opposite wall.

"Mr. Mannion?" called Jonas's voice as he rapped on the library door.

Vanessa swung around, wild-eyed. "Where can I hide?" she silently mouthed, desperation in her eyes. Hugh was surprised by the intensity of her desire to avoid Mr. Wilmot, and he felt a rush of feeling to be of assistance. Coming up beside her and catching her elbow in his hand, he propelled her toward the desk.

"One moment, Jonas," called out Mr. Mannion, uncertain what his daughter and guest were up to.

The door opened a few inches and Jonas scurried inside. "Mr. Wilmot desires to see you, sir. Immediately," said the butler, his voice quavering slightly. In openmouthed awe, he watched Mr. Talverton shove Vanessa underneath the desk, then lightly vaulted it to sit in a chair in front, slouching and crossing his long legs out in front of him to obscure any sight of Vanessa hiding on hands and knees.

Mr. Mannion just shook his head at his daughter's antics, then a thoughtful expression stole over his face, and he rubbed his hands together with glee. Making an abrupt decision, his lips parted in a smile, and he strode over to stand by Mr. Talverton and aid in the deception.

"Well, Jonas, show him in, of course," said Richard while he struggled to control a corner of his mouth from lifting in amusement.

Old Jonas's eyes rolled in his head and his lips split into a broad grin. "Y-yes, sir!" he said emphatically, backing out into the hall.

From inside the library, they heard the butler tell Mr. Wilmot in a very austere tone that the master would see him now. Mr. Mannion's iron-bar brows rose as one. Jonas never referred to him as the master, and with that supercilious air, he ventured to think Jonas could outshine a quality London butler any day.

He leaned casually against the desk and looked down at Hugh Talverton expectantly. Somehow he knew that if anyone could bring their ship safely to port, it would be this gentleman.

"So, Richard, you think I'll be able to secure the high-quality cotton I need for my mill in England?'' Hugh said loudly as they heard Russell Wilmot approach.''

''Without a doubt. You understand, however, why I can't quote you a price immediately?''

''Of course,'' Hugh said, his face a study of serious intentness.

''Good. Ah, Russell, come in. Hugh Talverton and I have just been discussing the magnitude of his cotton needs,'' Richard Mannion said with brash heartiness, his eyes darting about, not quite meeting Mr. Wilmot's.

Hugh stood up, inwardly cringing at Richard's tone, for it was a little too hearty and welcoming. ''Hello, Wilmot,'' he said neutrally, curious to judge the gentleman's reaction to his presence.

Wilmot nodded with bare civility before turning to address Richard. ''Where's Vanessa? You know I desire a word with her.'' His eyes narrowed and slid in Hugh Talverton's direction. ''In private.''

Hugh raised a sandy brow and crossed his arms over his chest.

''You have some objection, Mr. Talverton?'' Wilmot asked, his grating voice heavy with challenge.

''Objection?'' Hugh returned slightly before a comical expression of petulance pulled down his features. ''Why, dash it, yes, I suppose I do. I'd be in a devil of a pucker if she agreed to see you after turning down Trevor and me.'' He dropped his hands to his sides and turned toward Mr. Mannion, his posture and demeanor suddenly stiff. ''Sir,'' he protested lugubriously, ''surely you would not allow Miss Mannion to deliver us such a backhanded turn.''

Mr. Mannion coughed suddenly and looked down at the floor while scratching the side of his nose. The alteration in Mr. Talverton's manner was astounding, and he was trying very hard to maintain his serious expression. ''Uh—no, of course not. No daughter of mine would display such ramshackle manners,'' he said gruffly, clearing his throat again.

Under the desk, Vanessa shook her head ruefully, amazed at her parent's participation in a blatant prevarication. She was astounded that her usually sober father could hold his own in the mini-play he was enacting. Mr. Talverton's performance drew a wry smile to her lips. It seemed he was a natural dissembler. He should have trod the boards. She leaned closer to the floor to better hear their dialogue through the narrow gap between the bottom of the wood panel end piece of the desk and the floor.

"Forgive me, Richard," Hugh said. "You'd be right to consider me the veriest lobcock for my ill-chosen words."

A sound suspiciously like a snort came from Mr. Wilmot. "Richard, you assured me—"

The library door opened abruptly, cutting off his words as he swung around to see who entered.

"Excuse me, dear," Mrs. Mannion said sweetly, ignoring the dark scowl on Russell Wilmot's face, "why don't you gentlemen join us in the parlor?" Her eyes flickered down, catching sight of white cloth figured with trailing flowers peeping out from under the desk. Her eyes opened wide. Vanessa? Though flustered and confused, she knew immediately her daughter would not be quick to forgive, if her hiding place were revealed.

Amanda Mannion's eyes flew up and fixed upon Mr. Wilmot. She came toward him and hooked her arm in his, a stiff, broad smile on her face. "Come, sir, let's provide an uplifting example and lead these two errant gentlemen to the parlor." She pulled him forward, leaving him no recourse but to acquiesce gracefully. She patted his arm and strolled slowly out of the room. "It is too bad Vanessa won't join us. The child is dreadfully embarrassed by that bruise on her face. It really is not that terrible, but she is adamant in her refusal to see anyone. She has been keeping to her room. Pouting, I think, poor dear. Oh, but just listen to me, my tongue is carrying on like a fiddlestick. If I'm not careful, you'll soon be likening me to Mary Langley," she said with a laugh, her voice fading from Vanessa's hearing as she led Mr. Wilmot into the hall.

"I'll follow behind you, just let me get my glass," Vanessa heard Hugh say loudly.

She started to back out of her hidey-hole on her hands and knees, only to bump into Mr. Talverton's shins and sit down on his foot. Mortification stained her cheeks cherry red, and she bolted upright just as he leaned down to assist her. Her head collided violently with his chin and she toppled forward again as Hugh bit back an oath, a hand coming up to nurse his sore jaw.

"What are you doing here?" she whispered savagely while blinking back the tears caused by the sharp pain on the top of her head. She grasped the edge of the desk and pulled herself up.

"I wanted to be sure you were all right, but I didn't expect you to wallop me," he whispered back.

"What? I think, Mr. Talverton, you have the wrong end of things," she declared, tenderly touching the sore spot on the top of her head.

They stood and glared at each other. Eventually the humor of their attitude percolated through to Vanessa, and she started to giggle. Quickly she compressed her lips to stifle the sound. She waved a hand toward the door.

"You'd best join them before Mr. Wilmot becomes suspicious."

"Becomes!" he retorted caustically. "I thought that was his natural state of being."

She swallowed another laugh and pushed him toward the door. She was rapidly revising her impression of Mr. Talverton. Truly, he displayed wit, intelligence, and understanding—all traits she admired. If it wasn't for his unfortunate habit of causing her injury and embarrassment, she could even come to like the gentleman.

* * *

Adeline opened the French doors of the parlor and walked out onto the gallery overlooking the gardens. Trevor followed behind her and placed a hand lightly on her shoulder. She turned to look up at him, a melancholy sadness touching her delicate features.

"What are we going to do, Trevor? Everyone believes you wish to marry Vanessa." She gave a tight little laugh. "I even told Vanessa that last Friday."

"I know," he said softly, "and last Friday I believed it, too. But then I thought I would never love another woman as I loved Julia, and I was looking for second-best—someone to be a companion to me and a mother to my children."

He turned her around to face him, taking both her hands in his. "I cannot believe I was blind for so long."

She pulled her hands from his and grasped the balcony railing. "This has all happened too fast. We must be mad."

"I realized that night at the theater that I loved you. I realized then it was a love that had been growing for some time, only in my blindness I didn't see it for what it was." He grinned. "Do you know when it really hit me? It was when Wilmot touched Vanessa. I was angry—angrier than I can ever remember being. But what went through my mind was that my anger was like that of a brother. After Hugh's antics I looked down at you and it hit me with a hurricane's force that if it had been you he touched, I would not have hesitated as I did. I would have milled him down immediately because I *love* you."

"Oh, Trevor," she said, smiling wistfully, "I knew the night of the Langley Ball when we danced. I don't know why or how. I can't explain it. I felt awful about the theater because Vanessa asked me to keep you occupied for the evening so she could allow Mr. Wilmot to be her escort. I felt, I don't know, almost rebellious, for I knew Vanessa was busily comparing you and him. It was as if I could see her making up lists of the good points of both of you."

He chuckled and gave her a little hug. "We're both very lucky."

"Yes," she said slowly, then backed away a step and looked at him earnestly. "But we can't tell anyone of our attachment yet, and you must continue to act as if you are courting Vanessa."

He frowned but nodded. "I agree. Vanessa is ripe for marriage, but if her heart is not entangled, I don't wish her to fall into Wilmot's grasp. The man is up to something. I can smell it, but for the life of me I don't know what it is."

"Father has been acting very strangely, too. He knows of the incident at the theater but has virtually ordered Vanessa to forgive Mr. Wilmot his transgression."

"That doesn't sound like Richard."

"It's true. He had a long talk with Vanessa about it yesterday."

Trevor leaned against the balcony railing, a thoughtful expression on his face. "I've told Hugh I would start some discreet inquiries into Mr. Wilmot. There have been rumors of a connection with Laffite."

Adleine paled but remained silent.

"Hugh and I have had doubts about Wilmot. Hugh has even volunteered to be cannon fodder to draw Vanessa's attention away from Wilmot."

Adeline smiled. "I don't believe that will be difficult."

Trevor cocked an eyebrow in inquiry.

"I think my sister is more than halfway in love with Mr. Talverton."

Trevor's eyes gleamed. "Oh, really. I feel the same interest in her from Hugh. Perhaps my continued show of interest in Vanessa may be just the trick to get him to appreciate his feelings."

"Why do you say that?"

"Because long ago he and I were both suitors for Julia's hand, and Hugh has never been one to take defeat easily. This time he just might exert himself to be certain he doesn't lose again." He looked down at Adeline tenderly. "Oh, but I would like to declare myself for you."

She smiled back. "Soon, my dearest love, soon," she said, choking slightly.

Trevor pulled her into his arms and kissed her.

"I cannot find her anywhere!" proclaimed Paulette, sweeping into the parlor.

Trevor and Adeline sprang apart.

"Now, where is everyone?" demanded Paulette.

Adeline sighed with relief and looked ruefully at Trevor. "Mr. Danielson and I are out here."

Paulette came to the door. "Oh, is she in *le jardin*?"

"No," Adeline said, moving past her into the room, "we didn't see her out there." She sat down by the quilting frame and bent her head to set some more stitches.

"*Mon Dieu*, where can she be?" Paulette asked.

Trevor shrugged and sauntered over to stand by the fireplace. Just then they heard voices from the hall, and Paulette turned expectantly toward the door.

Amanda Mannion was still chattering to Mr. Wilmot as they came into the room, chastising herself for her runaway tongue. She hastily rang for refreshments, sat down next to Adeline, and waved everyone else to dispose themselves at their leisure.

Paulette sat down, then bobbed up again. "But where is Mr. Talverton?"

"Right here, Miss Chaumonde," he said from the doorway. He crossed the room to her side and sat down.

"It is unfortunate Miss Mannion will not make an appearance," he said to the room at large, seemingly oblivious to the various tensions in the air. "I really am quite interested to know how well the raw beef worked."

CHAPTER
NINE

♥

Late the next afternoon, Hugh Talverton sat slumped in a scarred wooden chair in the barroom at Maspero's Exchange, absently contemplating the sawdust clinging to the toes of his boots. Blessedly, the slave auction was over and the clientele sparse. In another hour, the cavernous room would burgeon with merchants, town tulips, and swash-buckling filibusters. Then there would be a raucous energy throughout the building as the rafters sang with loud voices filled with hilarity and anger, or creaked with the whispered plans for some illegal or noble endeavor. Now it was quiet; the few who sat at scattered tables, far apart from others, talked in hushed tones.

Hugh sat there the better part of an hour, attempting to sort his thoughts into some semblance of logic. His frown deepened, and his eyebrows pulled together creating furrows across his wide forehead. Hugh didn't like the strange maze he walked. It lacked the formal elegance and precision of an English garden maze. There was an unseemliness to its twisted paths, an unseemliness relieved solely by the brightness of Vanessa Mannion. Her father did well to call her his

bright star. There was a vibrancy about her that heightened
Hugh's senses and stirred a heretofore unknown protectiveness
within him.

He grinned sardonically as he realized Shakespeare's *All's
Well That Ends Well* might be the source of Mannion's
phrase. He looked up at the ceiling and silently mouthed the
lines:

> *'Twere all one*
> *That I should love a bright particular star*
> *And think to wed it, he is so far above me...*

He was certain Shakespeare would appreciate the irony,
for those were the words the lowborn Helena said regarding
the highborn young count she loved. In the reality he faced,
Hugh felt those were his words; in these United States, he
was the interloper without position.

The tenor of his own thoughts stunned him. Love? Wed?
What paths were his mind and heart taking? He shook his
head and straightened in the chair, looking about to signal a
waiter for another drink. His maudlin thoughts on the dark
maze tricked his senses. He was not hanging out for a wife.
To entertain himself in New Orleans with a dalliance was
acceptable, but a wife— He shuddered convulsively. She
was Trevor's chosen and they'd deal admirably, he told
himself forcibly as he caught the attention of the waiter and
conveyed his request. It was his duty to aid his friend in
clearing the path, not clutter it as he had with Julia. Years in
the military had taught him well the responsibilities of doing
one's duty.

Now, it was also his duty to untangle the skein of Mr.
Wilmot's plans and save the Mannions if he could, for that
had to be Richard Mannion's reason for confiding in him.
He held that confidence dear, and not readily would he
divulge his knowledge—not even to Trevor. For some reason, he had been given a mandate, a sacred trust, to lead the

family out of the maze. It was a trust he would honor. The question was, how?

He accepted another glass from the hovering waiter and took a long drink. He closed his eyes, bringing his hand up to pinch the bridge of his nose as he thought. His other hand dangled by his side, the glass loosely held in his fingertips. He drew in a deep sighing breath and expelled it slowly.

His best course was still perhaps the one he laid out for Trevor. Mannion felt his best recourse was to prevent a relationship from developing between Vanessa and Wilmot, without arousing Wilmot's suspicion and thereby causing him to force matters to his satisfaction. If he could do this during the time prior to their summer departure, Vanessa would then be removed from Wilmot's grasp for the duration of the summer and by the time she returned, Mannion expected to have the funds to repay the purchased notes.

There was one major aspect of Mannion's plan that was faulty, and Hugh could not believe Richard did not see it. Vanessa now held Mr. Wilmot in fear and disgust. He saw that yesterday in her father's library. Hugh doubted the gentleman could overcome her newfound abhorrence. Vanessa operated within her own very strict sense of personal rules. They could be bent but not broken, and Wilmot quite effectively broke those unwritten rules by his behavior the night of the play. Not for the first time did Hugh wonder what possessed the man to so ill judge an action.

As Hugh did not believe Wilmot was likely to win the fair Vanessa with honeyed words—he doubted the man was even capable of uttering such speech—then his only recourse, if he was truly determined to control Mannion's business, was through blackmail. He could threaten her father and therefore blackmail her into marriage to obtain financial safety for her family. Knowing Vanessa, Hugh would be surprised if she did not succumb to that type of coercion. He doubted, however, that Wilmot would play his hand too soon; a willing bride would be preferable to an unwilling one. In the meantime, he may rethink his strategy and begin plying his charm with a trowel. But he could only do this if he was in Vanessa's orbit, preferably alone. In company, he could not achieve his ends. Consequently, Hugh's first priority was to be constantly upon the Mannion's doorstep.

It may also be wise to continue to adopt his slightly jovial, quick-to-temper-and-hurt demeanor. It will be interesting to see what Wilmot makes of the mien, Hugh thought sardonically since he could not see himself cowering and bowing prostrate before the man—a circumstance Hugh was confident Wilmot was unused to. It would put him slightly off stride.

Hugh's second order of business would be to subtly encourage Trevor to press on his investigations into Wilmot's character and dealings within the town. He needed to know the extent of the man's clout. It may end up being wiser to move Vanessa farther afield than a summer home, and send her to some other part of the United States.

He shifted in his chair and stretched languidly. The level of noise in the barroom was increasing, its haven for thought evaporating. He rolled his head to get the kinks out of his neck and opened his eyes.

"I was beginning to wonder if you'd fallen asleep," said Russell Wilmot sitting in the chair opposite him, his lips curled in a travesty of a smile.

Hugh started, nearly dropping his drink. What was the damned man doing here? Hugh faked a yawn to play for time to gather his wits. "I almost was," he said ruefully, his agile mind wondering what the man's game was, and how long he'd sat opposite him. He didn't enjoy surprises like that. They set his teeth on edge. What was damnable was the fact he'd not heard the man approach. He'd not been out of the service a year and already his instincts were failing him. Time was when he slept so lightly he heard the slightest rustle of fabric, footfall, or expelled breath and leapt to his feet.

He smiled congenially at Wilmot, though inwardly his thoughts were hardly friendly. All his senses were janglingly alive, as if to belatedly make up for the lapse that had led him to be surprised at Wilmot's appearance. The man's expression was feral as he sat before him, idly swinging his leg. His black clothes were austere, but expensively made, and the diamond winking at him from the folds of his cravat was no cheap bauble. He had a powerful frame, his hands showing a roughness that proved the man was no stranger to hard work. Hugh's nose twitched slightly as a strange, sweet scent wafted his way. He sniffed, thought for a moment, then almost laughed, for the heavy rose scent emanated from Wilmot's clothes. Obviously the man had not spent his entire afternoon locked up in an office perusing account books. He idly wondered about the woman who pressed herself up so close against him that her scent lingered. A mistress, more like. It might be amusing to turn Trevor's investigation in that direction. Some mistresses could prove distressingly possessive and vindictive.

Hugh sat straighter in his chair, raised his port glass, and silently offered a salute in Wilmot's direction. The man's eyebrows twitched in dubious disbelief of Hugh's action, yet acknowledged the salute with his own, and a half smile ghosting his lips.

Wilmot pulled a thick cigar out of his coat pocket and arrogantly waved the passing waiter to supply flint and tinder. The man rushed to obey. Hugh's eyes narrowed. He realized Wilmot was well known at Maspero's. He wondered if he came here to conduct his legal business, or if he was—as Trevor suggested—one of the filibusters who gathered to plot revolutions.

Wilmot clamped his teeth around the cigar and leaned back in his chair. "So, tell me, Mr. Talverton, what do you think of New Orleans?'' he queried aggressively, without preamble.

Curious as to the man's purpose, Hugh responded easily. ''It is a fascinating city, sir, unlike any I have ever encountered.''

Wilmot barked a short laugh. ''From what I have seen, Europe pales in comparison, my friend.''

''You're a traveler?''

''Only by necessity. I have not the time for frivolous entertainment.''

''Ah, yes, hard work and all that,'' Hugh said airily, aping the manner of some of the more flighty aristocrats of his acquaintance. ''Trevor tells me you have made quite a successful business for yourself here.''

Wilmot's brow furrowed at Hugh's tone, yet he could not detect a trace of malice. ''I have been fortunate.''

''Indeed,'' murmured Hugh, touching his fingertips together in a steeple as he silently regarded the man.

''How long do you intend to remain in our city?'' Wilmot inquired.

''Probably a few weeks more, at least until society retires to the country to avoid the contagion I understand is yours every year.'' He shuddered deliberately, then warned himself against overplaying his hand when he saw Wilmot's eyebrows twitch again. ''I shall return come harvest, however.''

''You have plans?'' An ash from his cigar fell to the table. Wilmot absently brushed it to the floor.

Hugh shrugged. ''None formally. Unlike you, I think I shall travel for entertainment, see a bit of this country of yours. I've been thinking of heading up the Mississippi on one of those new riverboats and stopping at St. Louis.'' He paused for a moment, the image of the congenial London rattle. ''You certainly can tell the French influence in this area, can't you, with names like New Orleans, Baton Rouge, St. Louis. Your government made quite a deal when it purchased this land." He smiled in his most charming fashion and took a drink.

"Yes, that rankled with you British."

Hugh scratched the side of his head. "I'm not up on the political ramifications of all that. Think I'll reserve judgment till I see this land of yours. I admit I'm interested in this peltry trade. Beaver fur is dear in England."

"Do you care to try your hand as a trader or trapper?"

Hugh looked aghast. "Mc? Neither, sir. But I don't rule out buying. Might be able to make a tidy little sum on the side, other than the cotton."

"With your interest, I'm surprised you don't go upriver now. Mannion knows your requirements, so there can't be much for you here until fall."

This was the nub of the matter. Wilmot wanted him away from the Mannions. Was he also considered a threat? "True enough," he answered easily, "but I'm staying on to bear Trevor company. It's been eight years since we last spent some time together. We've a lot of catching up to do."

"Ah, yes, the balls, the gossip, the women—"

Suddenly Hugh realized he played his role so well that Mr. Wilmot really had no notion he was other than a rackety London beau. Nonetheless, Hugh ventured Wilmot still did not know how to play him in the scheme he was hatching. He wagered he was still the wild card, and that made Mr. Wilmot a trifle nervous. Good. A nervous man makes mistakes.

Hugh nodded absently to Wilmot's observation, then glanced around the room, as if suddenly aware of it. "Getting to be a sad crush in here, isn't it?" he asked as a gentleman squeezed between his chair and the one behind.

"Maspero's is a gentleman's resort," responded Wilmot as suavely as his gravelly voice permitted.

Hugh nodded again, tossed off his drink, and dropped some coins on the table. "If you'll excuse me, Mr. Wilmot,

I've promised to meet Trevor near the marketplace. He promised to introduce me to another facet of New Orleans society.''

"Oh? And what might that be, the camp houses on Rampart Street or the stews of Girod?''

"Haven't heard of those yet. I'll have to ask Trevor," Hugh lied.

"Where's your spirit of adventure? Investigate them on your own. It will broaden your education.''

I'm sure it would, thought Hugh savagely. But he was not a man to be so naive, though he was amused at Wilmot's clumsy attempt to trick him into endangering his own life in that rough part of town, haven of the keelboat men. His smile broadened, though his eyes narrowed slightly. ''Mayhap I will," he returned lightly. ''Right now, Trevor's to lead me on your equivalent of a stroll in Hyde Park.''

"Ah, yes, Chemin des Tchoupitoulas.''

"That's it.''

"Perhaps I shall see you there later.''

"Delighted, and thank you for the company.''

"Anytime, Mr. Talverton, anytime.''

"Right," mused Hugh as he turned to leave. It took all his considerable presence of mind to stop from turning around, or running for the door in fear of a knife thrown in his back.

Hugh followed the Rue de St. Louis southeast to Chemin des Tchoupitoulas, or King's Road as it was commonly known. Across the way was the levee dotted with wood benches beneath graceful willow trees. Beyond lay the port where beautiful tall-masted sailing ships cast long shadows across squat ugly keelboats docked nearby. The wharf was quieter now than during the prime of the day, when people of seemingly all nationalities scurried about, shouting, as they directed business at the docks, handling such commodities as hemp, cotton, coal, food, tobacco, lead, and pelts.

Activity on the levee also assumed a slower pace, its face changing as the day changed. Elegant gentlemen, couples, and families strolled the levee, or sat beneath the willow trees. A few Negro women, with baskets on their heads, still wound their way through the people, offering refreshments and flowers, but on the whole, the mercantile activity of the day might only have been some far-away dream.

Hugh looked down the path, searching for Trevor's lithe figure. He spotted him a block away, standing near one of the willows, talking to someone seated on a bench. He sauntered toward them, a broad smile lightening his features when he realized his friend's companion was a veiled woman in an elegant apricot-colored walking dress trimmed with blond lace. He'd wager the woman was Vanessa, still hiding the small, mottled discoloration on her face. She was lucky, actually, that the bruise was so slight—though he doubted she would have believed it a good fortune at all.

She looked up as he drew near, a slight tension in the set of her shoulders. Hugh wished he could see her face to read the feelings registered there.

"Miss Mannion," he said, briefly clasping her hand in both of his, "it is delightful to see you are no longer prone to hiding."

The laughing lilt to his voice told Vanessa he was thinking of her sojourn under her father's desk, not the polite excuse given to Wilmot for her absence. A flare of red stained her cheeks, and she was grateful for the face-obscuring veil. It was merely another example of his self-centered arrogance that he could take enjoyment from another's discomfort, she told herself petulantly. Then she relented, realizing she was not being fair. Twice now he had saved her from embarrassment at the hands of Mr. Wilmot. All he asked in return was that she laugh with him in the aftermath. It was quite petty of her not to, she decided, and the situation truly had been humorous. She and her family had laughed over it long after the gentlemen had left.

"Hiding has its own rewards, Mr. Talverton, though it sometimes makes for strange alliances," she said archly, delighting in his start of surprise followed by a hearty rich laugh.

"Something tells me I am missing the joke," Trevor complained good-naturedly.

"It was at my expense, my friend, so vanity prohibits me from explanation," Hugh said ruefully. He smiled down at Vanessa. "I am pleased to see your good humor restored, especially as I was the cause of your unfortunate accident that has heretofore robbed us of your charming company."

"Very prettily said," Vanessa responded dryly, cocking her head to the side. "I shall have to take care that you don't turn my head by your flattery."

"Whoa! I should say, Hugh, she has put you decidedly in your place," Trevor said, laughing.

Hugh shrugged laconically. "It is not a position to which I am unaccustomed," he said with a smile. "One can only account oneself fortunate when it is done by as beautiful and gracious a lady as Miss Mannion."

Vanessa started to answer, but Trevor interrupted. "Be done, Miss Mannion. I warn you, you shall only encourage him to become more outrageous. Any more and he will be near to waxing poetical."

"Oh? Well, it might be an improvement," she said teasingly.

Trevor groaned theatrically. "Not when it is *his* poetry. He sounds as melodious as a cawing crow."

"Now, Trevor," admonished Hugh, "I must protest. I fear you're confusing my singing with my poetry."

"No I'm not. They're both awful," he assured Vanessa, "and something to be avoided ere he has you running for the alligator swamps."

"Why, Mr. Danielson, I don't believe I've ever heard you so ardent," Vanessa said, laughing freely.

"That's because you've never heard his bleating. I have."

"Bleating!" protested Hugh.

"Bleating," affirmed his friend grimly, a pugnacious expression on his face.

Hugh looked at him silently for a moment, then burst out laughing, clapping Trevor on the back as he did so. "You have a decidedly unfortunate memory, my friend."

"Unfortunate for you, maybe, not for Miss Mannion and me. I would call it provident."

Vanessa laughed. "I am surprised you two have not seen each other in so many years, you act so close. Why the long absence?"

Hugh's face wore a melancholy smile. "He married the woman I thought I loved."

"Oh," she responded weakly.

"And it was the happiest day of my life when I realized she preferred me to him," Trevor interjected cheerfully.

Vanessa looked down at her hands resting in her lap, feeling awkward and at a loss for what to say. It pained her to think Mr. Talverton's life had been blighted by his friend. She remembered Julia Danielson. She had been an elegant and charming woman, full of warmth and sincerity. She fidgeted on her seat and abruptly stood up.

"Adeline and Paulette should be here shortly. They went for a short stroll toward the marketplace." She turned away from the gentlemen, straining on tiptoe to see down the path. "Oh, look, there they are now, and Charles is with them!" She hopped up and down, waving broadly at them to catch their attention, caring little how undignified she looked.

Hugh touched her arm to halt her antics, wondering what had made her so suddenly skittish. "They see you. Be careful else you fall and bruise another portion of your anatomy."

"Mr. Talverton!" she said, scandalized, a hot blush flooding her face.

Hugh raised his eyebrows when he noted a telltale sliver

of red below the edge of the veil and above the blond lace at
her throat. "You have a vivid imagination," he drawled,
causing her to blush anew.

The man was infuriating, Vanessa fumed, caught between
embarrassment and chagrin. Just when she was beginning to
like him or feel some sympathy toward him, he invariably
reminded her he was totally devoid of gentility—whatever
his birth!

"Monsieur Talverton!" cried Paulette, releasing her brother's arm and skipping toward them "*Je suis—*"

"Paulette," warned her brother ominously.

She looked back at him and wrinkled her nose distastefully
before turning back to Hugh. "I am so happy to see you,
for you will never guess what has transpired. Charles,
Charles, tell him!" she said excitedly, grabbing her brother
by the arm and urging him forward.

Charles rolled his eyes in dismay at his sister's hoydenish
behavior, but he could not totally repress a smile. "Don't
you mean *ask him* rather than *tell him*?" he inquired.

"Oh, Charles, don't be a gudgeon," Paulette said petulantly.
She looked up at Hugh. "Louisa is planning a party."

"I'm very pleased for her, but who is Louisa?" Hugh
asked caustically.

"My wife," said Charles.

"My sister," said Vanessa simultaneously

"My apologies, I did not mean to sound so abrupt."

Charles laughed. "It is Paulette's fault. She would always
start a story from the wrong end. My wife misses the New
Orleans social life, so she is planning a small soiree for this
weekend. She has invited some of the people from neighboring estates to ours in the country, and has asked me to
extend a few invitations in the city. She would be honored if
you and Trevor could attend."

"Well, I—"

"Oh, you will say yes, won't you? It will be *très
amusant*! We can all go down Saturday morning and return

Sunday afternoon. It cannot possibly interfere with your business," said Paulette.

"Paulette," said Vanessa, "Mr. Traverton may have other plans."

"Surely you do not," exclaimed Paulette.

Hugh laughed and looked over at Trevor, who only smiled and shrugged.

"All right," he relented. "I should like to visit a Louisiana country estate."

Paulette clapped her hands. *"Merveilleux!"* she squealed.

Vanessa kept quiet, but privately she was pleased with the proposed weekend and the knowledge that Mr. Talverton would join them. She was confident that with his wry sense of humor, he would help enliven the affair.

"Trevor," Charles said, "Louisa asks that you bring the children, too."

"Please do, Mr. Danielson," said Adeline, laying a gentle hand on his arm and smiling warmly up at him. "I should love to see them again, and I am sure they would love the outing."

He patted her hand, and smiled intently at her, but no one noticed, for Mary Langley bustled up to the group claiming their attention with her chatter, wild gestures, and twinkling brown eyes.

"Vanessa, oh Vanessa!" said Mary, after all the formal greetings were exchanged. She crossed to her side and patted her arm. "I just saw your parents down the way, and your mother told me of your unfortunate accident. I'm glad to see you're getting about, dear. That veil is charming. You'll probably start a new fashion for strolling in the park!" She turned toward Hugh standing next to her. "Though the Mannions did not go about in society much before Louisa met this rascal, Charles here," she said, throwing him a teasing look, "they were always envied and copied for their sense of style. Now, la! There are many who wish they still were hermits in that charming home of theirs."

Vanessa laughed. "You are too kind, Mrs. Langley."

"Stuff and nonsense. I'm not kind, I talk too much to be kind. I do like your veil, though. Only, don't hide behind it too long; I like your pretty face better." She patted her arm again, then turned to address Adeline.

"I agree with her," Hugh murmured for her hearing only.

"I beg your pardon?" Vanessa said, feigning incomprehension. Hugh was not fooled; he saw the telltale blush on her neck. He grinned.

Paulette squealed again, and Vanessa looked toward her with relief. Mr. Talverton caused the strangest feelings to arise within her, feelings she didn't want to analyze or investigate.

"There is Monsieur Wilmot. Did you not say, Charles, that he is also to be invited?" Paulette enthused.

"Yes. Where is he?"

"Down there, see?" She pointed toward the Rue de St. Louis. "He was just talking to a keelboat man, I think. Yes, see, as he walks away, he has a red turkey feather in his cap."

"Wilmot appears to be headed in our direction. Good," said Charles.

"And there's Mr. and Mrs. Smythe," rattled on Mary Langley. "Excuse me, I must go say hello and see if I can find out when his new steamboat will be in. I don't know what got into me—probably just grandmotherly affection— but I promised my grandson a tour." Trotting off, she lifted her hand in a little wave of farewell.

Vanessa, her shoulders slumping slightly, scarcely noticed her departure. She was not prepared to greet Mr. Wilmot. Hugh placed a supporting hand under her elbow and leaned toward her as Charles hailed the man and extended him the same invitation.

"Do not fret, Miss Mannion. I will see to it that the man has no opportunity to embarrass you further," he whispered hastily before Paulette claimed his attention.

Vanessa looked at him in blank surprise, but he did not notice because of her veil. She recovered in time to hear Mr. Wilmot smoothly agree to join them, then turn to look at her with an intense, unfathomable expression in his dark, considering eyes.

CHAPTER
TEN
♥

Saturday morning dawned clear and rain-washed fresh. The Friday night rain—which it was feared would leave the roads a sloppy, muddy morass—lasted only long enough to settle the dry dust and dampen the earth. The very air seemed to sparkle, and the light breezes were redolent with the scent of fruit and flowers from heavily laden trees, bushes, and plants along the Bayou Road.

Vanessa Mannion inhaled deeply and smiled, a wide smile that set her eyes twinkling, brightening her face. She laughed delightedly as she rode her high-stepping chestnut mare between Hugh Talverton and Russell Wilmot. Both gentlemen looked at her in silent inquiry, but she only laughed again and shook her head. She didn't think she could share her heady feeling of exuberance at the day. Not even Mr. Wilmot's presence could dampen her spirits, though in truth, this day he was the epitome of gentlemanly regard. She felt gloriously alive and therefore generous with her forgiveness.

The disfiguring bruise, which she had used to such good advantage all week, was now no more than a slight dark spot high on her cheek, almost hidden in the shadow cast by the rakish tilt of her blue riding hat with its gray plumes curling down the side of her face. She was elegantly attired in a pearl-gray cloth riding habit, ornamented and frogged with blue velvet. Though her countenance was not beautiful to a critical objective eye, her vivacity of manner, her delight in the world around her, gave her an aura of comeliness to rival any studied image of female pulchritude.

Hugh Talverton was enchanted with her sprightly manner; her aspect of prim propriety left farther and farther behind in the city with each passing mile. This was a part of Vanessa he knew was always lurking behind her formal mein. He'd love to see her in London. More likely she'd take the city by storm and turn society on its ear, if she allowed herself to follow her natural inclinations. He was amazed that Mannion had been able to keep her heart-whole and retired from society for so long.

He glanced over at Wilmot, nodding to that gentleman, an artificial social smile on his face. Hugh admitted Wilmot was on excellent behavior this morning. He was neither demanding Miss Mannion's attention, nor scowling when she turned to speak to him. Wilmot was suspiciously mellow, an odd aspect for a man of his dark temperament.

Hugh was thankful Paulette did not ride well, forcing her to journey to the Chaumonde estate in the carriage with Mr. and Mrs. Mannion and Adeline. Trevor had left the night before for his country home to organize the children, Alex and Mary, and their governess for the weekend jaunt. Hugh was curious to meet Julia's children and wondered if either bore her tranquil beauty.

Hugh trotted contentedly beside Vanessa, his quick eyes darting all about him as he studied the landscape of the area. It was an exotic land, full of tall cypress trees above stygian swamps, wide-spreading oak trees heavy with Spanish moss, pomegranates, bananas, and fig trees, hedges of Spanish dagger, glossy bushes of camellias, crepe myrtle, and olean-ders. Set back from the road, among lush settings, stood pristine white mansions with columns, piazzas, and covered galleries. In the fields they rode past, the glistening sweaty bodies of the slaves shone in the clear light of the morning sun. Their dark brown bodies were in marked contrast to the bright bits of clothing they wore, from the turbans twisted around the women's heads to the loose shifts and the baggy trousers that clothed their nether regions.

Hugh shook his head as he absorbed it all. New Orleans was truly a fascinating city, so fresh and alive—a decidedly far cry from the jaded and stifled atmosphere of London. But England was home, and in all his travels, regardless of where the military sent him, he was always thankful to leave and return to England. This was the first time he had ever returned to a battlefield area, or even wanted to.

He thought about that miserable time of the Battle of New Orleans as he looked with awed eyes at his surroundings. Everything seemed so different now from then. He remembered the sheeting rain during the day, the thick mud cleaving to the dead and dying, and that cold, dead-of-night, nine-mile retreat through a quagmire path. His had been one of the last companies to quit the battleground area. For them, the journey was a nightmare, for almost all trace of a path had disappeared. By then the mud, tramped on by hundreds, was knee- and thigh-deep. With a shudder, Hugh remembered witnessing one unfortunate wretch sink into the liquid muck until he disappeared from sight.

It was curious, when he thought about it, that he should desire to return to the scene of an ignominious defeat, but it was the very reason England strove for New Orleans; the talk of those he met who knew the city, the sight of the fabulous plantations, they had all pulled upon him to journey back to see the city in her natural state, far away from the threat of war and death. He had been well rewarded by his decision. The cotton he was to purchase would feed the new mill to capacity and earn him a handsome profit. The people he met, and the wonders he saw, would give him pleasant memories to last a lifetime—memories far different from those garnered through seven years of military service. And now, he thought—watching Vanessa guide her horse past a cart loaded with produce for the marketplace and exchange a pleasant word with its driver—if he could deliver the Mannions out of the dark maze of Mr. Wilmot's making, and happily settle Vanessa and Trevor, he would account himself well satisfied with his New Orleans venture.

His reverie had caused him to fall behind his companions. With a start, he realized Wilmot was drawing near to Vanessa for private conversation, and he remembered his promise to her that he would prevent this occurrence. Pressing his heels into his horse's flanks, he encouraged the bay gelding to catch up with them.

"Miss Mannion, surely your father has told you of my desire for private conversation," Wilmot said softly, his grating voice like pebbles underfoot.

Vanessa swung her head toward him, a polite smile on her lips. "Yes, Mr. Wilmot, he has informed me of that request." Her voice was low and pleasing, but distinctly neutral.

His horse sidled closer and Vanessa's fingers clenched reflexively tighter on her reins, causing her mare to dance skittishly. She quickly brought the animal under control, once again establishing distance with Mr. Wilmot.

A brief frown of annoyance crossed his lips, but it was immediately replaced with a tight smile as if he were amused by the movements of her mount. He rode closer again. He started to lean down to grasp her bridle but a sidelong glance at her visage forestalled him and he rocked back in his saddle.

Vanessa's breath came out swiftly when he moved his hand back. If he had touched the rein, she was afraid she would have reacted spontaneously by laying her crop along his broad shoulders. She was more skittish than the mare at his presence, and she was sure it was part of her nervousness, transmitted to her horse, that caused the animal to dance away.

She had always detected a certain rough-and-tumble masculine power in Mr. Wilmot. It was part of his attraction
with the ladies. This power emitted an aura of danger and
excitement, and it had led her and other women to dream of
harnessing that power for themselves alone. The truth was
he was not a man to consider a woman's gentler nature, nor
allow his own dark nature to be brightened by a woman.
Vanessa feared any woman marrying him would descend
into his darkness rather than pull him to the light.

The amusement he'd had at her feeble struggles to pull
her hand free from his taught her much about him—and
power. Her knowledge was refined when he came to confess
his misdeed to her parent and somehow persuade her father
to let him continue in his courtship. The true cap to her
understanding came, however, when he returned to her
house on Wednesday, after being told she was indisposed,
and then demanded to see her. The mere thought of his
audacity shook her to the soles of her calfskin riding boots.
The man frightened her, and she wished she knew how to
turn his attentions elsewhere; nonetheless, she was determined to hide her fear, with brash bravado if necessary.

The sound of pounding hooves at her left drew her attention
from Mr. Wilmot. With sudden, staggering relief, she saw Mr.
Talverton rein in beside her and she smiled brightly at him, her
eyes glittering with an unnatural feverish light.

"Hello! I'm sorry, I'm afraid my mind was wandering as
I observed the countryside," he confided ingeniously while
his intelligent eyes noted her heightened color and shimmering
nervousness. He slid a glance in Wilmot's direction and
found the gentleman regarding him with a disquieting glint
in his eye. Hugh decided it was time for more of the sad
rattle guise.

"By Jove, but this is a magnificent ride. Wouldn't want
to be cooped up in a carriage if I knew all this was about,"
he said, making a grand sweeping gesture with his arm. He

rested his hand on his thigh and looked past Vanessa over to Wilmot. "Do you also have a country place?"

"No," Wilmot responded shortly, then seeing Vanessa's arched eyebrow he relented, his voice nearly a growl: "My business precludes too much time away from the city, but I have plans for a mansion on the other side of Canal Street."

"I have heard, though I can't recall where, that many prominent Americans are moving in that direction," he returned conversationally.

"Excuse me, gentlemen," interrupted Vanessa, "but if you're going to converse, please allow me to get out of your way." She spurred her horse forward before the last words were out of her mouth, then reined back to settle on the far side of Hugh Talverton.

"Excellent idea, thank you!" said Hugh, before turning back to Wilmot. He was pleased with Vanessa's quick thinking, and wondered if she was even aware of his hand in manipulating the situation. His lips twitched and his eyelids drooped, nearly covering his eyes, but he was obliged to keep his expression one of keen interest directed toward Mr. Wilmot. Now with that gentleman a veritable captive audience by his side, Hugh began a campaign of small talk as countermeasures to Wilmot's claiming Vanessa's attention. Wilmot fidgeted restlessly for a few moments; however, he did not know how to break free from Hugh's steady dialogue politely. His answers became shorter and shorter, but Hugh never seemed to notice. His equanimity unruffled, he continued to smile benignly. Wilmot finally reconciled himself to foregoing a private conversation, when both he and Talverton were hailed by Vanessa.

"We're here, gentlemen," she said breezily, rising up in her saddle and pointing.

Hugh turned his head to follow the path of the finger and saw one of the most beautiful homes he had ever seen.

"My sisters' raised cottage," stated Vanessa whimsically.

"Cottage?" Hugh asked.

"Yes, cottage," she said, laughing at his puzzled expression. "Houses built raised off the ground to deter unwelcome visits from snakes and other animals are called raised cottages, regardless of size."

He studied the structure. It did appear to be raised, probably some six feet from the ground. It was a massive, square building with a hipped roof overhanging the house and supported by turned wood columns. Large dormers jutted from the roof on all sides and a curious little cupola with wrought-iron railings surmounted the roof. The wide, covered gallery, created by the overhanging roof, ran completely around the house and was also fronted by wrought-iron railings. The steep steps leading up to the gallery were edged with wrought iron as well. Two wide windows stood on either side of the massive entrance to the house with its elaborate Georgian-style moldings framing the doorway.

Four young men ran from the side of the house to take the horses and assist those in the carriage just now coming up the drive. The front door opened and a willowy figure in white dimity picked up her skirts and ran down the steps, mindless of the flash of slender calf she displayed.

"Louisa!" called Vanessa in obvious delight. She kicked free of her stirrups and, gathering her skirts about her, slid off her horse before either of the gentlemen with her could move to assist.

Smiling at the two women similar in height and facial features, Hugh ruefully acknowledged Vanessa's precipitous action of dismounting unattended probably saved them all from an embarrassing confrontation. He handed the reins of his horse to one of the young men and stood off to the side as the carriage drew up and the Mannion family descended. The family was quickly engulfed in hugs and kisses, oblivious to Mr. Wilmot and himself. Curious to see how Mr. Wilmot accepted this occurrence, Hugh glanced in his direction. The man stood leaning on the step railing, his expression one of boredom. Hugh grinned, realizing an opportunity to further the play and Wilmot's discomfort. Sauntering over to him, he gave him a hearty clap on the back.

"Reminds me of my family—it almost makes me homesick. If a member has not been seen in a while, it always was family first and hang the guests," he said chuckling as they watched the Mannions. "How about your family, Wilmot?"

Wilmot sneered slightly at Hugh but could not refuse to answer under Hugh's steady regard. "We're not that close," he said simply, pushing away from the railings as the Mannions appeared to be recollecting their surroundings and about to approach the house.

Hugh nodded, well satisfied with what he'd observed. During the ride to the Chaumonde estate, he wouldn't have been surprised if Wilmot had snubbed him. The fact that he didn't might have been because of Vanessa's presence; now he knew differently. Wilmot lacked the ability to deliver a direct cut. A man who could not do so was a man who feared one being turned in his direction. Interesting, Hugh mused, as the family came up beside him.

"Louisa!" cried Paulette excitedly, dancing up beside him and taking his arm. "This is Monsieur Talverton. He is an aristocrat from England," she confided artlessly.

Hearty male laughter drew their attention to the steps. At the top stood Charles Chaumonde, his arms across his chest, laughing at his sister. Trevor Danielson stood at his side.

"Trust Paulette to cut to the heart of the matter to where her interest lies," said her brother as he descended the steps.

Paulette pouted at him, which only caused Charles to laugh more. Coming up before her, he chucked her under the chin.

"You lack tact, my little sister. You should try for more of Vanessa's sangfroid."

His sally drew smiles from all and a light blush to Vanessa's cheeks, but she rallied admirably.

"And you, dear brother, could do well to follow your own advice," she said primly.

He shrugged expansively, then placed a chaste salute upon her cheek. "Ah, but I, little one, am a man," he responded enigmatically before turning to shake hands with Hugh Talverton and Russell Wilmot while his wife sputtered indignantly.

Louisa shook her head in vexation, the deep red of her hair catching the morning sun. "Come," she said, gesturing toward the house, "let's go inside before he becomes too outrageous." The arch look she cast her husband was full of exasperated love.

She led them into a large foyer with a magnificent freestanding curved staircase flanked by two servant women dressed primly in dove-colored dresses with starched white aprons. "Mr. Talverton, Mr. Wilmot, Ruth will show you to your rooms while Bessie and I lead my family to theirs. When you have freshened up, we will be serving a light repast in the dining room, and we can talk much more comfortably then. Ruth will show you the way when you are ready," she said, smiling graciously. Behind her came the sound of the men taking the trunks and portmanteaux from the carriage.

"We'll await you in the parlor," Charles said, leading Trevor away.

Vanessa burst out laughing after Mr. Wilmot and Mr. Talverton disappeared upstairs. "Gracious, Louisa, you play the grand lady of the manor so elegantly!"

"One has to if one is going to socialize with and be accepted by the Creoles," she conceded wryly.

"*Mais, naturellement*," said Paulette, her expression perplexed that Louisa should even need to make such a comment. "How else would it be?"

"Thus is the Creole conceit," murmured Louisa, exchanging glances with her mother and sisters.

"Where is *Tante* Teresa?" asked Paulette.

Louisa laughed. "She follows Celeste's example—she's napping."

"Is she still as big as a house?" Paulette demanded, laughing.

"Worse!" Louisa replied in horrified tones, causing all of them to laugh.

Richard Mannion harrumphed. "Enough nattering. What rooms are you going to put us in this time?"

"The same as last time," his eldest daughter responded tranquilly.

He grunted acknowledgment and started up the stairs, followed by the women still talking. On the landing Amanda Mannion stopped and laid her hand on Louisa's arm.

"Were you able to arrange matters for this evening satisfactorily?" she asked softly.

Vanessa, who was a step ahead, faltered, then proceeded slowly, straining to hear her sister's response.

"Definitely," she said, and there was a gleeful note to her voice. "And if I know our players right, it shall work out admirably."

Amanda smiled and nodded.

"Coming, Mrs. Mannion?" Mr. Mannion called back as he stood at the entrance to their room.

"Yes, of course, dear. Louisa and I were merely discussing seeing little Celeste after luncheon."

Vanessa's jaw dropped slightly, but she closed it firmly as she looked between her mother and her sister. She knew perfectly well they were not discussing the baby, and she was very curious to know just what they were discussing. Her mind whirling, she dazedly followed Adeline and Paulette into the room they would be sharing.

"I'm impressed," Hugh Talverton told Charles Chaumonde later that day as the gentlemen rested their horses under the shade of a large oak tree.

Charles leaned back on his saddle cantle and smiled

contentedly. "I am a very fortunate man, sir," he admitted. He turned to Richard Mannion. "And I account myself the most fortunate to have married Louisa."

Richard grunted and scratched the side of his nose. "The gal is fortunate herself," he said self-consciously.

Charles cocked an eye at Trevor, Russell, and Hugh. "Any other man who weds a Mannion will find himself likewise blessed."

Hugh laughed. "You talk like a marriage broker."

Unabashed, Charles nodded. "Can I help it? These sisters are very special to me. Ah, but with my own sister, I have a problem. That one is a hoyden and needs a strong hand."

Trevor grinned at Hugh, but he ignored him and pointed to the field before him. "Is all your acreage planted in indigo?"

"Mostly, to my father-in-law's everlasting dismay," he said, casting a teasing look his way. "But I am thinking of switching over to sugarcane. Monsieur Baligny, my neighbor, and I are discussing the merits of sharing the cost of a sugar mill and refining our own sugar and that of other small plantation owners as well. There is talk in the government circles of imposing a three-penny tariff on imported sugar to boost local production and profit. I think it will pass; consequently, this would be a good opportunity for us."

Behind him he heard Richard Mannion grumbling under his breath. Charles laughed. "Now, Richard, don't take offense. If everyone grew cotton, we'd flood the market and ruin the land. Besides, you know it is much too wet here and someone has to grow these other crops, or their scarcity would make their price too dear."

Hugh looked out across the well-ordered fields and shook his head. "I'm still amazed. You are a lawyer and a plantation owner. What other trades are you involved with?"

"I've part ownership in a sailing vessel and am heavily involved with banking," he said as he gently urged his horse out from under the shade of the tree and led the party back to the house.

Trevor laughed at Hugh's slightly bemused expression. "Not at all like England, is it?"

Hugh shook his head as he followed the others. "No," he said slowly, "but I admit I find myself a trifle envious," he said as he kicked his horse into a loping canter, "for here it is the *gentleman's* trade."

Trevor rode easily beside him. "You should consider staying here. As you said to me last Saturday, there are fortunes to be made."

He shook his head regretfully. "No, my home is in England." Then he wondered why he said that, for he'd spent little time there since 1808. Was it force of habit that called him home, or desire? He didn't seem to know anymore.

As they approached the stables, they spied Adeline and Vanessa running and playing a form of tag with two small children, while on the gallery surrounding the house sat Louisa, Amanda, and a rotund Teresa Rouchardier, Charles's and Paulette's aunt. Amanda was cradling a white-swathed form in her arms.

Trevor reined in and sat a moment on his horse as he watched Adeline with his children, a loving smile hovering on his lips. Hugh and Russell Wilmot noted his expression and looked in the same direction to see Vanessa laughingly pretend to miss a towheaded little girl she was supposed to tag.

Vanessa looked up to see the men dismounting, dismayed to feel her heart beating faster and a faint flush creep up her neck. She could not forestall it. She watched Trevor and Hugh approach, followed by her father, Charles, and Mr. Wilmot, and her breath clogged in her throat. In wonder she realized she had never really looked at Mr. Talverton before, so ready was she to condemn his every action. Now her breath was swept away. He was so handsome with the sun glinting off his sandy blond hair and the faint afternoon breeze lifting and gently ruffling its golden waves. His shoulders were broad and his legs showed well-defined muscles through the tight fit of his buckskin breeches, yet still he moved with a fluid, catlike grace. Suddenly that strange tingling she felt before in his presence rippled through her, and she felt light-headed. To hide her confusion, she pulled Trevor's daughter, Mary, into her arms and sank down on to the green sward. She looked down at the little girl until her cheeks cooled and the tingling subsided.

Unaccountably, Hugh felt his heart sink to the soles of his feet when he saw the look Vanessa gave Trevor. He wanted them to be together, he told himself savagely. But a small voice asked him if that was true, why did he feel an aching emptiness at the thought? Then he realized if he saw that ardent exchange, Wilmot did also. He looked back to see Wilmot scowling darkly, a dangerous gleam in his narrowed eyes that were pinned on Trevor's back. Hugh took a deep breath. Tonight, he would have to claim Miss Mannion's attention as best he could lest Trevor and Wilmot come to blows.

"I had to see you, to talk to you. This farce is becoming extremely painful."

Adeline turned with a start, then smiled. She laid her basket down at the edge of her sister's flowerbeds and extended her hands toward Trevor. "I, too, am finding it grievously difficult," she admitted softly, her fingers curling into his.

He lifted one hand and then the other to kiss, faintly caressing her knuckles with his thumbs.

She blushed, then gently pulled her hands free. "We mustn't be seen in this way," she murmured, distressed.

"Hush, love." He dropped her hands. "I am being selfish and unfair. I should know better and desist from plaguing you."

Her head flew up. "Oh, you are not plaguing me!" she assured him, then blushed anew and smiled shyly.

He smiled fondly at her. "Yes, I am, but happy am I to hear you so ardently tell me nay. Well, for propriety and prying eyes, may I assist you in collecting flowers?" he suggested, picking up her basket.

She nodded, and they began to walk the garden paths, stopping occasionally as Adeline selected a bloom.

"By the length of stem you are cutting, I would gather you are not collecting for your flower art," Trevor finally said, breaking the strained silence between them.

"No, you are correct. I'm collecting flowers for vases. I think a room looks so much prettier with flowers around, and by my sister's own admission, she is no dab hand at it." She laughed slightly. "When I offered to create the bouquets for the parlor and hall, she agreed with unsurprising alacrity."

"When we are wed, I vow our gardens will rival any in the state," he said sincerely.

She smiled shyly again. "I liked the sound of that."

"What, my love?"

She stopped and stood in front of him. "Our," she answered, her eyes sparkling.

"Oh, Adeline," Trevor said, closing his eyes tightly, then opening them and sighing deeply. "You make me want to pick you up in my arms and carry you away."

She skipped away from him. "Remember where we are," she said teasingly. Then she sobered. "We must discuss this evening. I have been watching Mr. Wilmot very closely. He does not notice me for he holds me to be a drab slip of a woman."

"The man is blind."

Adeline smiled and nodded her head in thanks but went on: "His eyes follow Vanessa everywhere, and he scowls deeply when any man talks to her—even Charles! He desires private conversation with Vanessa, but so far he has been thwarted by you and Hugh. He is growing increasingly restive. Perhaps we should allow him his time with her.''

Trevor's dark sable brows pulled together across the bridge of his nose as he thought. ''I don't know. Hugh and I had an opportunity to talk earlier. He seems to feel Vanessa is afraid to be alone with Wilmot.''

''Vanessa, afraid? I find that difficult to believe of my sister.''

''Well, perhaps afraid is the wrong word, but she definitely is uncomfortable.''

Adeline nodded. ''I would venture to say that if she is afraid, she is afraid he will declare himself and demand an answer from her. She is well aware of Father's needs for his warehousing this year and would be loath to be the cause of any problems for him.''

Trevor agreed. ''I get the feeling there is more to it than that, but what I cannot say. I have started some discreet investigations into Wilmot's activities, and I hope to have some information on Monday.''

''So, for now, we are left with our original idea,'' she said forlornly.

''To continue the ruse of my courtship. Is that truly fair to Vanessa?''

Adeline smiled wanly. ''It will not matter ultimately. Her heart is not involved as mine is. Here, I think we have gathered enough flowers. I'll take the basket now.''

He handed it to her, capturing her hand in his as he did so. He held it for a moment and both stared mutely at each other. It was the sound of a dog barking that broke the magical moment, and they parted self-consciously. They started up the well-manicured path toward the house.

A lone figure, watching from the shadows of the gallery, slipped silently back into the house and out of sight.

CHAPTER
ELEVEN

♥

Madame Teresa Rouchardier rolled into the room while Paulette held a pot of rouge in her hand, contemplating the delicate placement of its contents.

"Paulette!" she admonished, shock written plainly over the woman's round countenance. She wheezed and drew another breath.

Vanessa grimaced and closed her eyes, wincing at the impending storm. She'd tried to dissuade Paulette from the use of any cosmetics, but her young friend had airily dismissed her words, certain, she said, that the judicious use of such artifice was common in England. Vanessa doubted her, though she had no proof to gainsay her statement. She looked helplessly at Adeline and shrugged. When Adeline entered the fray to attempt to convince Paulette of her error, Paulette arrogantly informed them they were hopelessly provincial. At that, both retired from the lists, leaving the battle to those better able to handle the situation. It appeared one such person had now appeared, and Vanessa wished she were elsewhere.

Paulette slammed the rouge pot on the vanity top and rose

swiftly, turning to face her aunt, her natural blush garishly augmented with the red touches she had carefully contrived.

"What are you about? *Une jeune fille*—it is *incroyable!*" her aunt sputtered, her arms waving in wide circles in counterpoints to the swaying rolls of fat on her arms. She stalked over to Paulette.

"But Aunt Teresa," began Paulette mulishly.

"*Non*, I do not listen to you. You, you are a child. I should never have let you stay with the Mannions," she proclaimed as she whipped a lace-edged handkerchief out of the voluminous folds of her red gown.

"What?" protested Vanessa.

"*Non, Tante*, listen to me, *s'il vous plaît!*" Paulette cried, trying to fight off her aunt to prevent her from sweeping the handkerchief roughly across her cheeks.

Her aunt backed her against the vanity, her massive form pinning her in place. "I should have known my first duty was to you. You are but an *enfant*." One massive hand clamped around Paulette's chin to hold her steady. She clucked her tongue and shook her head as she wiped at the offending rouge. "I should have insisted you stay here with me instead of letting you stay with the Mannions." She turned Paulette's head to cleanse the other cheek. "I was weak, but no more!" she declared, wheezing heavily.

Vanessa and Adeline looked at each other in alarm. They were concerned for the woman's health; her breathing sounded labored to their ears. Vanessa glided forward, her arm outstretched. "Madame Rouchardier—" she began.

The woman let go of Paulette, who sagged down against the vanity, and turned on Vanessa.

"You! It is your fault. You have filled *ma petite's* head with fast ideas. You should be ashamed of yourself, a woman who should be married now and have a home of her own *avec les petits bébés*," she spat, her large bosom heaving.

"Me!"

"Madame, you are unfair!" protested Adeline.

Vanessa stood riveted, wide-eyed shock leaving her help-less. Dazed, she looked beyond Madame Rouchardier to Paulette, who was struggling to stand upright and straighten the fall of her lavender skirts. Paulette caught her eye, mortification written plainly across her features. She bit her lower lip and looked contrite but remained silent.

"Paulette?" queried Vanessa softly.

"You shall not talk to my *bébé*!" Madame said adamantly, turning to enfold Paulette in a crushing embrace.

"What is going on in here?" demanded Amanda Mannion from the doorway. "Guests are arriving and your voices are carrying clear down the hall."

"I am surprised at you, Amanda, or did you not know you were nursing a viper to your beast?"

"Teresa, what are you talking about?"

"Your daughter, she has been poisoning my Paulette, she—"

"*Non! Non, Tante*," cried Paulette, tears streaming pretti-ly down her cheeks as she fought her way free of her aunt's enfolding arms. "It was not Vanessa or Adeline. In truth, they tried to dissuade me, but in my conceit I would not listen."

"I do not believe this, and with *Le Comte* arriving momentarily," wailed Teresa Rouchardier.

"It is true, it was all me, I thought—I thought the rouge would make me more worldly and— What count?" Paulette suddenly asked, her aunt's last words filtering through. The tears stopped as quickly as they began.

"Why, Monsieur Baligny's nephew of course, *Le Comte* Andre Baligny de Sachire."

"He is a real count?"

"*Mais, oui!* He's over here visiting, but he has extensive properties in France."

Vanessa relaxed and slouched against the large canopied

bed, exchanging amused glances with her mother and sister.

Paulette's eyes gleamed brightly, and she captured her aunt's pudgy fingers in her hands. "*Tante* Teresa, I am sorry to be such a trial to you. In truth, the Mannions have been very good to me. I regret to say this, but—" She paused, throwing back her head and looking her aunt squarely in the eye. "I am a Chaumonde and I will be honest. You owe the Mannions an apology. The rouge was truly my idea and they tried hard to dissuade me, but me—" She shrugged and relaxed, smiling roguishly. "Sometimes I do not listen that well. You will no longer be mad at me or them, will you?" she wheedled soothingly, her large dark eyes luminous with her regret.

"Ah, *mon enfant*, you are the image of your *maman*—and just as cozening in your manners. All right. For you, my pet, I forgive and beg the Mannions' pardon."

"Thank you, best-of-all-aunts," enthused Paulette.

Her aunt laid a hand against her chest. "But now, I fear I must lie down, all the excitement—"

"Of course, my dear," agreed Amanda Mannion, slipping one arm around her ample waist and signaling Vanessa to do likewise. "We will help you to your room."

"Yes, yes, that would be best," Teresa Rouchardier agreed weakly, tottering between the two women. "Just a little rest; my nerves, you know."

"Of course," soothed Amanda. "Adeline, fetch my sal, please." Over the woman's sagging head she met Vanessa's eyes and winked at her. "Just a little rest and I am positive you will be as right as rain and grace the gathering with your presence."

"Oh, yes, *la soirée*," murmured the woman.

"I shall send Bessie or Ruth up to you later to see how you go on."

"Yes, perhaps that would be best," she conceded weakly.

They met Madame's maid at the door to her room and turned her over into her brisk and capable hands. "We shall see you shortly," cajoled Amanda soothingly as she and Vanessa left and returned to the girls' room.

"Well, young woman, what do you have to say for yourself?" asked Mrs. Mannion when they reentered the room.

Paulette sat before the mirror, patting the curls by her face into place. She frowned in vexation. "Aunt Teresa mussed my coiffure, and Leila isn't here. She is the only one who can work miracles on my hair. What am I to do? A count is here!"

Adeline, seated on the edge of the bed, looked over at her mother and sister. "She has been like this since you left," she explained cheerfully, her hands folded in her lap as she watched Paulette with amusement.

"*Sacré bleu!* How can you joke? There is so little time. Vanessa, your fingers are clever, could you not help with these curls, *s'il vous plaît*?"

The last was said so sweetly that Vanessa nearly burst out laughing, but she recovered herself. "I shall try my poor best," she said with mock solemnity, crossing to Paulette's side.

Adeline's mouth curved in a ghost of a smile, her mind contemplating the implications of Paulette's probable desertion of Mr. Talverton due to the count's arrival. She sighed contentedly, well pleased with the turn of events.

Amanda pursed her lips and shook her head in consternation. "Hurry up, girls," she said briskly, then turned her head to hide her own sly smile.

That evening, Paulette fairly ran down the staircase before Adeline and Vanessa, her pale lavender skirts billowing softly behind her. Near the bottom she stopped and looked about her, but the foyer was free of people save the servants stationed near the door. From the double parlor came the rise and fall of voices, punctuated with restrained titters of laughter.

At the top of the stairs, the Mannion sisters watched Paulette shake out her skirts, lift her head, and thrust her small high breasts forward before continuing down the stairs in a stately manner, gliding along the polished floor.

"I do believe Mr. Talverton may find himself bereft of company," Vanessa observed dryly.

Adeline giggled. "Somehow I don't think he will mind."

Vanessa hooked her arm in her sister's. "Come, let's hurry. I would like to witness Paulette meeting her count. I have the distinct impression that this evening may prove more entertaining than a play."

Adeline murmured her agreement, secretly hoping Vanessa was right.

Due to Paulette's stately progression across the hall, Vanessa and Adeline were not far behind her when they, too, entered the front half of the large double parlor, the back half cleared of furniture to provide a good-sized ballroom. They were astonished by the multitude of people gathered, conversing predominately in French. Vanessa looked at her sister and made a slight moue of dissatisfaction.

"Remember, Louisa has had to work hard to win these people's respect. Please do not think to turn this party on its ear."

"Me?" asked Vanessa, mockingly scandalized.

"Yes, you," whispered her sister furiously. "And don't smile so idiotically at me, either. Now where's Paulette?"

Vanessa, the taller of the two, looked around and over heads of milling people. She saw a brief flash of lavender heading for the French doors leading to the gallery. "This way," she whispered, pulling her sister across the room. *"Pardon. Pardon. Excusez-moi,"* she rattled out absently as she threaded their way through the throng.

"Why is it everyone seems to congregate in one area?" Vanessa whispered. Adeline only giggled in response.

"Miss Mannion!" hailed Mr. Wilmot, stepping across her path.

Vanessa halted abruptly, her sister nearly colliding into her. "Excuse me, Mr. Wilmot," she said, attempting to steer clear of his formidable black form.

"Surely you will not refuse me a few moments of your time," he persisted.

"No, no, of course not. But we are late descending, and we must find Louisa. I am certain she wishes to introduce us to her guests."

"It would be very rude of us if we only talked among ourselves," Adeline offered timidly, looking past Vanessa. She spotted Hugh Talverton's tall figure and threw him a speaking glance.

As luck would have it, Hugh was looking in their direction and Adeline caught his attention. He was surprised by her ardent look of entreaty and casually started toward her, absently making his excuses to those he was talking with. He took but a few steps when he spied Vanessa's glossy brown hair near Mr. Wilmot. His sandy brows lowered and his eyes narrowed as he made his way toward them.

From his position amid a group of plantation owners gathered near the fireplace, Trevor Danielson also saw Wilmot and Vanessa. He bowed out of the group, edged around several women settled on a sofa, and approached his friends.

Inexorably, Trevor and Hugh made their way from opposite ends of the room to Vanessa's side, each determined to rescue her from any unnecessary unpleasantness.

"I have been waiting for days to speak to you, and surely you would be forgiven a small conversation with a suitor," Mr. Wilmot coaxed, not quite able to keep the undercurrent of threat removed from his voice.

"Suitor! La, sir, you take me by surprise," she returned airily, hiding behind her fan, though her hand shook betrayingly.

"Don't take me for a fool!" he said harshly, his face darkening and his voice rasping against her nerve endings. Then his face relaxed and he spoke softly, winningly. "You must know, Miss Mannion, of my heartfelt intentions."

"Sir, you put me to the blush. Not now, please," she pleaded, stepping back a pace. Around her, she noted people beginning to turn and stare.

Trevor and Hugh both saw the little retreat and the blush staining her cheeks, and each grimly began formulating a comment to interrupt and cut through the tension between Vanessa and Wilmot. Unfortunately, their mutual, immediate reactions were not to do it with joviality.

Adeline saw them both, and though daunted by their expressions, she was relieved, and turned quickly from one to the other to smile welcomely.

"*Vanessa!*"

The intended auditor snapped her head up and glanced away from Wilmot with some little relief.

"Vanessa!" called Paulette enthusiastically, waving her hand to catch her friend's attention as she plowed through the people around her with a devastatingly handsome young man in her wake.

Shocked gasps were heard at the hoydenish impropriety of her call, soon followed by a surge of rapid, scandalized French from those same souls. Paulette ignored them all.

"Vanessa! Here is someone I wish you to meet. You, too, Adeline," she added gaily. She pulled the young man to her side, clasping her hand possessively around his forearm. "This is the Comte Andre Baligny de Sachire. He has been telling me the most remarkable things about France and his *estates*." Her eyes sparkled with mischief, the curls at the side of her face dancing, for she could not be still.

Trevor and Hugh stopped where they stood on either side of Vanessa, wondering how to proceed. They had both worked such malice into their thoughts that it was difficult to reorient their thinking. They glanced, up, seeing each other at opposite sides of their goal and glowered, each realizing the other's intent, and how they might not have been the one to extricate her. An irrational jealousy gripped both as their gazes locked.

"Oh, but where are my manners? *Comte, celles-ci Américaines sont mes amies Mademoiselles Vanessa et Adeline Mannion.*"

"Do not feel you must converse in French. I would improve my English, if you please," the young man said graciously.

Vanessa looked up into his dark, soulful eyes and smiled. He was truly a handsome man, with his slender build and glossy black waves of hair that allowed one lock to fall and curl across his brow.

"It is a pleasure, Comte Baligny," she said simply, followed by Adeline. Somehow, she noticed, Paulette had managed to elbow past Mr. Wilmot and edge him out of their circle while Hugh and Trevor edged closer. Mr. Wilmot's face was a thundercloud. Turning on his heel, he stalked off.

Paulette peeped over her shoulder after him and giggled.

"He was the one?" the Comte asked.

Paulette nodded.

"The one what? What are you about, Paulette?" demanded Vanessa.

"Saving you, of course. You, you do not think I know anything, that my only interest is frivolity." She smiled smugly and tapped her brow with a forefinger. "But I see much. I know," she said, nodding her head sagely.

"Egad," murmured Hugh. "How the deuce— Miss Chaumonde," he began again, pausing to bow over her hand, "I have wronged you.'

She shrugged whimsically. "Not really, only a little."

"Be that as it may," protested Trevor, "we would most likely have made a mull of it."

"What is this?" demanded Vanessa, suddenly very annoyed. "Does no one think I may take care of myself?" She backed out of the little circle and turned. "If you are all quite through managing my life, I will now find Louisa, as I told Mr. Wilmot I should." She turned her back on them and walked away, denying the gathering of tears in her eyes with an angry shake of her head and a quick little audible sniff.

"I do not understand," protested the young Comte Baligny, "did she not wish to be rescued?"

Hugh Talverton smiled sardonically. "Yes, she did, my dear sir, however not quite so obviously. Excuse me, I will see if I may make amends for us all," he stated softly, his lips twisting up in one corner with amusement as he followed Vanessa.

She fled out of the parlor and across the foyer to slip into the dining room. Curious, Hugh walked faster and opened the dining room door in time to see her slip out the French doors on the other side of the room. He rounded the long table and stopped, peering out onto the heavily shadowed gallery. He could just make out her slender figure slumped against a column, her shoulders heaving.

Silently, he slid out the partially open door and glided to her side. His heart pounded and tore at the confines of his chest. He stared down at her. "It's all right, love," he murmured, taking her shoulders in his hands and turning her to face him. It agonized him to see her in such pain.

She turned easily, and in the pale moonlight he searched her face. His jaw slackened. She wasn't crying, she was laughing!

His surprise must have been clearly evident upon his face for her laughter increased until she was nearly hiccupping with wild hysteria.

"I—I'm sorry," she finally managed. "In some ways, I feel I should still be crying; however, as I ran from the parlor, the humor of all your actions did not escape me, and belatedly I recalled your and Trevor's expressions when you

realized Paulette had beaten you at your own noble game!''
She laughed freely again, her eyes shining up at him.

Hugh looked down at her, the moonlight softening her
features beautifully. His breath constricted in his chest.

"You think it funny, do you," he growled deep in his
throat. His hands were shaking as he grabbed her shoulders
and roughly pulled her against him, his breath now coming
rapidly, echoing the pounding of his pulse. He lowered his
head, claiming her lips in a bruising kiss.

Vanessa struggled against his sudden onslaught. She pushed
at him, pounding on his chest. Panic engulfed her as the
strange tingling she sometimes felt in his presence began
singing along her nerve endings.

His arm went around her to still her struggles, the other
creeping up to caress the back of her neck, holding her head
still and urging her closer.

A sensual weakness robbed Vanessa's limbs of strength,
her writhing and pounding growing weaker as Hugh stole
her very soul through his lips. She relaxed against him, a
little mew of helpless enthrallment rising up in her throat.

He felt her relax, felt her give herself into his care. His
senses soared with masculine power, glorying in her feel
and the quick tightening in his loins. Then he heard her little
whimpering sound, and his heart stopped. His breathing
ragged, his eyes glazed and glinting feverishly, he gently
released her, setting her a foot away, his hands sliding
slowly down her arm, capturing her hands.

Vanessa staggered before she could force her pliant knees
to hold her upright. With an odd, remote part of her mind,
she was aware of a cool breeze blowing between them,
evaporating the heat of their embrace. Louisa and her
mother were correct, whispered a distinct little corner of her
mind. Love soared in her and through her, beyond description. She understood her sister's dreamy reflection on the
emotion. In reality it wasn't one emotion, but a myriad of
bright, coruscating feelings; light through a prism.

She looked at Hugh in wonder. She saw him inhale deeply, close his eyes, and turn his head up to the bright moon as he slowly exhaled. He opened his eyes, his hands convulsively clenching hers.

"Oh, God, Vanessa, I'm sorry," he whispered raggedly. "I had no right—" He dropped her hands and turned to lean against the gallery railing, fighting to regain his sanity. Never before had a woman shaken him to the core as Vanessa had. He was lost, and ashamed. "If you choose now to avoid me as you do Wilmot, I'll understand." He turned back to look at her, a slight self-deprecating smile on his lips. "I won't like it, but I'll understand and I'll not trouble you as he does."

A vague smile touched her lips. "Please, enough of your nobility."

"But you belong to Trevor," he cried, anguish resonating in his voice.

"Do I?" she asked in a faraway dreamy tone touched with humor.

"Yes!" he affirmed harshly, turning away from her again.

"Why is it that everyone around me feels the necessity to make my decisions for me and assign themselves the thankless job of my protector?" she asked whimsically. A pensive little frown wrinkled her brow. "It is very lowering, you know. I have always prided myself on being a thinking, rational woman, with an even above average comprehension of the realities of life." She blinked, struggling with the sensual haze that remained swathed about her.

He laughed shortly, a harsh, heavy sound. "You are all that and more. Your father's called you his bright star." His tone lowered until it was a mere whisper that Vanessa could barely hear. "And you are my bright particular star. Shakespeare had the right of it," he said with a grim smile.

Vanessa frowned sharply as her mind cleared. The last threads of the sensuous haze were blown away by the freshening breeze. Anger and confusion rushed to overcome her. "So what is this all about? Did you just seek to take something before Wilmot got it? Is this a game of masculine superiority?"

He whirled to face her. "What? Vanessa, no. On my honor, no."

"Well, what then?" she asked, her voice breaking as tears welled in her eyes. "I'm so confused! You raise feelings and fears and joys inside me that I've never felt before."

He grabbed her shoulders and shook her gently. "They're feelings you're meant to feel—but not with me," he said softly.

"Why?" she demanded. "It's been coming. You can't tell me you haven't felt the pull between us."

"Yes," he admitted harshly. "But in this maze we tread, Trevor is your salvation, not me."

"Why?" she demanded again, her voice rising as she struggled with her tears. They were tears of loss and tears of embarrassment, and they flowed from her very soul.

He raked his hand distractedly through his hair and shook his head to clear his thoughts. He sighed heavily, his broad shoulders slumping. "Once before Trevor and I courted the same woman—Julia," he recited flatly. "I thought I loved her, but she showed me my love was only a toy, a prize at the end of a game. She was right, and she chose Trevor. Now, again I am attracted to the same woman as Trevor, and I want her with an even greater hunger. Luckily, Julia showed me how false are my affections, something I am too close to see."

Vanessa stared at him in shocked surprise, then a shimmering anger curled and roiled through her. "I don't believe what I am hearing," she gritted out. "You would bow out of a courtship because of Trevor and some dead woman?" It was incredible. How could he be so blind and so—so naive?

"You don't understand," protested Hugh.

"Yes, oh, yes, I think I do understand. You've carried

Julia's rejection around as some sort of armor, a convenient excuse for shallow emotions and amusing little dalliances. For all your great military service and courage under fire, you haven't shown courage where it really counts. This country of mine was founded on risks and the people willing to take them. That takes a special kind of courage, a courage you can't even begin to know," she blazed, her eyes sparkling like jewels. She paused, glaring at him, then gave it up in disgust and turned, fleeing the gallery, the moonlight, the sharp tingling, and him.

Stupid, stupid, stupid. The single-word litany resounded in her mind as she made her way back to the parlor. She was the naive one. Imagine thinking an English aristocrat could be interested in her. Hadn't she despised him for days after their first meeting? Her initial reaction to the man bore more truth than the subsequent softening of her ideas and feelings. She had merely been surprised by the debilitating and exhilarating feelings he aroused, for they were alien to her. Now that she knew and understood more about love, she was confident another gentleman could rouse her to the same emotional state if she allowed him.

The quartet Louisa hired for the evening was playing a sprightly contredanse. Vanessa wondered how long she had been gone, and if her absence went unnoticed. Though she asked herself that question, she realized she actually didn't care. Suddenly the party seemed as appetizing as flat champagne. She slipped inside the parlor behind a guest nearly as rotund as Madame Rouchardier, then sidled around the edge of the room toward the back section of the large double parlor where the quartet was playing and the dancers bowed and moved through the figures with more arrogant elegance than competence.

On the dance floor, Paulette was being led out by the Comte Baligny, and Adeline by a young man who displayed more awkward angles to his limbs than lines. Vanessa winced when she noted him accidentally jabbing her sister in the shoulder as they executed siding. Trevor came up beside her, standing silently.

She smiled and waved her hand in Adeline's direction. "My sister displays more forbearance than I could manage."

He nodded. "Hers is a gentle soul, and she would not hurt or embarrass anyone by her actions."

She looked up at him, an arrested expression in her eyes. "I've always known that, but I don't believe I've ever put it into words before. You're very right."

"Where's Hugh?" Trevor asked abruptly.

Vanessa's face twisted into a grimace. "He is busily employed with fabricating rationalizations for his actions that have nothing to do with his emotions."

Trevor cocked an eyebrow. "Oh?"

She shook her head. "It is not important. They are his demons, and I for one refuse to allow someone else's deficiencies to cause me pain."

"And could they?"

"Could they what?"

"Cause you pain."

She laughed shrilly. "La, Trevor, you are reading too much into a short conversation."

He looked at her solemnly, then quickly smiled warmly at her when he spied Wilmot making his steady way toward them. "Would you care to dance?" he asked with stiff pleasantry.

Vanessa's brow knit at the abrupt change in conversation, then she, too, saw Mr. Wilmot. She smiled brilliantly up at Mr. Danielson and nodded, tucking her hand in his arm. "I shall be delighted, and I promise my bad temper shall not resurface."

'I have no fear of your temper," he said, "for you are nothing if not fair."

Vanessa thought of her words to Hugh Talverton, and a

brief feeling of remorse swept through her. "Sometimes I wonder, Mr. Danielson, sometimes I wonder."

He looked at her strangely but, leading her out onto the dance floor, he did not question her further. In truth, she was in an uncertain temper. He was curious to know what had transpired between his friend and her; however, his manners were too polished to inquire.

Vanessa danced, smiled, and adopted a deliberate carefree demeanor. If her laughter was a trifle shrill to her own ears, and her eyes overly bright, it did not seem to be noticed by others. She even allowed herself a mild flirtation with this or that young man who squired her to a dance, and bent so far as to allow Mr. Wilmot to partner her for a set.

Hugh Talverton entered the makeshift ballroom in time to see Vanessa lead down through a set on Wilmot's arm. He watched them perform the intricate figures of the dance, an arrogant mask hardening his features. He had promised he would protect her from Mr. Wilmot's unwanted advances. The irony was he afforded her no protection from himself. He was the veriest cad to take advantage of her trust—and Trevor's. Yet he could not deny the curious allure she exuded, and now he was uncertain who was the spider and who the fly.

Remembering the warmth and gentle pliancy of her body against his, the taste of her kiss, the sweet essence that was hers alone filling his nostrils, he hated himself and, God help him, he hated Trevor. The jealousy he bore his best friend ate at his soul, but he steadfastly vowed he would not make the same mistakes he made with Julia. Now that his business dealings were near completion, and there was no need of his presence in the city until the cotton harvest, perhaps he should do as he told Wilmot and leave and explore this raw, untamed land.

His eyes restlessly followed Vanessa's every move, ignoring the dark-eyed Creole women who wished he'd look in their direction so they might claim his attention. The dance was ending. He stiffened, fighting the urge to rush to her side and claim the next, thus removing her from Wilmot's orbit. But he did not trust himself, and he told himself he would importune her no further.

"Miss Mannion," murmured Russell Wilmot as he led her off the dance floor, "I regrettably am not, by nature, a patient man; yet with you I have exhibited a marked degree of patience. I have desired private conversation with you this past week."

"I know, sir, and I apologize." She fidgeted with her fan, her eyes downcast. "But I find I have no words of encouragement to offer you, and in my weakness, I found avoidance easier."

"You will not forgive my presumption?"

"It is not that! Truthfully, I now know that your actions were not so forward as to be beyond forgiveness," she said weakly, coloring slightly at the memory of Hugh's kiss. Desperately she looked around for Hugh, for now she felt like a damsel in distress and would have him rescue her. But it was not Hugh she spied making his way across the crowded room toward her but Trevor. Her face cleared, a faint sigh of relief passing her lips.

Wilmot noted her blush and followed the direction of her eyes. His eyes narrowed, and a scowl darkened his countenance. "You would have me understand that your heart is otherwise engaged?" he growled.

She looked back toward him, startled. The truth of his statement pierced her heart. She loved Hugh Talverton, but it was a love doomed to frustration. She felt helpless, gripped as she was in the throes of her emotion. Gripping her fan tightly, her face pale, she nodded slowly, her tongue cloying to the roof of her mouth.

"Your pardon, Miss Mannion," Wilmot said stiffly, a particularly feral gleam flaring in his eyes. "For the moment, I shall relieve you of my presence." He bowed, then cast Trevor a malevolent glance, before turning to walk away.

Vanessa silently watched him leave, confusion and sorrow evident in her face. Her grip on her fan tightened until she heard a snap. Looking down at her hands, she was dismayed to see a stick of her beloved New Orleans fan splintered beyond repair.

"You are troubled," said a soft, melodious voice. A gentle hand touched Hugh's arm.

He looked down into the delicate visage of Adeline Mannion. She smiled sweetly at him. He stiffened. He did not want sympathy, or even knowledge of his desires.

"So is my sister," she added, looking to where Vanessa stood irresolute at the side of the room.

Wilmot was saying something to her. She nodded slowly, her face a canvas of tortured emotions. A sharpening of his features conveyed Wilmot's ill will toward Trevor. Vanessa appeared to be attempting to placate him with little success. He bowed stiffly and walked away. A momentary anguish wrung her features as she stared down at her hands, but she recovered swiftly and donned a brilliant smile for the world.

"I cannot help her," Hugh said harshly, hating the words as they left his lips.

Adeline looked at him piteously, then sighed. "For now, Trev—I mean, Mr. Danielson, shall offer such protection as she will allow; however, I greatly fear my sister will stubbornly tread her own path. At least Mr. Danielson has secured her company for supper."

Hugh nodded. "That was to be expected," he said loftily.

"Was it?" queried Adeline.

He looked at her sharply, momentarily shaken out of his stoic attitude. She was attempting to convey some message to him, a message he declined to comprehend.

Recognizing the absurdity of his pose, Adeline's mouth twitched then lifted into a smile as she gave into her inclinations. "And Paulette," she continued airily, "has quite effectively claimed the attentions of the Comte Baligny."

She paused and looked at Hugh steadily. "I have a request to ask of you, Mr. Talverton, that I realize is highly improper on my part."

He looked at her quizzically, her soft features unusually intent. He bowed. "Your servant, Miss Mannion," he murmured.

She drew a deep breath. "It is nearly time for supper, and I have no partner. I confess these Creole gentlemen quite overwhelm me." She grimaced slightly. "Their form of gallantry puts me so to the blush, I hardly know where to look. Many have the mistaken idea that American women are shockingly fast, you know."

"I had no idea, Miss Mannion. I should be delighted to escort you and count myself fortunate that you should trust me."

She laughed. "It is no mean request, Mr. Talverton, for I know you are enamored of Vanessa."

"You quite mistake the matter, Miss Mannion!" he said abruptly, glaring at her.

She continued smiling. "Am I?" she said with feigned vagueness. "Oh, dear, I hope I have not embarrassed you, sir."

He shook his head curtly and relaxed. "Not at all, Miss Mannion. I suppose my solicitude for your sister could be mistakenly construed."

"Of course," she murmured.

But she didn't look at all convinced, and he chafed under her steady, calm regard. Drawing upon his vast store of presence and arrogance, he looked down upon her haughtily.

She clapped her hands together, delighted. "You do do that so well. Come, they have rung the bell for dinner."

Hugh's breath expelled in a whoosh. "Are all you Mannion women so truthful?" he asked in exasperation.

"Oh, Louisa and Vanessa are much more discerning than I. I am quite the shyest of the lot," she assured him.

"Indeed," he murmured, caught between his initial exasperation and his natural inclination to see the humor in life. In jest, he once asked Trevor if he was being thrown to the wolves, and in jest his friend had agreed. But some jests bear a striking similarity to reality, he thought wryly as he offered Adeline his arm, the beginnings of his own smile turning up his lips.

CHAPTER
TWELVE

♥

Trevor Danielson came into the dining room the next morning softly whistling through his teeth, his face alight with good humor. Hugh Talverton was before him, filling his plate from the broad selection of meats, fruits, and pastries spread across the sideboard. His face bore a shuttered expression, and his complexion held a muddy cast accentuated by dark smudges under his eyes. He glanced once in Danielson's direction then looked away, settling himself at the far end of the table.

Trevor noted the dissipated appearance of his friend, and his concomitant surly behavior. Chuckling, he filled a plate for himself and grabbed a cup of coffee, seating himself across from Hugh.

Hugh barely glanced up, looking at him through heavily hooded eyes before returning his attention to his plate where he absently shoved his food around.

"Got foxed, did you?" said Trevor jovially. "You must be showing your age. I remember the time—"

"Enough," growled Hugh. His face contorted as various emotions surged through him. "I'm sorry, Trevor. I do want to say though—'' He paused, bringing his napkin up to dab at the corners of his lips, then laying it very precisely beside his plate. ''I do want to wish you happy.''

''You do? You know?'' asked Trevor, nonplussed.

Hugh nodded his head heavily, wishing he were anywhere except sitting before his friend and witnessing his happiness.

A slight sound, like a muffled scuffing, attracted his attention. He looked up. Wilmot was leaning against the door molding. How much had the man heard? He watched cagily as the man unfolded his arms, pushed himself away from the door, and strolled into the dining room.

''I hope I'm not interrupting a private conversation?'' he inquired politely, pouring himself a cup of coffee.

''No, no, not at all,'' assured Trevor. ''My friend here,'' he said, casting a jaundiced eye over Hugh, ''is still recovering from tipping his elbow too much and is sorry company. I welcome your appearance.''

Hugh's scowl darkened. *I bet you do*, he mocked silently. He pushed a few more pieces of food around on his plate, then rose, nodding his head curtly in Wilmot's and Trevor's direction.

''If you'll excuse me, please, gentlemen,'' he murmured, striding toward the door. At the doorway he passed Richard Mannion and Charles Chaumonde, ignoring them both. He shoved past them, as if all the demons of hell were nipping at his heels.

Richard and Charles looked after him, bemused expressions on their faces.

''Is something the matter with Hugh?'' inquired Charles.

Trevor laughed. ''Nothing that time and black coffee won't cure. He has a devilish head this morning.''

Richard grunted as he placed a succulent section of capon on his plate.

''My compliments to Louisa, Charles,'' Trevor continued. ''That was an excellent party.''

"She has a flair for entertaining, my Louisa does," affirmed Charles, seating himself at the table.

Russell Wilmot set down his coffee cup and dabbed his mouth with a fine linen napkin. "I should like a word with you, Mannion, before I leave this morning," he said curtly, his dark brows twitching.

Charles set his fork and knife down abruptly. "You're leaving, Russell? It was my understanding you were all staying until late this afternoon."

Shaking his head, Wilmot smiled slightly, his eyes nearly closed. "The press of business. I'm sorry," he said deprecatingly. "It has been, however, an enlightening weekend."

Richard Mannion looked at him sharply, then back at his plate and resumed eating.

"Bonjour!" called Paulette gaily as she swept into the room, the train of her forest green riding habit draped over her arm.

"You are up early," observed her brother.

"Who could be abed on such a wonderful day?" she asked rhetorically before leaning over to bestow a kiss on her brother's cheek.

His eyebrows rose. This behavior was not typical for Paulette. He turned his head to watch his sister take a thick sweet pastry for her plate.

"I suppose I need not ask what your plans are for this morning," he said dryly.

"Comte Baligny is taking me riding this morning," she managed between bites. "I must hurry or I shall be late."

"What are Vanessa and Adeline doing?"

"They are helping with the children," she tossed out, as if bored with the topic. "I think they are planning a picnic for them."

"Indeed!" put in Trevor. "Dashed good notion. I don't spend enough time with my two. I believe I will go see if I may be of assistance. If you gentlemen will excuse me," he said, hurriedly using his napkin and pushing back his chair. "If you're firm in your decision to leave this morning, I doubt I shall see you again, Wilmot, so I'll say my good-byes now."

He held out his hand to Russell Wilmot, who looked at it a moment before offering his own in return. Richard Mannion and Charles Chaumonde were surprised at the blatant insult, and stirred uneasily in their chairs. Trevor chose to ignore it, and bidding the others good morning, he left in search of the women.

"Now see here, Wilmot," began Richard.

Wilmot cut him off, his face coldly neutral. "We will talk later, Richard. In private," he promised.

Paulette looked from one to the other, her eyes wide. Finishing the last bite of her pastry she, too, rose to leave.

She hurried to the stable to order the gentlest horse available to be saddled. She knew herself to be an indifferent rider; however, that was not something she wished to confess to the count. Nonetheless, a little helplessness would not be amiss.

After giving her orders she questioned the servants on the location of Mr. Talverton and set off to find him.

She was aware that her family and friends considered her a pretty ninnyhammer and hoyden. That didn't bother her; it was a useful excuse, and it permitted her much freedom. And in truth, she knew herself to be disgracefully self-centered. But if she was not, how might she achieve her goals? Vanessa and Adeline could use some self-consideration. Bah! Everyone was tripping over each other to help and nothing was being accomplished.

Impossible, these *Américaines*, making everything so complicated! Shaking her head, she headed purposefully down the path the stable boy had indicated, contemplating her course of action.

When finally she spied him, he was standing on a small levee at the side of a canal, studying its construction.

Silently she came to stand beside him. He looked down at her, the top of her saucy hat just reaching his shoulders. Some of the haggard grayness had left his complexion, and the deep furrows across his brow had eased. He was surprised and a little wary of her presence.

She sighed dramatically, which brought a smile to his face.

"I don't know what I should do first," she said conversationally as she looked down at the still waters, "beg your pardon, or call you *un imbécile*."

Hugh blinked, at a loss for words.

"I am very fickle, you know, and I did lead you a merry dance," she said seriously, pursing her lips. "My situation, it is *très tragique*, for I am neither fish nor bird."

The corners of Hugh's lips lifted up again. "I believe," he drawled, "you mean neither fish nor fowl."

She shrugged. "*N'importante pas*. The Creoles, they are not happy with *mon père*, they say he is too *Américain*. They do not wish their sons to marry his daughter for they feel I shall taint them in some manner, despite all I do to prove I am a true Creole."

"Is that why your speech is often heavily accented, while your brother speaks near perfect English?"

"*Oui*."

"Miss Chaumonde, I fear you refine too much on the matter. Your brother appears perfectly well accepted, and his wife is an American."

"Phtt! You do not understand. He is a man, and he can do manly things to prove he is Creole at heart, like fight duels and gamble till dawn. He is also rich."

Hugh threw back his head and laughed. "And does he do these things—duel and gamble?"

She frowned. "*Non*, for he says words are his sword, and he gambles every day he invests."

"Wise man."

"Do you really think so? I don't know," she said

consideringly. "It seems so tame and not at all romantic. But what was I saying before?"

"That you are not accepted by the Creoles."

"*Oui, merci.* It is very true, I shall most likely die a spinster if I wait upon a Creole husband. So I said to myself, Paulette, you must marry an aristocrat and then thumb your nose at the Creoles. Therefore, even before I met you, I decided I would marry you."

"You did?"

"*Naturellement*, so long as you possessed wealth, of course."

"Ah, now I know why Trevor teased me about being raised to the manner born."

"He did that?" She shook her head dolefully. "Regardless, I regret to inform you, you will not do at all."

"No?"

"*Non.* Now, my pardon is done and I will tell you why you are an *imbécile*."

Hugh crossed his arms on his chest. "By all means, please continue," he said, amused by Paulette's disclosures.

"You are an *imbécile* for you do not realize Vanessa will never love Mr. Danielson."

"Perhaps she doesn't yet," he said stiffly, "but with time—"

"Phtt! There is no help for you. I tell you one more thing, and then I go. Mr. Wilmot is leaving this morning." She gathered up the train of her skirts in her arm and turned to leave. "*Au revoir*, Monsieur Talverton. I must not keep the count waiting. I have a mind to be the Comtesse Baligny. It has a nice sound, *non*?"

Hugh laughed. "Enjoy your ride."

She wrinkled her nose. "Me, I am not fond of horses, but one does what one must. Oh, I nearly forgot. Vanessa, Adeline, and Trevor are planning a picnic for the children. You might find it—umm, enlightening." She giggled and turned to run down the path toward the stables, her hand on head to keep her hat in place.

"Enlightening?" Hugh echoed, but she was already out of earshot. He shook his head. Sometimes Paulette truly had lamentably poor English. He wondered what word she had meant.

"Is this a private party, or may a father join?" Trevor Danielson asked, standing in the doorway to the bedroom allotted Alex and Mary.

"Papa! Papa!" Mary yelled, twirling out of Adeline's grasp and launching herself at her father.

He crouched down to catch her and hug her tight. When he looked up, he observed Alex coming closer in a properly reserved manner, though he could tell by the expression on his face that he longed to copy his sister's spontaneous action. Trevor smiled and opened his arms, waving Alex to join in the embrace.

The little boy didn't need further encouragement before he, too, launched himself into his father's arms.

Vanessa, rocking back in her chair and folding her hands in her lap, smiled complacently at the familial scene. It was heartbreakingly tender. Trevor knelt on the floor without regard for his buckskin breeches or the tails of his coat brushing the floor. His arms encircled his children, their heads resting lovingly on his shoulder. Mary's hair was a pattern card of his own glossy sable-brown locks; her brother's hair more closely resembled their mother's. They were prettily behaved children and delightful company.

Vanessa looked over at her sister to see her reaction to the family tableau. She was surprised to note tears on her sister's eyelashes while a gentle smile hovered on her lips. She opened her mouth to comment only to be forestalled by the expression she noted on Trevor's face. He was looking over his children's heads at Adeline, the light of love evident in his eyes. Vanessa blinked and shut her mouth abruptly. She stared at Adeline and Trevor in silence. They were oblivious to her regard, so wrapped were they in their lovers' roles.

They were perfect! Why couldn't she see that before? Did they know? Yes, of course they did, though they tried hard not to show it, she thought, remembering their shared glances, long conversations, and time spent together. Why were they trying to deny their relationship? It was obvious they were in love. Or was it only obvious to her because she was now familiar with that heady, confusing emotion?

Vanessa compressed her lips in an amused smile as she studied them. She cleared her throat noisily and gently asked, "Am I the last to know?"

Guiltily, Adeline turned toward her sister, a pink blush surging over her features. "Oh, Vanessa, I'm sorry—"

"For what, you ninnyhammer?" asked Vanessa, sliding off her chair on to the floor beside her sister. She took Adeline's hands in hers, squeezing them gently. Behind them, Trevor gently extricated himself from his children's embrace, and taking their hands in his, led them from the room, closing the door behind them with a soft click.

Copious tears now trailed down Adeline's cheeks. "Oh, Vanessa," she murmured.

Vanessa's eyes sparkled with unshed tears. "Is that all you can say to me, *Oh, Vanessa*? And stop that crying! Here, take my handkerchief," she said, removing a small square of embroidered linen from the neckline of her dress and handing it to her sister. "I swear, Adeline, you're a watering pot. Now stop this lest you have me in tears as well."

"Thank you," Adeline murmured, sniffling slightly, though her eyes shone like jewels.

"Tell me all," insisted her sister, an admonitory expression on her face.

Adeline gave a watery chuckle and did as requested, though mindful of her sister's temper last evening when she discovered their attempts to protect her from Wilmot, she prudently skirted the subject of the reason for the continued deceptions.

"So, when is Mr. Danielson going to declare himself to Father?"

"Well," Adeline hedged, "he feels Father has some weighty business matters plaguing his mind at the moment that need resolution first."

"Stuff and nonsense! Tell him to speak to Father at once."

"No! No, please, Vanessa, allow us to handle this in our own way—after all, it wasn't long ago Trevor was your suitor, and we don't wish the transition to be a shock."

"So, what may I do to help, marry Mr. Wilmot?" Vanessa tossed out whimsically.

Adeline blanched. "Don't joke about that! Please, promise me you won't agree to marry Mr. Wilmot out of some misguided emotion of—of rescue."

"Rescue?" Vanessa chuckled. She rose to her feet, extending her hand to help her sister to rise. "I believe, dear sister, you're picking up Paulette's melodramatic tendencies. Come, let's find Mr. Danielson and the children and get this picnic organized. I can't wait for the opportunity to twit that gentleman," she teased.

"Oh, Vanessa," sighed Adeline again, earning a raised eyebrow and twisted smile from her sister as they left the room in search of the Danielson family.

For the better part of an hour Hugh Talverton wrestled with himself on the advisability of, versus his desire to, join the picnic party. He had made a mull of it last evening by kissing Vanessa, breaking all her strict unwritten rules for acceptable behavior. Perhaps it would be best to follow Mr. Wilmot's example and make an early departure—not that that would be the easiest solution, for he was staying in Trevor's lodgings above the offices of the Danielson and

Halley Company. It might raise more questions than he was currently willing to answer.

Truthfully, he was uncertain as to the reception he would receive in Vanessa's company. He was loath to face the same skittish behavior she directed toward Mr. Wilmot. It would twist his soul to endure such a reception from her as was his due. Why had he played the incontinent fool last evening and given in to his temptations? He was not some callow schoolboy.

His thoughts churned, and he remembered her pliant body in his arms. After her initial shock, she'd succumbed willingly to his kiss, reveling in it as much as he. Why? She never accepted Wilmot's clumsy, arrogant machinations. Why had she responded to him? Was it possible that she felt a modicum of feeling for him? She'd spoken of the pull between them. He'd recognize the feeling within himself but had not realized, and, in truth, verily denied, that she should feel likewise. Was it so unheard of? Could he now be the chosen over Trevor? The questions reverberated in his mind as he paced the canal, searching for peace and answers.

Finally, drained from the efforts of a virtually sleepless night, he made his way back to the plantation house to seek out the company, stoically preparing himself for rejection but feeling he had to see Vanessa again.

The servants directed him to a corner of the property where the vegetation resembled a forest glade versus the ubiquitous swamp. The little party he sought was encamped on blankets under the shade of a large tree. They were all laughing and looking up to where Trevor's six-year-old son was swinging from a thick branch and little Mary sat in the crook of two massive limbs. Adeline stood beneath her, urging her to climb down, but the little girl just shook her head defiantly, inviting Adeline to join her.

Vanessa urged her sister to climb the tree, her face alight with mischief. Hugh saw Adeline steadfastly shake her head, a false frown remonstrating her sister for making the suggestion. As he drew near, Hugh heard Trevor add his voice to Vanessa's, and offer to give her a boost. Laughing, Adeline acquiesced, and Trevor gave her a leg up onto a low branch of the tree.

Adeline swung her legs and chatted animatedly with Mary. Hugh saw her sweep her arm wide to indicate the view, her gaze following a moment later, catching sight of him on the path.

"Mr. Talverton!" she called.

Vanessa swung around, a deep rose blush staining her cheeks. Deliberately she looked away, unable to maintain eye contact with him lest she show where her heart lay.

Hugh understandably interpreted her action as rejection. He would have turned on his heel if Trevor was not approaching him and the children not screaming with delight.

Reluctantly, he joined in their merriment. Alex dropped to the ground and ran to his side, tucking a trusting hand in his arm. Mary squealed and called for him to help her down. Laughing more freely now, he pinched her cheeks and lifted her off the branch.

"Help Miss Adeline, too," the young girl instructed with curiously grown-up presence.

He bowed over her hand. "It shall be my pleasure," he promised earnestly. But when he turned to face Adeline, Trevor's hands were already on her waist as he gently helped her down. Hugh frowned darkly when he noted his friend's hands resting longer than was seemly in polite company. Embarrassed for Vanessa, he cleared his throat loudly.

Adeline and Trevor looked over at him but just laughed. Vanessa's face bore a curious expression of equanimity. Curious, because it was not a typical emotion for her. She felt things swiftly and heavily, with all emotions registering on the canvas of her face. Because of her usually mobile features, it was odd that she should sit so still and not display her feelings. He was certain she could not have observed the scene with quite the serenity she was displaying.

"Feeling better now?" Trevor asked, his arm still around Adeline. His smile was hearty as it had been earlier that morning.

"I was," he muttered darkly, his brows drawing forward again. How could his friend treat Vanessa in this fashion, ignoring her and reserving his attention for another woman.

If Vanessa could not come to love Trevor, then it would be on that gentleman's head. If Trevor did not appreciate her, then damn it, he certainly did, and he was not about to let any man give her slipshod treatment.

Trevor's arm slipped from the small of Adeline's back. He came toward his friend, smiling ruefully. "What ails you, Hugh? You are as blue as megrim."

"It is not what ails me, it is what ails you," came Hugh's acid rider, putting his back to the ladies and children so they might be spared his righteous anger.

Trevor's eyebrows snapped together. "Don't stand on points with me. Quit behaving like a Tragedy Jack and tell me what has you by the tail," he said with asperity.

"Your behavior," Hugh ground out.

"My behavior?"

"Your behavior toward your intended is deplorable."

"What?"

"The bonds of affection we share are strained by your unprincipled actions."

The glint of sharpening anger showed in Trevor's eyes. "Now see here, Talverton," he said, maintaining a bare degree of civility, "my intended and I have a comfortable understanding, and I'll thank you to keep out of our affairs."

The gentlemen's rising tones captured the attention of Adeline and Vanessa. They exchanged worried glances.

"Let's go see what different wildflowers you may find for me," Adeline hurriedly suggested to the children, leading them away.

Vanessa rose from her seat on the blanket and took a step nearer Hugh and Trevor, a concerned frown pulling at her features.

"Understanding—is that the best you have to offer a wife?"

"I repeat, what I offer is not of your concern," Trevor answered tightly, his face flushing.

Hugh glared at him helplessly, his tawny eyes glowing like cut gems. His fist clenched, his arm swung back then out, to connect squarely with Trevor's jaw.

The force of the blow spun Trevor around, knocking him off balance. He landed heavily. Hugh stood over him, his hands balled into fists.

"Trevor!" yelled Vanessa, dropping to her knees beside him.

"Oh, is there to be a mill?" asked young Alex excitedly.

"Of course not," snapped Adeline, picking up her skirts and running toward Trevor.

Alex and Mary looked at each other. "Adults," Alex said with disgust. Mary nodded her solemn agreement.

"Talverton, you must still be foxed," said Trevor, nursing his jaw. "I haven't the foggiest what you're about. If the children and ladies weren't present, I'd give you the mill you're so obviously looking for—and don't be so cocksure of its outcome."

Vanessa glared at Hugh. "Barbarian!" she cried, throwing back at him the word he'd once used to describe New Orleans. She drew a handkerchief from a hidden pocket of her dress and dabbed at a slight cut on Trevor's lip.

"Trevor! Are you all right?" demanded Adeline, sinking down to the ground and placing his head on her lap.

"I'd liefer be a barbarian than a shocking loose screw," vowed Hugh, but his tense posture eased, though his face was still dark with emotion. "If I were marrying Vanessa, I'd show her more respect than to cavort with her sister."

"Vanessa!" exclaimed Trevor, struggling up on his elbow.

"Me!" squeaked the subject of discussion.

"Oh, dear me," exclaimed Adeline weakly before she was overtaken by a paroxysm of laughter.

Thunderstruck, Hugh stared at them all.

"I thought— By your words this morning, I thought you knew," said Trevor, the beginnings of a laugh welling up in him. He put his hand back to his face. "It hurts too much to laugh, but by Jove, Hugh, you're a cork-brained fellow. I want Vanessa for a sister, not a wife!"

"A sister?"

"Yes, I want to wed Adeline."

"Hurrah, hurrah!" pipped in two little voices behind him.

Trevor sat up just in time to avoid being trampled by his own children as they threw themselves at Adeline, entwining their arms around her neck.

Hugh slumped down to the ground, holding his head in his hands. "This is a devil of a muddle. I must be worse than cork-brained for I'll confess I don't understand."

"I'll admit I once contemplated wedding Vanessa, but that was before I realized I was in love with Adeline. After we realized our true affections, we, Adeline and myself, decided it would be best if I were to continue to court Vanessa publicly for the reason we discussed: Wilmot. I'll admit there was another reason, too, but I didn't realize the strength of your feelings and commitment not to be thwarted again," Trevor said wryly.

"What do you mean?"

"We reasoned you and Vanessa had the potential for more than an antagonistic relationship; you just needed the proper incentive. I thought if I continued to court Vanessa, you'd see the parallels to the courtship of Julia and get jealous enough not to want to lose again."

"Oh, he saw them all right," said Vanessa, rising and brushing the dirt and grass off her gown. "But that's not the lesson he came away with."

Tears shimmered at the edges of her eyes, blurring her vision. "I cannot believe the lengths you all have gone to to protect me from something I may not wish to be protected from. I would just like the opportunity to find out for myself. Is that so much to ask? Now if you'll excuse me, I'll take my leave of you. I find I have a splitting headache." Her voice caught in her throat as she whirled away to stumble down the path.

"Vanessa! Please!" called Hugh, rising to his feet and starting after her.

"No, don't, Mr. Talverton. Give her some time. I know my sister. Though she may be quick to anger, she does come around to seeing the humor in life. Let Vanessa work her frustrations out of her system."

Hugh looked at Adeline and then back to Vanessa uncertainly. He exhaled deeply and shook his head. "Truly, I don't know what is the proper course any longer." He laughed shortly, remembering Paulette's words. The minx knew exactly what she was saying. Joining the picnic had been an enlightening experience.

CHAPTER
THIRTEEN

♥

"Hugh!" Trevor cried, bursting into the small study where his friend sat writing a letter to his family. "Russell Wilmot is the worst type of vermin to crawl upon the earth. You would not believe what my contacts have discovered."

Leaning back in his chair, his quill held lax between his fingers, Hugh looked up. Trevor's countenance conveyed a deep agitation. His sable hair, normally neatly waved back off his high forehead, spiked outward at the sides of his head, augmenting his wild-eyed appearance.

Despite his own low spirits and depression, Hugh was moved to listen to his friend, albeit dully.

"Mannion took some loans out this spring, and guess who holds the notes?"

"Wilmot," Hugh said flatly.

"How did you guess?"

Hugh snorted. "I've know that since Wednesday."

"Wednesday! That was nearly a week ago. Why didn't you tell me?" Trevor expostulated.

"I believed the information to be given into my trust in strictest confidence."

"But how— Who would know such a thing?"

"Richard himself."

"Richard!"

"Please Trevor, must you continually sound like an echo? Soon you'll have me believing I'm back in the Alps."

"The Alps!"

"See what I mean?"

Trevor shook his head, his mouth set in a grim line. "This is not a time for levity."

His friend sighed. "If I don't laugh, I vow I shall be consumed with a burning anger or quaking sadness."

"This maudlin mantle you wear is not like you, Hugh."

"I don't think I know what is like me anymore," he responded whimsically.

"Hugh!"

"All right. All right," he placated. "Tell me. There is a chance Richard did not disclose all, and there may be more to be gleaned from the matter."

Trevor pulled a chair around in front of Hugh and straddled it, resting his forearms on the gracefully carved wooden back. "Word has it Mannion's invested almost all of his blunt on this year's cotton harvest. Overextended himself, in fact, so he was forced to seek loans—tweren't from the gull gropers, but might as well have been for the rates he's to pay are usurious. They say he didn't borrow conventionally because he wanted his dealing kept private in order to instigate some sort of coup in the marketplace come fall. Funny, I'd never have taken Mannion for that type of gambler. Thought he was a straight, conservative fellow, actually.

"Anyway, it seems Wilmot somehow found out about the loans and bought them up—paid top dollar, too, I heard. Now he's using his possession to put some sort of pressure on Richard. It's true he wants to marry Vanessa, but it's not as if he's possessed of a grand passion for her or anything. They say he's got a quadroon mistress in a nice house on

Rampart Street that he's not about to give up. Evidently she's pure class. But back to Vanessa. For some reason Wilmot's blackmailing Richard to try to force him to grant him Vanessa's hand in marriage—as a willing or unwilling bride. I'll tell you, though, a number of heads are scratching to figure out just why. I mean, it's known Louisa's dowry was hefty, but there are plenty of other debutantes whose dowries are plumper. Vanessa's can't be that different from her sister's.''

Hugh laughed shortly. ''Ah, but that's where you and all your contacts are wrong. It is quite different.''

''What do you mean?'' Trevor asked, straightening in his chair.

''Mannion's settled half his business on her.''

''What!''

''My sentiments exactly. It is a long story, so I won't bore you with all the details. Suffice it to say, one other gentleman in New Orleans knew about the arrangement and has held it over Richard's head for four years. And he's the only one Wilmot could have learned it from.''

''Who?''

''Jean Laffite.''

Trevor swore viciously. ''I suspected Wilmot's overnight success in business might be due in part to that pirate. They must have been working far closer than I ever imagined, to share that kind of knowledge.''

Hugh shrugged. ''''Whether they were close or not, there is no honor among thieves and, from some things Richard's said to me, I'd be willing to bet a pony Laffite has no notion of Wilmot's machinations.''

Trevor nodded. ''Laffite has been too busy attempting to reclaim what is rightfully his.''

''So Richard alluded.''

''What was Laffite's stake in all this?''

''He got to choose the bridegroom and therefore gain control of another legitimate front operation.''

"But why hasn't he done so before now?"

"I suspect because things began to get a little unsettling for him in 1814, the year Vanessa turned eighteen."

Trevor agreed. "At that time," he said thoughtfully, "he was more concerned with saving his own hide than worrying about further aggrandizement."

"Precisely."

"Let me see if I understand this correctly. If Wilmot marries Vanessa, he gets half of Mannion's business, and right now he holds notes worth the other half of his business."

"Correct, because Mannion is an honorable man and could not, in good conscience, pledge his daughter's dowry for the loans," Hugh added.

"So right now," Trevor mused, "if Wilmot marries Vanessa before the harvest, and Mannion defaults on the notes, which I'm sure Wilmot has in some way orchestrated— probably by demanding a payment just prior to the harvest— Wilmot walks away with the entire business."

"Exactly."

"Neat. But what's to prevent Mannion from borrowing the money elsewhere?"

Hugh shrugged. "A large part is probably pride, though I'd also wager Wilmot's fuzzed the cards some way."

"If only there was a legitimate way for Mannion to get the money prior to the deadline, something Wilmot couldn't even question. If Mannion was able to pay Wilmot off, the man might also lose his interest in Vanessa if he doesn't stand to get control of the entire business."

"You know the city better than I. Any ideas?" Hugh asked.

"None, I'm afraid. The only recourse I can offer is to continue to investigate Wilmot, see if we can discover any unsavory skeletons in his closet that he'd liefer remain hidden," Trevor suggested.

"Hmm— Yes, I agree we should pursue that avenue, but it

is a chancy thing at best,'' Hugh said, absently tapping the end of his quill against the letter to his brother, his eyes staring blindly down at the squiggles and curls of his handwriting. Slowly his eyes focused, caught unconsciously by one phrase. Straightening in his chair, a devilish smile curved his lips upward, shooting sparks into his eyes.

''What is it?'' Trevor asked, lifting his chin off his folded arms.

''This,'' he answered, tapping the letter. ''I was just telling my brother I might take some time and tour this country, take a trip up the Mississippi on one of those new steamboats. I told the same thing to Wilmot last week.''

''So?''

''If I am to be on a protracted journey, I will be facing unknown conditions of travel. What if I were delayed in returning to the city at harvest time? Then perhaps, to insure myself the best of the cotton harvested, I should prepay. I don't fear being gulled, for it's well known that a New Orleans businessman's word is his honor-bound vow, and certainly Mannion has an excellent reputation. The prepayment is not a demand of Mannion's, but a convenience to me, and of course, I am just a crazy Englishman.''

Trevor laughed. ''I like it, and it might work. Unfortunately, I hate to see you leave the city in order to give credence to your story.''

''At this point, Trevor, with the mull of things I've made with Vanessa, it might be my best course of action.''

''Don't underestimate her.''

''I don't. That's the problem,'' he said wryly.

Trevor laughed sympathetically. ''Regardless, I feel we should move to put your plan to work immediately. We'd best see Richard today. Wilmot pulled him aside for another of his private discussions yesterday, and afterward Richard looked decidedly gray. He may have upped the date again.''

Hugh scratched the back of his neck. ''Unfortunately, I agree with you, but the mere thought of possibly facing

Vanessa makes the hair on the back of my neck tingle. I daresay she'll be out for blood.''

"Oh, come now, I've never known you to shirk from danger."

"That's because the danger has always come from other men. Coming from a woman, it's a decidedly different matter."

"Meddling. You all are the aristocrats of meddling! I am shocked. What must be your collective opinion of me? I cannot rate very high in your esteem if all of you find it necessary to manage and order my life for me. What words do you use to describe me? 'She's a little ninnyhammer, silly widgeon, pea-goose, hen-witted, paper-skulled—' "

"That's enough, Vanessa. You've made your point," interrupted Mrs. Mannion with more asperity than was her wont.

"Now see here, Vanessa, you don't know all that's involved," put in her father.

"You're right, I don't. But whose fault is that, may I ask? If you would be a bit forthcoming, Father, instead of treating us like so many baubles to decorate your home, you might discover we have a modicum of brains and could be of assistance."

"There have been reasons for that, too," Mr. Mannion said heavily.

"And pray, what might they be?"

"Vanessa, you are becoming unseemly."

"Pardon me, Mama, but I find I have lost all control over my baser self. Who knows what I might do in this temperament. Perhaps throw myself at Mr. Wilmot and shockingly drape myself over his broad figure."

"Vanessa! That will be enough!"

Mr. Mannion sighed heavily. "If we are not to find ourselves in seriously straitened circumstances living off Vanessa's beneficence, she may have to do just that."

"Mr. Mannion," his wife said, "I do wish you would speak plainly without roundaboutation."

"I overextended myself this season and faced the necessity of taking out some loans to tide us over until harvest. I used half my business as collateral. Mr. Wilmot purchased my vowels and is now demanding payment by the end of the week. He will trade Vanessa's hand in marriage for an extension."

"Why? Why does he so desire my hand in marriage?"

"Because you are the true owner of the other half of my business."

"What?" she whispered, sinking down into a chair by the fireplace.

Very quickly he told them his machinations of the past four years, often casting entreaties for forgiveness in Vanessa's direction. When he completed his tale, he looked old and drawn, and for a moment, no one in the room moved or spoke.

Vanessa's mind whirled at the implications of all he had said and also left unsaid. She shook her head to clear her dazed mind, then rose and crossed to her father's side, laying a gentle hand on his shoulder. "Thank you, Father," she said softly. "You have given me much to think about. Why don't you go lie down and rest, or sit in the library and read one of your beloved histories, while I wrestle with these realities. Do not worry, I shall see our ship come in."

"Not at your own expense!"

"Father, consider this. If Mr. Wilmot was a truly evil man, he would not have even attempted to court me. My distaste for him is derived mainly, I think, from the liberties he took at the theater. I have since had cause to learn that my reaction under the circumstances was extreme. Perhaps I should now offer him an apology."

"Never!"

"Calm yourself, Father, and allow me to ruminate further on the matter. I'm sorry if I appeared unduly sarcastic earlier. But I don't believe pairing me with a—a wastrel such as Mr. Talverton is an answer either."

He sighed again, and rose from his dejected position on the sofa. His blue-gray eyes, so like Vanessa's, were glassy. Vanessa's soul cried at seeing her stalwart father a mere shadow of his usual self. She put her arms around him in a hug. He was surprised, but a faint trace of a smile eased the harsh, sad planes of his face.

She let go and stood away. He walked slowly, almost in a semblance of Jonas's old, bent scuffle, to the door. Amanda rose to follow him, hooking her arm in his and laying her head on his shoulder as they went out of the room.

With her parents' exit, Adeline laid aside all pretense of working on the quilt. "So, sister, where do we go from here?"

"I suppose I marry Mr. Wilmot."

"No, Vanessa, you can't!"

"Don't fear, I believe I have a few tricks I may play. When is Charles returning to town with Paulette?"

"I believe early Wednesday morning. I will admit, I myself am astonished to discover Mama corresponded with Louisa about Paulette's infatuation with Mr. Talverton and between them they orchestrated last weekend just so Paulette could meet Count Baligny," Adeline said. "Do you think two extra days in the country will solidify Paulette's relationship with the count?"

"If it can be managed, she shall do it," Vanessa said, leaning her head back against the sofa. "The young man lacks Mr. Talverton's worldliness and ability to adroitly step out of the line of fire. Mama and Louisa signally failed to take that into account in their matchmaking. I was most surprised to learn Mama considers Mr. Talverton an appropriate suitor for me."

"There is a touch of bitterness in your tone," observed Adeline.

"Do you blame me?" she asked.

"I think it is your pride that is smarting, not your heart," her sister bluntly observed. Vanessa look at her disgustedly, causing Adeline to chuckle. "So, tell me, what do you think you might do to spike Mr. Wilmot's guns?"

"Have Charles draw up some documents as part of the bridal settlement. I don't know how, but I'll see to it Mr. Wilmot pays a pretty penny for me," Vanessa vowed. "And me, in my innocence of business affairs, shall act as if I don't understand the matter at all."

Adeline shook her head. "That still has you married to Mr. Wilmot."

"I know, but truly, would that be so horrible?" her sister asked lightly.

"To marry where you heart is not involved? Definitely."

"From my study of it, I don't believe I'm capable of such fervid emotion."

Adeline snorted in disgust. "You, my dear sister, are a brass-faced liar."

The sky was dark blue woven with threads of purple and red along the western horizon as Trevor Danielson and Hugh Talverton set out for the Mannion residence. The streets possessed an eerie stillness in that twilight time after the business and shops closed for the day, and the bustling throng of people repaired to their homes to rest, eat, and prepare for their evening's entertainment. City workers were beginning the task of lighting the street lanterns, though they had not reached the street Trevor and Hugh traversed, heavy with black shadows. Their boots made a hollow echoing sound on the wood planks, punctuated by the tap of their elegant walking sticks.

They did not speak, each man alone with his thoughts.

Trevor's mind dwelt on Adeline and the twenty-four hours since they'd parted company. He knew a warm feeling in the pit of his stomach, expanding throughout his body as he thought about her. He had been ecstatic to discover his children loved her as he did, and he hoped to be blessed for many years with her companionship and love.

Hugh's thoughts remained tangled in a maze of uncertainty. He was no longer in the military where safety came with battle's end until the next day's engagement. What else did a man call safety? Love, home, and hearth? Those were terms he wasn't sure he could relate to after years in service. He felt rootless, uneasy with his lot in life, but uncertain what, if anything, should be done about it.

And what of Vanessa? Just the thought of her sent a ripple of feeling through his body, jangling his senses. The emotions Vanessa aroused were far different from the courtly love he bore for Julia. Curious that he should finally label it that—courtly love—as in the ballads sung by wandering minstrels of long ago. It was no more real than the love Titania bore for the ass-costumed Bottom, inspired by Oberon's love-in-idleness juice, the lowly pansy. Vanessa made his body sing, as it did in the heat of battle, his stomach churning as if he'd swallowed whole a thousand butterflies, and his head light, disconnected from his body. He could not rationalize his feelings, find precise little reasons why each occurred; it was the sum of her existence that played upon his sense like a fine-tuned harp. He was finding it exceedingly difficult to cope with her rejection. He fought the urge to use helping her father as leverage for another chance with her. He was *not* in the market for a wife! Or so the lying litany sang in his head.

"There he is, the dark-haired one!"

The whispered ghostly voice, barely sighing on the wind, alerted Hugh. He grabbed Trevor's arm, jerking him away from a particularly noisome and dark patch of shadows. Tossing his walking stick straight up, he caught it in the middle as four burly keelboat men dressed in buckskins and dirty linens, sprang out of the shadows. Held tight in their hands were massive cudgels and wicked knives catching what little light the coming night offered on their silver surfaces.

Hugh's stick caught the first one squarely underneath the chin, sending him staggering backward, clutching his jaw. Without sparing the man a glance, Hugh lengthened his grip on the stick, wielding it like a sword as the other three ruffians charged.

Regaining his balance and wits, Trevor entered the fray, his walking stick sweeping out to tangle the legs of his closest attacker and sending him sprawling to the ground. With the flick of a hidden button, he released the wooden covering of his walking stick, sending it clattering to the ground, revealing a wicked rapier.

Hugh grunted in pleased surprise at his friend's weapon as he fended off the glancing blow of a cudgel. His effort was rewarded with the sharp splintering snap of his walking stick. He stared for a bare moment, disconcerted at the broken walking stick, then held out its jagged end before him as the biggest and brawniest of the attackers came barreling toward him. Hugh stood his ground until it seemed the man would mow him down. Then he threw the stick into the man's face, dropped to the ground, and rolled into his assailant's legs. He grunted in pain as the man's heavy boots connected with his ribs, his foe tripping and falling heavily. Hugh staggered to his feet and knocked the man down again as he started to rise. Clutching his injured ribs, Hugh looked up to find Trevor.

Trevor's rapier was making little headway with his two assailants, who were dancing just out of reach of its wicked end, circling, looking for an opportunity to rush him. Whipping around, Hugh saw they were distancing themselves for an attack from either side of Trevor. They were both muscular, strong men. His friend would likely fall before one or the other. Bending his head low, Hugh charged into the small of the back of the man closest him. Surprised, the man crumbled, twisting as he did so, his heavy, raised cudgel falling. Hugh dodged, but not quickly enough to avoid a sharp blow to his head. He staggered, his head exploding with pain. Trevor quickly lunged forward, sending his needlelike rapier through the upper chest of the remaining attacker.

From down the street, they dimly heard voices shouting assistance and running in their direction. The three injured attackers scuttled back into the shadows at the sound. The brawny fellow, bellowing his rage, was up and rushing Hugh. Blood ran down Hugh's face, blinding him as he lurched sideways. The giant man was not fooled twice and came toward him, pushing his defending arms sideways as if they were feathers, and wrapping him in a bear hug. He picked Hugh up, squeezing.

A flash of steel swam before Hugh's eyes, the point resting on the bulging neck vein of his attacker.

"Let him go, or you'll feel my steel in your throat and you'll gurgle blood until you die," Trevor threatened, his arm back to ram the blade home.

The man's eyes rolled as he looked about him for his compatriots. Trevor let the sword pink the skin.

"If you are looking for your fellows, they have slunk back into the hell from whence they were spawned." Trevor increased the pressure. The man released his grasp, and Hugh fell to the ground. Two young men, clerks judging by their attire, came running up. Trevor slowly lowered his sword.

"Yo! What's going on here?"

"Heard the scuffling, came running as fast as we could."

"Are you all right, Hugh?" Trevor asked.

Hugh rose painfully to his feet, clutching his left side. "Handy toy you have there," he wheezed hoarsely, each breath sending pain shooting through his side. He winced.

Trevor grinned. "It's de rigueur here in New Orleans."

"Now you tell me," Hugh managed.

"Oh, you're a visitor, thought you must be, unarmed as

you were," said the youngest of the newcomers. "I never go anywhere without my sword stick, or a pair of poppers."

Hugh blinked, struggling to stay upright and focus on the men who helped scare off the attack by their approach, while his head screamed in silent agony. The younger one was a short, round fellow; his partner was tall and angular. Both were holding slender sword-stick rapiers in their hands. Hugh looked back at his attacker who almost seemed to cower into himself. "What are we going to do with him?" he asked.

Trevor frowned. "I suppose we'd best let him go. He's only the hired help."

"You think this was intentional?" asked one of the strangers, whistling through his teeth in wonder.

The other young man nodded sagely. "Stands to reason. His type don't come out in this area unless he's in a pack and drunker than a monkey. Then they come roaring down the streets."

"How do you know?" Hugh demanded of Trevor, not paying attention to the two men.

"The fellow with the red turkey feather in his cap, he'd be the leader. It's a sign of status for the toughest member of a keelboat crew, or all crews.'

Hugh shook his head foggily. "I don't remember a turkey feather." His breathing was becoming shallow, and his body was drenched in a cold sweat.

"It was worn by the fellow you charged and pounded with a kidney blow. But we'd best get you home. You're bleeding like a stuck pig, and I'd say those ribs need binding."

His words drew all attention to Hugh's condition. The big man, seeing his opportunity, turned and fled.

"Hey!" yelled one of the men, primed to give chase.

"Don't bother," said Trevor. He looked aghast at Hugh's white complexion and dilated eyes. "Hugh, put your arm

around my shoulder. Can you make it as far as the Mannions'?
It's just around the corner.''

"Oh, well, we'll accompany you, sort of a rear guard,"
the taller angular young man then offered, excitement evident in his eyes. He wanted the blackguards to return. Hugh
vowed he would have laughed at the lad's enthusiasm if his
head and side didn't hurt so much.

"Trevor," he said suddenly, "I'd liefer go elsewhere than
the Mannions—" The thought was surprisingly clear in his
muzzy mind.

"You're in no condition to make choices or give orders.
Besides, the Mannion women acted as nurses after the
Battle of New Orleans to American and British alike. You'll
be well tended until we can get a sawbones to look at those
ribs and that head wound."

"The Mannion women?" piped in the short young man.
"One of them did a bang-up job of bandaging my burned
hand after that battle."

"Yeah, burned without even firing a shot at them damned
British 'cause your gun exploded. You never did know how
to keep a gun properly cleaned," his friend accused.

"That ain't so!" flared the first one.

"Gentlemen, please," snapped Trevor, "let's not fight
among ourselves." As spoiling for a fight as they were, he
wondered what would be their reactions if they realized
Hugh was British?

The two young men glared at each other but remained
silent.

"Here, this is the Mannion house," Trevor said, stopping
to bang the heavy knocker. He turned his head to address
their allies. "Thank you, gentlemen, for your help."

"Tweren't nothing, we just scared them off. Next time,
carry your own sword stick," one of the men seriously
advised Hugh.

"Or a popper," put in the other.

Hugh nodded groggily, willing his thoughts to make it

through the sand that seemed to be filling his mind. "I will take your advice with good heart," he said dryly, then coughed.

"Well, we'll be off then."

Trevor and Hugh watched them head off arm in arm down the street, strutting as if they'd vanquished the devil himself. Hugh's head began to loll sideways, and he could feel a churning sea of blackness threatening to drown him. Determinedly, he held it at bay, fighting his body.

Jonas opened the door and the bright light of the hall spilled out over their dirty, blood-streaked figures. "Mr. Talverton! Mr. Danielson! Come in, come in! I'll get the Missus immediately."

Vanessa stood on the last step, about to join her family in the parlor when she heard Jonas's exclamation. On first hearing Mr. Talverton's name, a simmering anger surged through her, and it was on her lips to tell Jonas to refuse him admittance. In the next moment, Jonas backed away from the door and she saw him.

"Oh, my God! Hugh!" she cried.

Hugh looked up, blood and sweat blurring his vision, her image only a white-clothed figure glowing with an angel's golden aura. His lips twisted into a travesty of a smile. "Hello, Vanessa," he managed, before the churning blackness finally engulfed him.

CHAPTER

FOURTEEN

♥

"The ribs will give him discomfort for quite some time, but I venture to say it's his head that'll ache the most when he wakes. Nasty bump and cut. Concussion most likely. You know what to look for."

The words came filtering through a great fog to Hugh's mind. He lay there trying to make sense of them. Memories of a pallet in Spain swirled in his mind, but surely they were only memories. Yes, memories, for then it had been his shoulder on fire. He realized he heard water pouring, the rustling of fabric. He wanted to open his eyes, but they were still so heavy, recalcitrant to his desires.

"Lucky fellow he didn't take a direct hit. I've seen my share beyond hope. There's a man I tended ain't much better than an idiot now after taking a bad blow," the voice went on conversationally.

There was the gentle murmur of a softer voice, but the words were indistinct.

"He'll come around soon, and when he does, give him that sedative draught I've prepared. Eh? Yes, a cool compress would probably help. Keep him quiet for a few days,

though by the looks of him, I'll grant you that might be difficult,'' the voice said, chuckling.

Concentrating, Hugh heard the snap of a lock and footsteps walking away. Somewhere a door opened and closed. Hugh sighed deeply, then grimaced at the painful pull to his side. A rustle of fabric followed his action, and he felt something cool touch his brow. He also smelled lavender water. There had never been any lavender water in Spain. His thoughts were fuzzy, impeded by the incessant pounding in his head. This was absurd. There were no soft pillows and mattresses in Spain. Dreaming.

"Devilish business. Had two horses shot out from under me," he said seriously, struggling to sit up despite a wave of giddiness sweeping over him. His eyelids fluttered weakly, but resolutely he ordered them to open.

Gentle hands on his shoulders pressed him back down among the pillows. "Rest now, it's all right."

The soft, warm words came from a blurred image. Hugh blinked, willing his eyes to focus despite the increasing pain pounding his temples at the effort. His vision refused to clear, but he knew the form to be female.

"Nonsensical," he stated flatly.

"To be sure," said the pleasing voice. "Here now, take this." A supporting arm lifted his head and helped him drink an evil-smelling concoction.

He made a face at the taste of the medicine, drawing a watery chuckle from his ministering angel. Angel. There was something about an angel, but the thought eluded him and tracing the thought increased the pressure in his head. He reluctantly gave it up. It didn't seem to matter now anyway; he couldn't keep his eyes open. Blissfully he slid into sleep.

Tears clung to Vanessa's lashes though a smile gently curled her lips. She leaned forward, brushing her lips across his brow in a whisper of a kiss, then sat back in the Windsor chair she'd drawn up beside the bed, her eyes never leaving Hugh's still form.

Vanessa woke abruptly. The blackness of night had deserted her room for the gray gloom of dawn. She lifted her head, peering at the ormolu clock on the mantel. It was but a few minutes after six. Hurriedly she rose. Pulling her crisp, white, lawn nightdress over her head, she let it fall carelessly to the floor as she rummaged in her armoire for a dress she could don without assistance. She settled on a blue printed cambric with creamy lace trim. Dressed, she sat in front of her vanity and frowned helplessly. At midnight, when Leila had come to relieve her at Hugh's bedside, she'd fairly stumbled to her bed; the perturbation she'd felt at seeing Hugh bloody and battered inordinately fatigued her.

She had not possessed the energy to lay a hand to her hair, and this morning it showed to no good effect. Ruthlessly she pulled pins from her hair until it tumbled down her shoulders. She brushed it vigorously, finally twisting it into a resecured knot on top. The hair that was cut shorter in front of her ears, which she dressed in curling papers every evening, looked smashed and limp. Deftly she coaxed and teased each curl into a semblance of its normal shape, pinning a few recalcitrant ones in place.

When she was finished, she glanced again at the clock, pleased to see how swiftly she'd dressed. Rising, she left her room, moving quickly down the hall. She stopped in front of Hugh's door and knocked softly.

Leila opened it and frowned at her. "What are you doing about so early, Miss Vanessa?"

"I came to relieve you."

The older woman snorted. "I bet you ain't even had yore breakfast."

"No, but I'm not hungry. How has he been?"

"He was a mite restless earlier, but now he's sleep'n restful like, and not likely to wake real soon. So, chile, you just take yoreself off and git some food in that belly lest you git too weak to do anybody any good." Her arms akimbo, her features set fiercely, the woman spoke with the authority of a longtime family retainer.

Despite her concern for Hugh, Vanessa was forced to smile. "All right, Leila. I'll be back shortly. But if he should wake—"

"Yes, Miss Vanessa, I know. I'll come a bustl'n after you just as I said I would last night."

Vanessa had to be content with that and agreed. Leila watched her go down the hall, then slowly closed the door. She turned to look at the man sleeping on the bed and clucked her tongue.

"Young man, you best appreciate my girl or may the spirits plague your soul," Leila said decisively, then crossed herself and returned to her seat at his bedside.

More than an hour passed before Vanessa could return to the sickroom. Trevor Danielson came by early with the expressed intention of remaining until Hugh awoke. He ate a hearty breakfast with the family and regaled Vanessa with the details of the assault for she'd not heard them the night before, busy as she was with Hugh's welfare.

Vanessa's face turned white when she heard how he'd tackled the man about to attack Trevor, earning him the sharp blow to the head. She remembered the doctor's words on the effects of such blows and shivered. The entire affair created a feeling of unresolved terror within her breast. Incidents as befell Mr. Danielson and Mr. Talverton occurred at the dark of night in alleys and in rough sectors, not at dusk along normally well-traveled roads. Something wasn't right, but she despaired of figuring out what that elusive something was.

Shaking her head in confusion, she poured herself a cup of strong coffee and carried it upstairs.

This time when Leila opened the door to her knock, the

older woman met her with a good heart. "Come in, chile," she said, smiling broadly. "You come in good time. I think he's nigh near wak'n." She took Vanessa's cup and saucer from her and set them on a table. "See, his color's much better—he don't look like no advertisement for an undertaker no more."

"Leila!"

"I calls it as I sees it," the woman warned her.

Vanessa laughed. "That's all right. I suppose he was a pretty sorry case last night. Dr. Kirby said he doesn't know how he made it this far before collapsing, yet Mr. Danielson says he chatted with their would-be rescuers quite naturally."

Leila nodded sagely. "His type be hard to fell. They keep fight'n until the danger's gone or they're dead. Then sometimes they fight on, Miss Vanessa, like the undead," she finished in hushed voice. Rocking back on her heels, she clasped her hands primly over her starched white apron.

Vanessa's merry laugh dispelled Leila's words of doom. She squeezed the woman's shoulder, silently thanking her for her vigilant care of their patient, then firmly escorted her from the room. Alone with Hugh, she shyly crossed the room to stand by the head of the bed. With a light touch she lifted a guinea-gold lock of hair off his forehead and pushed it back among the deep waves of his hair. He stirred slightly at her touch. She froze, uncertain what to do. Hesitantly she removed her hand until it lay by his head on the pillow.

He stirred again restlessly, his head turning to rest on her hand. A soft sigh of peace escaped his lips; for a moment his struggles to pull himself out of the deep well of sleep subsided.

Slowly she pulled her hand out from underneath his face, biting her soft inner lip in anxiety as she did so. Her reckless urges had nearly pitched her into trouble. She pulled her chair up closer to the bed and retrieved her coffee, sitting down next to her patient while she drank. Her mind wandered for a moment as she considered her feelings for Hugh Talverton. What she told Russell Wilmot was distressingly true. She was in love. Unfortunately it wasn't likely that her love would be returned. Her eyes teared slightly. Now she was learning about some of the negative aspects of love, the aspects that twisted one's insides into gordian knots.

She looked up to find Hugh's clear, tawny eyes on her. She flushed slightly. "You're awake. Good," she said smiling down at him.

It was the same voice, the same blurred angelic image from his chaotic dreams. He blinked his eyes, willing his sight to clear. Slowly, the flesh-tone image took shape.

"Vanessa," he murmured.

She smiled down at him. He might have been mistaken, for his sight was still none too clear, but he could have sworn her eyes were misted with unshed tears.

She placed the cup she held on the bedside table. "Well," she said crisply, rising and pushing the Windsor chair away from the bed, "how do you feel?" With brisk efficiency she laid her fingers on his wrist.

Her light touch was cool, but a faint trembling of her hand revealed a tumult of feeling at odds with her efficient, reserved manner.

"For a while I thought I was back in the field hospital in Spain."

"Oh, is that how you received that scar on your shoulder?"

"Yes," he answered, grinning.

She blushed bright red, remembering how she'd had difficulty attending the doctor's words while her eyes roved hungrily over Hugh's broad chest with its fine mat of golden hair. It had taken all her fortitude to wind the cloth around his chest in the manner the doctor prescribed, while he held him upright. She'd tried to ignore how low the sheet rested on his hips, for she knew Jonas and Mr. Danielson had stripped the soiled, bloody clothes from his body and Leila, with Jonas's help, had sponged the sweat and blood away. The colored woman had come out of the room clucking her tongue and declaring what a fine figure of a man he was. It was then Vanessa decided she would assist the doctor and assume the role of nurse, for she was suddenly possessed by the snake of jealousy winding itself around her heart!

"I assisted Dr. Kirby in the binding of your chest—" she said primly, casting a glance in his direction. His smile was broader. "I—I could not help but notice—" she foundered, her blushes increasing though Hugh made no response other than to continue to smile. "After all, I did do service as a nurse during the war. Dr. Kirby took advantage of that fact," she finally declared with more force than her words warranted.

"Naturally," he responded neutrally.

Vanessa looked at him suspiciously.

"But you asked me how I felt. In truth my ribs feel as if they've been run over by an ordinance wagon, and my head feels like a cannonade is going off inside."

Vanessa nodded brusquely. "Dr. Kirby feared as much. He left some medicine for you. Let me prepare it—"

He grabbed her wrist as she turned to leave the bedside. "Wait, please. The medicine will put me to sleep again."

She did not refute his statement. She stared down at the spot where his hand clasped hers. "Sleep is what you need right now," she managed huskily, all her nerve endings tingling at his touch.

"I know, *Nurse*," he said. He squeezed her hand, delighting in how her cheeks pinked. He dropped her hand. "What time is it?"

"About eight-thirty I believe. Why?"

He looked up at the covered windows, discerning slivers of sunlight through the shutters. He frowned, his expression one of serious contemplation. "It is just the day after our melee, is it not? I mean, I haven't slept for thirty-six hours, have I?"

She smiled at his concern. "No, you have not slept the day around."

He nodded, some of the furrows in his brow easing. She watched him, fascinated by the evidence of some inner turmoil and concentration.

"Is Trevor here?" he asked suddenly.

She jumped at the unexpectedness of his question. "Yes."

"Send him in, please."

"I don't think you're in any condition to—"

"Please, just for a few moments, and afterward I'd love a light breakfast, then I promise to take my medicine like a good boy."

"I don't believe you were ever a good boy," she returned archly.

He grinned. "That's probably because I never had you nearby to make sure I was. I'm sure you could have taught my old nurse a thing or two."

"Mr. Talverton," she said repressively.

"Miss Mannion," he returned equally serious, then his face took on a meek look. "Please?"

Vanessa sighed. "It's against my better judgment, but I suppose if a man is beginning to think of food, he's well enough for company. Nonetheless, he may visit for five minutes only!"

He nodded slightly and closed his eyes. "Thank you," he said simply.

Vanessa looked at his still form doubtfully, her lips set in a straight line, then she turned and hurried out of the room with a swish of her skirts.

Hugh opened his eyes after she left, raising his hand to massage his temples. He was almost surprised to find a bandage there, until he remembered the blow he took to the head. He was in severe pain and in truth he needed to sleep; however, he could not show Vanessa how debilitated was his condition lest she refuse him time with Trevor. He remembered the words he heard moments before the attack, identifying Trevor as their target. The question was why?

He heard Vanessa and Trevor arriving moments before the door opened. He took his hand away from his head and willed the lines of pain on his face to ease, compartmentalizing his agony to another corner of his mind. He knew he couldn't do it for long, and when he released his tremendous willpower, the pain would come rushing back tenfold, but that was a risk he had to take.

Vanessa opened the door and stood aside so Mr. Danielson could enter, bearing with him a breakfast tray for Hugh.

"Now remember," she remonstrated him, "five minutes, that's all."

"Yes, ma'am," Trevor said smartly.

She glared at both of them a moment longer, then closed the door.

"Phew! I wish you happy, my friend, but I think you have a termagant on your hands," he said setting the tray on the bedside table and handing Hugh a bowl of thin gruel.

"My little general, more likely, not that she'd wish to be my anything." Hugh looked at the gruel with undisguised dismay, then he wryly smiled and accepted the food.

Trevor rubbed his chin. "I wouldn't be too hasty in that assumption. You were out cold and missed her fight to be your nurse.'

"She fought to assist me?" he asked before drinking the gruel. He found it surprisingly tasty.

"Determinedly," his friend assured him.

Hugh expelled his breath slowly. "Thank you for that. But we must speak, and quickly, before the general returns," he said, handing Trevor back the bowl. "Tell Mannion of my plan. He may cut up stiff that you know of the problem, but placate him as best you can. Convince him it's for the best. Tomorrow—or better yet, later today—if you're able, bring me paper, quill, and ink. I must write a letter to the bank authorizing the draft. I want this done as swiftly as possible.''

He paused, running his hand unconsciously across his deeply furrowed brow. ''It might be to our advantage to have Vanessa as my nurse, since it may keep her out of circulation. Second, ask Mannion now for Adeline's hand in marriage, then make as big and as splashy an announcement as you can.''

Trevor laughed. ''I'm not averse to that, but may I ask why?''

''Because our attackers were after you, Trevor.''

''What?''

''Just as they rushed us I heard you identified as the target. Also, if the fellow with the cap with the red feather was the leader, he was making a concerted effort to lay you out. That's why he didn't pay any attention to me.''

Trevor frowned, but reluctantly nodded. ''All right. I'll accept that, but again I say why?''

''I fear they were hired by our erstwhile friend Wilmot because he sees you as a threat to winning Vanessa's hand. Remember, Vanessa spent an unconscionable amount of time in your company at the ball.''

''And when he finds out I'm not courting Vanessa—''

''You'll be safer, and I won't worry so much about your damned hide.''

''But what about yours?'' Trevor protested.

''Remember, I volunteered to be cannon fodder, but I didn't volunteer to enter the fray unarmed. I won't be taken by surprise again,'' Hugh grimly assured him.

''You'll be lucky to get out of that bed to do much of anything.''

A soft knock on the door was followed by Vanessa's presence, interrupting their discussion. ''Time, Mr. Danielson,'' she said, holding the door open and pointedly staring at him.

''Right,'' he said, raising from his chair. ''I'll talk to you tomorrow, Hugh.''

Vanessa stood silently until he exited the room, then she closed the door with a decided snap. "Now, Mr. Talverton," she said, walking toward him with a determined air, "you will take your medicine."

"Yes, Miss Mannion, I will," he admitted tiredly.

Her cold demeanor melted like spring snow, and her heart went out to him. She handed him the glass and put her arm underneath his head to help him rise enough to drink. When he was finished, she took the glass from him, setting it on a tray by the bed, and reached behind him to fluff his pillow. Hugh's senses swam at her closeness, but he held himself rigidly in check. When she backed away and looked down at him with tenderness, his heart swelled. He couldn't take much more of her tenderness; the prim and proper nurse was a safer companion.

He looked up at her, a mischievous little twinkle in his eye. "So, do I get a sweet for being a good boy and taking my medicine? I suppose I'm past the age of a sugar plum, how about a sweet little kiss instead?"

Instantly she pokered up. "That blow certainly addled your wits. Go to sleep, Mr. Talverton," she said repressively, setting the Windsor chair a respectable distance from the bed and sitting down, her hands folded primly in her lap.

"Yes, ma'am," he returned promptly and closed his eyes. Surprisingly, he was sound asleep in a trice.

When next he awoke, Hugh was pleased to discover the incipient pounding in his head to have settled into a dull ache. Experimentally he levered himself up in bed, testing for the returning waves of giddiness and nausea. Happily they did not return. Wrapping the sheet around his nether half, he swung his legs over the side of the bed.

"Mr. Talverton!" exclaimed Vanessa from where she stood by the doorway, a luncheon tray clasped in her hands. She stood there transfixed, uncertain whether to leave or enter.

Hugh hurriedly tucked the sheet in closer about his body. "I feel as weak as a kitten," he admitted, covering her embarrassment.

"Whatever are you doing, trying to get out of bed?" she demanded as she set the tray on a bureau.

He looked at her askance, his lips twisting. "I must at some time, you know—answer the call of nature."

"Oh. Oh!" gasped Vanessa, now understanding the matter. Her cheeks flared brilliant red. "Of course, how silly— You must— I mean— Let me get Jonas," she said disjointedly, turning to flee the room.

She did not attempt to return for an hour, and this time she knocked discreetly at the door. Mr. Talverton was progressing so swiftly, it was probably no longer necessary to maintain a constant vigil on him. She regretted that. She wished he would be an invalid a while longer. But with his returning strength, her parents were sure to deny her nursing privileges, for such close, private proximity with a man was unseemly.

Her knock was met with a request to enter. She was astonished to see him out of bed and fully dressed.

"Mr. Talverton, I must protest! While you may be feeling better, that was a nasty blow to your head. Please, sir!" she admonished, waving him toward the bed.

He smiled and caught her hands in his own. "In truth I am still weak, but strong enough, I venture, to soon be denied your presence in this room without a chaperone."

Her cheeks reddening when she realized his thoughts followed the same paths as her own, she looked down at their joined hands.

"I have spoken with your mother, and she is in agreement that if I descend the stairs to the parlor and settle on one of the sofas without moving about further, I should come to no harm. Besides, I believe Adeline and Trevor may be planning an announcement, and I'd much prefer to be in attendance, than to hear it secondhand," he confided, a glinting smile lighting his eyes.

She looked up at him, momentarily speechless. Her heart ached to see the stark white bandage around his tanned brow, his blond waves in disarray, falling across the bandage or standing almost straight out away from his head. She heard his sharp intake of breath, and suddenly realized she was staring at him with all the love she felt for him showing nakedly in her face. She pulled her hands out of his, turning toward the door, her slight laugh high and strained. She was not going to give him another opportunity to throw her love back into her face. He didn't want her love, he wanted an amusing dalliance. He was uncomfortable around her due to her emotions, and that was the last thing she wanted him to be.

"Well, come then. I'll lend you my arm on the stairs, but you must promise to tell me immediately if you feel the least giddy or dizzy," she said earnestly, trying to cover her own trembling limbs with false bravado.

Hugh scowled at her briefly, concerned about her skittish behavior. He wondered what he'd said or done to set her off on such a high-strung course. He clearly saw the love she felt for him reflected in her eyes, lit from a source deep within her, a source he longed to discover. He was nearly at the point of sweeping her into his arms in answer and mutual discovery, when she'd abruptly turned out the lights, leaving her eyes blank clouds of blue-gray fog. The change was so abrupt that he wondered if he had again been hallucinating. But there, she stood by the door, patiently waiting. He decided he would allow her her head, so long as she did not grab the bit between her teeth. He smiled at her, extending his arm.

"Your aid and abetment would be appreciated," he allowed, offering her a small bow.

"Have a care, Mr. Talverton, lest you tumble down again," grinned Vanessa.

"Ah! But if I could be promised you as my nurse, it might be worthwhile."

Vanessa feigned a broad yawn as they left the room.

"You cut me to the quick, Miss Mannion."

"Such was my endeavor, Mr. Talverton," assured Vanessa archly.

They slowly descended the stairs. In truth, the walking did aggravate Hugh's headache, and a slight feeling of giddiness gripped the edges of his consciousness. They were halfway down the stairs when Jonas answered a knock on the door and was shown to be admitting Mr. Wilmot.

"Oh, bother," murmured Vanessa, a slight moue of dissatisfaction turning down her features. She quickly recovered and smiled as he looked their way.

"Mr. Talverton," his raspy voice called out as he crossed toward them. "I heard of your mischance and came to find out how you did."

"Yes," Hugh drawled, his eyelids drooping until he was nearly studying Mr. Wilmot through slits. He leaned more heavily on Vanessa, desiring to keep her close.

She looked at him in surprise, wondering at his sudden weakness and antagonistic manner toward Mr. Wilmot. Did he know of her father's predicament?

"I understand I fared better than most do who come up against a group of keelboat stalwarts, no matter their numbers. Excuse me, but might we not continue to the parlor, Miss Mannion? I feel the sooner I am again in a recumbent position, I shall recover my strength."

"Of course, Mr. Talverton. You may follow us, if you would, Mr. Wilmot."

"Yes, I believe I shall," grated Mr. Wilmot, his saturnine features closed, yet watchful.

Vanessa was exceedingly aware of Mr. Wilmot's presence behind her every step of the way. She felt his eyes boring into the back of her head and felt his heavy tread echoing her own lighter steps across the floor.

She paused at the parlor door. Though the room was shuttered against the hot afternoon sun, enough light filtered into the room to create a soft glow around Adeline and Amanda as they sat before the quilting frame, their brown-haired heads bent over the poppy-red and cypress-green design sewn on a cream ground. They presented an image of serenity that she was loath to shatter.

Her heart swelled with love for her family, and suddenly all the implications of Mr. Wilmot's actions hit her. He would destroy the basic fabric of her family with barely the twitch of an eyebrow, and still expect her to accede to marriage graciously. She did not believe he had come to her home to inquire after Mr. Talverton. More likely he'd come to importune her further. She wondered when he'd begin his threats to her family, or if he considered her too naive to appreciate the implications of his actions. A white-hot anger overcame her, and her body stiffened.

Hugh Talverton, leaning on Vanessa's arm, felt her stiffen. He looked at her face and noted the set rigidity of her features and the pallor of her complexion. He stood up straighter, wondering at the change in her demeanor. The marked change worried him She was on edge and likely to land them all in the basket if she took some distempered freak. He silently cursed Wilmot's presence, accurately guessing that in some way the man was responsible for her manner.

The moment was fleeting, for then Amanda Mannion looked up and saw them in the doorway.

"Mr. Talverton," she said, rising gracefully, "I trust you are not feeling too ill from moving about?"

"No, madam," he responded, smiling, as they entered the room, "though I must admit to a dashed weakness."

"Yes, but he refuses to remain abed," Vanessa said, leading Hugh toward a sofa.

Mrs. Mannion chuckled. "Gentlemen seldom care for their health, my dear, and generally maintain a stoic front.

Just prop him up with pillows and hope he has sense enough to return to his bed before he must be carried."

Hugh's answering grin was lopsided. "Have no fear of that, Mrs. Mannion. After embarrassing myself by fainting last evening, I'm not likely to repeat the incident. It can hardly be conducive to winning favors," he said, glancing at Vanessa's face as he eased himself down on the sofa.

"Very prettily said, Talverton," growled Wilmot from the doorway.

"Mr. Wilmot!" Mrs. Mannion exclaimed, swinging around. "I'm terribly sorry. I did not see you enter behind Vanessa and Mr. Talverton. Please, come in and sit down. Adeline, ring for refreshments," she said, hurriedly crossing to his side.

"Thank you, madam," he said, sitting in a winged armchair, his back to the door. He leisurely crossed his legs and, from under heavily lidded eyes, looked across the room at Hugh Talverton. "My visit will be brief. I merely came to inquire after Mr. Talverton's welfare and," he said, turning his head back toward Amanda Mannion, the hint of a smile on his lips, "to see if I might have a word or two with Richard."

Vanessa's lips set in a straight line. Hugh touched her arm, turning her attention toward him. "There is no need to stand over me, Miss Mannion. I promise I shall not swoon."

"Oh! Oh, of course, Mr. Talverton," she said, recalled to her circumstances. She sat down swiftly on a small chair near Hugh and as far from Mr. Wilmot as possible, without being obvious.

"Richard is in the library in conference with Mr. Danielson at the moment. They should be out directly. In the meantime, may I offer you a glass of Madeira?" Mrs. Mannion suggested, sitting in the chair next to his.

He inclined his head in acquiescence, while his eyes roved the assembled company, feeling the tension in the room.

"Jonas," Mrs. Mannion said when the butler arrived in response to Adeline's summons, "please bring in the refreshment tray, then see if you can inform my husband of Mr. Wilmot's presence."

"Mr. Wilmot," Hugh drawled, pulling the man's attention away from the nervousness in the ladies, "possibly you can help us. I understand you employ and are well acquainted with these ruffian river men. Maybe you can help us identify the four that attacked Trevor and me, to see that they're brought to justice."

"Perhaps, though it would serve no purpose," he grated, his voice the sound of stone on stone.

"Well, truthfully, we're not concerned for the river men. We're more interested in who hired them," he said coolly, ignoring the concerted gasps from the ladies.

"Hired them?" asked Wilmot, his eyebrow twitching. "Surely you're mistaken. That Nongela they serve in the saloons makes brave-hearts out of cowards."

"No, Wilmot, I'm not mistaken. Those men were hired and were after Trevor," he said crisply, all vestiges of the London fop, that he'd maintained before Mr. Wilmot in the past, falling away. His tawny gaze pierced Mr. Wilmot, issuing a silent challenge.

"Trevor?" asked Adeline weakly as she rose unsteadily from her chair, leaning heavily against the quilt frame.

Wilmot's brow twitched on seeing Adeline's pale complexion. Vanessa scowled at Hugh, realizing with a sick feeling in the pit of her stomach, just how determined Mr. Wilmot was.

The man shifted slightly in his chair and studied his fingernails for a moment before looking back at Hugh. "Interesting," he said noncommittally.

A small sound, like a groan, escaped Adeline's lips as she crumbled to the floor, pulling the quilting frame over on top of her.

CHAPTER

FIFTEEN

♥

"Adeline!" called Vanessa and Amanda, running to her side.

Hugh rose clumsily to his feet cursing his stupidity. As quietly as she sat at her sewing, he had forgotten Adeline's presence. He grabbed the side of the quilt frame, pulling it off Adeline while her sister cradled her head in her lap and her mother chafed her wrists. With black annoyance, he noted Wilmot had not moved but was watching them, a smile playing upon his lips.

"Let's get her to the sofa," he said to Vanessa as he bent down to pick Adeline up.

"Yes, yes," she said distractedly, relinquishing her position.

"Careful, Mr. Talverton," Mrs. Mannion said.

A sharp stab of pain pierced his ribs when he picked up Adeline, and he staggered slightly as his head spun for a moment.

Suddenly the door opened admitting Richard Mannion and Trevor Danielson.

"Hugh!" cried Trevor, swiftly crossing the room as Hugh

gently placed Adeline on the sofa. He knelt by her side. "What happened?"

Hugh flopped down into the chair Vanessa had vacated, his long legs splayed out before him. Around him he heard the jumble of explanations as everyone moved to speak, save Mr. Wilmot who still sat quietly in his chair. Adeline was coming around, her moans adding a counterpoint to the noisy exclamations of her family.

Hugh's head was pounding again. He ran his hand across his brow. "Your intended discovered the attack was not an accident."

"What?" Trevor demanded, glancing quickly in Mr. Wilmot's direction. That gentleman's brows merely twitched, and Hugh again cursed his forthright tongue. He must be more muzzy-headed than he knew.

Russell Wilmot slowly uncrossed his legs and rose to his feet. "I think, under the circumstances, I shall take my leave of you all. Richard, I'll call upon you tomorrow," he said sharply.

Mr. Mannion nodded, his iron brows lowering over his eyes, his face rigid. "I shall expect you around ten?"

Wilmot paused, taken aback by Mannion's ready agreement. "Yes," he said considering, "ten it is." He bowed to the rest of the company who stood in their places like a silent tableau, then turned to leave as Jonas entered with the refreshments.

His exit heralded an explosion of speech from the room's occupants. Hugh sat slumped in his chair, letting the exclamations and remonstrations lap over him like the ocean's tide. He sat apart, his head aching, yet feeling they were approaching the end of the maze and the resolution of their travails.

He looked up at Vanessa, arms akimbo, as she listened to her father's explanations. Her face was a study of astonishment and dismay. She was fairly sputtering her indignation, her face showing heightened color on her cheekbones in contrast to her pale complexion. She was beautiful in her own unique style. What had he dubbed it last week? Was it really such a short time ago? Did people really fall in love in that short a time? He didn't know. All he knew was that he felt as if he'd known her all his life. She had a vitality he'd never seen in a woman before, and she exerted a pull upon his senses he'd never experienced. He hoped her solicitous attitude was in some measure a sign of the depth of her regard for him. He'd faltered badly with his behavior at the Chaumondes'. He could not believe he was so blind as to think what he felt for Vanessa wasn't love. To deny the tug upon his senses that sent his blood pounding in his head was ludicrous. He wanted nothing so much as to enfold her in his arms and claim her lips once again.

Vanessa suddenly swung around to face him. "And you, Mr. Talverton, need to repair immediately to your bed."

Hugh blinked at her words, coming as they did on the heels of his erotic thoughts. He stirred uneasily in his chair, afraid he would soon embarrass himself before all by the evidence of his increasing arousal. Hastily he clamped down on his wayward emotions, his teeth grinding with determination. He allowed a slow smile to curve his lips upward in a lopsided manner.

"You are correct, Miss Mannion, and I should be grateful for your assistance."

Mrs. Mannion heard their exchange and broke off ministering to Adeline to address them: "Yes, Vanessa, please do. We do not want him passing out again, and I'm afraid he went beyond his limits when he picked up Adeline. I really should have forbidden it," she mused. "But Vanessa, as Mr. Talverton no longer appears to be in danger of delirium, we may dispense with vigilant nursing," she added pointedly.

Vanessa blushed at her mother's words, acknowledging the propriety, but realizing it warred with her desires. When she saw him smile up at her with his crooked grin and his golden blond waves falling across the white bandage on his head, the tingling surged rapidly up from her toes to shake her entire being. She offered him her hand to aid him in rising but wondered, as she struggled with the light-headedness his nearness created, who would be supporting whom.

Trevor, kneeling on the floor beside the sofa where Adeline lay, rocked back on his heels as he watched the silent drama being enacted between Hugh and Vanessa as she escorted him out of the room. He nudged Adeline to view the play as well, and noted Mrs. Mannion watching with complacency while holding up her hand to her husband to forestall any comment from him.

Neither actor noticed the attention they were receiving from the others in the room as they walked arm in arm toward the door. Vanessa was interestingly pale, and Hugh remarkably formal, yet each tried to maintain a covert regard for the other that was not lost on the rest of the company. Mr. Mannion turned to his wife, a question in his eyes. She nodded. He turned back to watch them exit the room and grinned, with a renewed spark in his eyes that had been missing for four years.

Vanessa quietly touched the door handle, then hesitated, looking up and down the hall before silently pushing the door open. Hugh was sleeping, the etched lines of pain erased from his brow. Vanessa smiled and tiptoed into the room, shutting the door soundlessly behind her.

She shouldn't be in his room now. She understood her mother's strictures well. Nonetheless, she chose to ignore them for she needed to see Hugh again, to drink in his presence and dream on what might have been. She crossed to the bed, her hand reaching out to gently brush a lock of hair off his forehead, her slender fingers trailing through his thick blond waves.

All of her life she had been so intent on understanding everything she came in contact with. It was a drive within her. She'd felt the world was run by logic, and all a person had to do was know the rules. Funny, she thought, how those twisted ideas rooted themselves in one's mind. She'd never dreamed there were emotions that defied rules, emotions that created chaos—a beautiful chaos—that nonetheless felt right.

Such were the emotions gripping her now. She loved Hugh, and her mind was in chaos. What was a person to do when love was not returned full measure? Louisa was lucky, it seemed, for she'd discovered a complete love that was returned. How uncommon was that occurrence, and why did life have to be so unfair as to create love that may not be returned? The trial upon her soul was great, yet it was a trial she bore with gladness for the knowledge she gained of herself and life.

She leaned over to place a kiss on Hugh's forehead.

Hugh woke the moment her hand touched his hair, the feather-light touch caressing his head like a gentle breeze. He didn't move but looked out through his lashes. His heart pounded. He was afraid she would hear it, so loud did it sound in his own ears. He was ecstatic at her attentions, and knew he had only to be still to claim what was his.

He felt her lean over him and his arms ached to rise and grab her, tumbling her into the bed beside him. He felt a quick, hot tightening in his loins and prayed the covers would not betray him.

"I'm going to see if I can speak to Talverton now, before Trevor returns with the documents." Richard Mannion's voice came from the hallway, just outside the bedroom door.

Vanessa jerked away from the bed and silently Hugh cursed, for his breathing had become labored, his body alive with anticipation of Vanessa's kiss. She looked around distractedly, then ran toward the large armoire that dominated a corner of the room. Opening its door, she stepped inside, pulling the door after her just as her father entered the room.

Hugh was delighted by Vanessa's precipitous action, and found it difficult not to smile.

"Mr. Talverton? Hugh? Are you awake?" asked Richard Mannion, slowly approaching.

Hugh stirred on the bed, feigning waking. His eyes fluttered open. "Oh, it's you, Richard. Yes, I'm awake," he said, yawning broadly.

"Good—good," Mannion said, dragging the Windsor chair closer to the bed. He sat down and leaned forward. "Trevor's presented your plan to me."

Inside the armoire, Vanessa started. *What plan?* she thought. She peered out through the crack in the door, maneuvering until the small slice of the room in view revealed her father seated at Hugh's side.

"Great," Hugh said hurriedly, "why don't the three of us discuss it further when Trevor returns?" He was very much aware of Vanessa's listening presence, and therefore wanted to shut her father up.

"Can't say I'm happy to be taking your blunt now, but I wouldn't be an honest man if I didn't voice my thanks," Richard continued.

Hugh ground his teeth. "My money?" he tried to say lightly. "It's what I owe you. Let's just leave it at that."

"No, no, I can't do that. Those funds could be invested and earning you interest rather than be used to bail out a foolish old goat from his dreams of grandeur."

"You did what you thought was best," Hugh said forcefully, exasperation edging his voice. He was expecting Vanessa to pop out of the armoire at any moment and confront the two of them. "Let's leave it at that."

Richard nodded heavily, then a smile curved his lips. "You didn't do it for me, anyway, did you?" he cajoled, poking Hugh in the ribs. "I've seen how you look at my daughter," he said sagely, rising to leave.

Hugh winced when Richard poked his bruised ribs, more from the man's words than from any pain he felt. He was

surprised Vanessa had not shown herself in a fit of righteous
indignation. She had more self-control than he would have
thought. He only prayed she'd maintain a modicum of that
self-control when she confronted him. Richard's words
sounded far more damning that the reality. He hoped he
could make her listen.

Richard took his hand in his, then clapped him on the
shoulder before he turned to leave the room. Hugh watched
him go with mixed emotions. The man had decidedly more
life in his step, and that was good. He only prayed he had
not completely ruined his chances with Vanessa. This was
one instance where her sense of pride would probably
overpower her propriety and passion.

The bedroom door closed with a sharp click, and Vanessa
exploded out of the armoire in a flurry of coats and shirts.

"Before you say anything, Vanessa, let me explain,"
Hugh said.

Vanessa blinked and stopped short. "You knew I was in
the armoire?"

"I wasn't exactly asleep," he drawled, his smile broadening
as he watched the play of color upon Vanessa's face when
she absorbed the implications of his words. She started to
draw back, but his hand shot out to capture her arm in a
viselike grip. She tugged and twisted to get free. He
laughed shortly. "No, you're not going to run away from
me again," he warned. "Not ever, if I have anything to say
about it."

His words halted her struggles. She stared at him, stunned.

He chuckled, and tossing the covers aside, sat up and
swung his legs to the floor. He gathered her closer to him.
She made a little mewing sound of protest and pushed
halfheartedly on his chest, but it was all for pride. Passion
soon swept pride aside and propriety never had a chance as
she melted into him while he rained kisses across her brow
and down her neck, nibbling on her ear as he passed.

"I love you, you proud, stubborn wench," he growled huskily.

She moaned again softly, and his mouth captured her parted full lips in a teasing kiss that sent quivers to the core of her being, heating her from within until she radiated a melting passion. She answered his kiss with the pressure of her own lips, and when his tongue teased the corners of her mouth, she parted her teeth to bid him enter.

He leaned back against the bed, pulling her with him, until they fell among the pillows and linens. Hugh's hand roved over her back and she arched to meet his body with her own.

"Vanessa," Hugh murmured as his lips left hers for a moment to trail kisses across her face. He raised a hand to her face, gently tracing the outline with his fingertips. He lifted his head to look at her, a thoroughly masculine, raffish smile on his lips. "You do realize, don't you, that we are in a highly compromising position?"

A delicate blush suffused her face, but she met his gaze squarely. "Yes," she returned simply, then nuzzled his neck and whispered in his ear, "It is a position I desire to investigate further." She lifted her head to look at him. "But not now," she said, sliding out from his arms and rolling off the bed.

He lay back against the pillows, his eyes mere slits as he watched her straighten her clothes and run a trembling hand over her hair, ineffectually patting wayward strands into place. "When?" he finally asked after the silence had lengthened and it seemed she no longer could meet his eye.

Her brow shot up at the hint of a challenge, and she turned to look at him coolly, her hand sinking to her side. "When I know your love is not the toy you mentioned at the ball," she said archly, then grinned, spoiling the effect. "But now I must leave, for you have effectively demonstrated that you no longer need a nurse, or anyone, to check up on you. You are a madman for whom there is no cure."

"Oh, yes?" he asked silkily, springing upright to grab her again. This time she sensed him coming and danced lightly out of reach. She backed up to the door.

"They say, Mr. Talverton, that patience is a virtue. It is a virtue it would be wise for you to cultivate if you truly desire me."

She opened the door and was out in the hall before the pillow he threw hit the door.

Hugh slumped back against the pillows of his bed, an appreciative smile on his face for his beloved's humor. She was correct. It was time he wooed her properly, time he treated his damsel in distress like the feisty princess she was. With Wilmot defanged, he would tend to his wooing with tender ardor before he risked all to formally request her hand in marriage. He looked forward to the day he would be taking her back to England with him.

"Paulette!" Vanessa called out gaily as her friend swept into the front hall the next morning in a flurry of lemon yellow froth. Charles crossed the hall more soberly in her wake, though a faint smile traced his lips.

"Vanessa! We must be off shopping immediately! There is so much to do, and so little time! I must have a new gown, and you, my friend, must help me to choose it, or I shall be lost."

Vanessa laughed. "Quick, tell me all, I am agog," she enthused, hooking her arm with Paulette's."

Hugh followed her into the hall and laughed at the meeting, exchanging a wry glance with Charles.

"Say, what is this?" Charles demanded, eyeing Hugh's bandage.

Hugh touched the white material briefly. "A minor misunderstanding," he said lightly. "More an inconvenience than a problem."

"Is Richard about?"

"He's in the library with Russell Wilmot at the moment."

"Ah—"

"Do you know the situation?" Hugh asked as they turned toward the parlor.

"Not entirely, though I have my suspicions," Charles admitted.

"Later I will be pleased to tell you the whole sordid details. But what of you, Paulette? How did you fare?"

Paulette giggled and squeezed Vanessa's arm before answering. "The count, he is a trifle young, for he is only four and twenty—"

"So says the ancient eighteen-year-old," said Charles.

Paulette stamped her foot. "You, you have done nothing but tease me. You know nothing of what it is like to be in my position. Now, I tell you, the count, he is young, but very gallant and oh so handsome. He comes to the city with the Balignys next week. There will be a theater party, and a card party to which we are invited."

"Louisa has even decided to bring Celeste to the city for a couple of days and join in the merriment," put in Charles.

"The timing could not be better," said Hugh as they neared the parlor, his eyes twinking.

"Why?" Charles asked.

"Because—"

"You'll regret this, Mannion!" swore Russell Wilmot as he threw open the library door.

The party in the hall stopped and turned toward the library.

"I don't believe so, sir," Richard returned coolly as the two men entered the hall.

"I'll see to it that you don't get a single inch of warehouse space in the city!"

"Well, you may certainly try, but I would warn you, I have been in this city longer, and though you are accepted, it will raise many eyebrows to wonder why you choose to blackball me."

"Remember those papers!" Wilmot warned.

"No one would find them more than a curiosity now, and I don't believe you'll discover much purchase from them." Richard looked up and noted the assembled company in the hall. "Now if you'll excuse me, Wilmot, my son-in-law is newly arrived, and I would pay my respects." He gestured Mr. Wilmot toward the door.

The man scowled and stalked after him, but he stopped when he came even with Hugh. "You'll regret your meddlesome interference, Talverton."

"I? But I am only a visitor to your city and do not expect to be here long. What purpose would it serve you?"

Paulette's eyes grew round and a fine dark eyebrow rose as Mr. Wilmot took his hat and cane from Jonas and flung himself out the door.

"Me, I think I have missed much in three days! To see Mr. Wilmot so routed, oo-lala, it does my heart good. He is a devil, that one, and you are well quit of him, Vanessa."

"You have the right of it," rasped Richard Mannion, striding over to the group. He shook his head as if to clear the last bit of ichor left by Mr. Wilmot out of himself. "Come, let us join Mother and Adeline, and you, you naughty puss," he said, chucking Paulette under her chin, "may tell us how you fared with your genuine aristocrat."

Paulette laughed gaily. "*Très bien*, but I feel I have missed much here," she said as they all entered the parlor.

"Only a tirade from Vanessa, an attack upon Mr. Talverton and Mr. Danielson, and Adeline's engagement."

Paulette clapped her hands. "*Vraiment!* Adeline is engaged?" She ran over to Adeline and hugged her closely. "This is so exciting! Me, I am speechless! Let me guess, it is Mr. Danielson, *non*?" I saw you in the garden at Louisa's, you know," she said slyly.

Adeline blushed bright red and all looked at her expectantly. "It was nothing; he merely helped me to gather flowers for the ball," she finished lamely.

Paulette swung around to Vanessa and Hugh. "And you two, have you also settled things between you?"

"Paulette," scolded her brother.

"What? When they left the estate, they were not speaking. So stupid, when everyone could see how they reacted to each other."

"Must you arrive and put us all to blush, Paulette?" Vanessa complained amid general laughter.

"Phtt! You still take yourself too seriously," she stated, sitting on one of the sofas. "But tell me, how have you left things, or have you waited to have me come and put you to right?"

Vanessa blushed anew. "You are impossible."

"We have agreed to a courtship. Beyond that, we wait and see," Hugh told her.

"Wait for what? A sign from God?"

"Paulette!"

"*Pardon*, but I do not believe this. Here are two people, so obviously in love to all who see them, yet they play at coy indifference like two children. It is *insupportable*," she said, sadly shaking her head.

"We have much to discover about each other," Vanessa explained softly.

"Yes, and I would like to learn all I can about this woman while we are still in New Orleans. I'd like to see it through her eyes and understand how it worked to make her the most marvelous woman in the world."

Everyone smiled and laughed, all feeling calmer now that Mr. Wilmot was properly defanged. While Paulette launched into a recital of her past two days, Hugh pulled Vanessa though the French doors onto the gallery.

"What do you mean, while we are still in New Orleans?" Vanessa asked as they strolled in the shade.

"In the time we have here before we sail for England," Hugh explained absently, more intent on threading her fingers through his.

"To live?"

"But of course to live. Where else would we live?"

"Here," she said flatly, stopping short.

He looked at her perplexed. "Here?"

"Yes, I have no desire to go to England. I thought you would stay here," she exclaimed aggressively while pulling her hand free.

"There is nothing for me here, Vanessa—" he began.

"There is me," she offered simply.

"But if we married, you would come with me," he said patiently, coming forward to gather her into his arms.

She pushed him away and danced backward. "Ah— Now you have just said the key word—*if*." She shook her head in amazement. "I cannot believe your blind arrogance, to suppose I would simply up and leave New Orleans just to be with you! No, I take that back," she said, holding up her hand as another thought occurred to her. She ignored the flare of fire in his tawny eyes and continued: "I have always known you were arrogant, I just thought it was a trait I could wean you of. Obviously I was mistaken."

"Blind arrogance!" he stormed, his body rigid.

"Yes, and aristocratic conceit as well," she flared hotly.

He pokered up. "It is obvious we were misled in our affections," he stated stiffly.

"Obviously."

"Most likely caused by the novelty each presented to the other," he went on.

"Precisely."

"I don't believe we should be wasting each other's time. It is obvious to me your affections are shallow—"

"Shallow!" she fumed.

"—and ephemeral. I thank you for your kind offices in nursing me. Now, if you'll excuse me, I'll go pack my portmanteau and return to Trevor's town house immediately."

"Yes," Vanessa said tightly, "I think that would be best."

He bowed stiffly. "Your servant, ma'am," he said softly, turned on his heel, and left.

Vanessa stood still for several moments after he left, emotionally stunned by the events that had just transpired. A tiny moan of despair finally escaped her lips, and she slumped down on a nearby bench and wept.

CHAPTER
SIXTEEN

♥

"This is idiotic," protested Trevor as he watched Hugh pack his portmanteau. "At least stay until after the engagement party."

"It would be to no purpose, and I would not have my presence put a damper on the festivities."

"Gammon. Your absence will do that quite nicely. Adeline will be distraught."

Hugh placed a stack of neatly folded cravats in the corner of his case. "Then I depend upon you to lighten her spirits."

"Damn it, Hugh, it's been a week. Don't you think the two of you could talk about it now?"

"There is nothing to discuss. Miss Mannion made her views eminently clear to me."

"Well, I'll tell you something that's not clear to me, and that's why you're so insistent upon returning to England to live. What's there for you? True, you have an easy competence that will allow you to live life comfortably without worry, but I can't see you as a man of leisure. What are you going to do? Tend fields? Enter politics? That's all you'll be able to do without risking ostracizing the *ton*. They might forgive this little foray of yours into trade as a lark, but become further involved and they'll shun you."

"I doubt that," Hugh contradicted without looking up, his movements as he packed the bag swift and efficient.

"Do you? Do you really? You can lie to me, but you'd better not lie to yourself," Trevor warned. "Remember, I lived in England, and coming from trade, I know what reception I received. You've been at war for so many years that England has become some Elysian Fields to you and bears little resemblance to reality."

"Our cases are different. You're an American."

"And you would take an American woman to live in England? You tell me our cases are different? Egad, but Vanessa was correct. You are arrogant," he said with disgust.

Hugh straightened, and one blond eyebrow rose in an otherwise impassive face as he looked at his erstwhile friend. "But as you once told me, no more so than any other Englishman."

"It appears I was wrong," Trevor said harshly, flinging the bedroom door open and stalking out.

Hugh stared at the door, then slowly crossed the room to close it gently, his hand resting for a moment on its carved paneling. Trevor was correct, there wasn't anything for him in England. Nonetheless, Vanessa should have loved him enough to go wherever he went. That she didn't ripped at his very being like the tearing claws of a lion. He'd been to the center of the maze and managed to come back out, but without the prize, and the wounds from the skirmish would take forever to heal.

His mind was dull, his only thought to travel upriver on a steamboat, and from there he hoped to explore a bit of the countryside, to let its untamed wilderness ease the pain in his chest. Perhaps it was for the best. Their cultures were diverse, and more than likely she would not be happy in

England. All the reasons he desired to see her in London society were tied to the fact that she would set the town on its ears, and such circumstance would invariably lead to her own ostracism by the beau monde. He was a veritable cad to wish to see her humiliated so, though she was worth more than any English miss who paid mere lip service to the society's rules themselves but categorically renounced anyone else who strayed from the proper path.

He had certainly made a mull of his relationship with Vanessa. He was worse than any callow schoolboy. He swore savagely under his breath, then turned back to packing his things.

"Vanessa, what do you think of this orchid-colored material?" Adeline asked, fingering a bolt of filmy muslin.

Her sister didn't answer.

"Vanessa?" Adeline called, dropping the bolt to look around the small shop. She spotted her sister staring at a magnificently attired quadroon woman. She laid her hand on her arm. "Vanessa?"

"What? Oh, I'm sorry, did you wish to show me something?"

"Yes, an orchid fabric over here," she said, leading her to the bolt of cloth. "But why were you staring at that woman?" she asked softly.

"Because she has been staring at me, and has done so in the past three shops we've entered."

"She's been following us?"

"So it would appear, but it's me who's captured her interest for some reason, for I've purposely separated myself from you and Paulette to see if she followed either of you. She hasn't. It's me who has her interest, so I decided it would be best to stare back at her and let her know I am aware of her regard."

"I don't like this, Vanessa. Perhaps we should return home," Adeline said nervously, glancing around the small establishment. It was filled with bolts of fabric creating hidden shadowed corners. "Where's Paulette now?"

"Purchasing some ribbons to refurbish her pink silk hat, I believe."

"Well, let's get her and leave," she suggested.

"No, I don't believe so," Vanessa said slowly. "I want to discover what this woman wants."

"But you don't know anything about her, and she looks like—like—"

"A man's mistress? No, don't blush so, Adeline. I agree. That's what has me even more curious. What could such a woman, and a woman obviously fashionably well maintained, want with me?"

"You don't think that Mr. Talverton—"

"Has taken her up?" A quick little pain pierced her heart at the mention of his name. She ruthlessly shoved the feeling aside, as she had pushed aside all errant thoughts of Hugh Talverton for the past week. "I wouldn't have said she suits him, but then, I don't know him all that well," she said bitterly.

"I'm sorry I said anything. I didn't mean to cause you pain," Adeline said lamely, a worried little frown creasing her brow.

Vanessa smiled lightly, a weary, wan smile that was all she had been able to manage on any occasion during the past week. "I know. Well, talking won't pay toll, so I suggest we find Paulette and be on our way. Or did you mean to buy this material?"

Adeline looked at the bolt in front of them. "No, no I don't think so. Now, somehow, it seems just too depressing a color."

"I'm sorry, Adeline. I am not good company for someone with happy plans on her mind."

"Oh, Vanessa, no, please don't say that. I wish—I just wish you would talk to Mr. Talverton. Trevor says he's determined to leave New Orleans today. I know he wouldn't go if you'd just talk to him.''

"Mr. Talverton and I have nothing to say."

"But—" Adeline protested.

"No buts. We would not suit. Hugh Talverton was an educational interlude for me, and I an amusing dalliance for him, that's all. I neither wish to see the man again, or hear his name mentioned."

"You may find that before this day is out, you have cause to regret your words, Miss Mannion."

Vanessa whirled around, shocked to hear a melodious, lightly accented woman's voice directly behind her. It was the quadroon woman. She was beautifully attired in a glowing turquoise silk gown and was redolent of a heavy rose scent. She smiled down at Vanessa, her wide mouth open, revealing pearly white teeth. She was a beautiful woman, and a woman obviously well versed in the pleasures of men.

Vanessa glared at her, and tilted her head up haughtily. "I beg your pardon?"

The woman merely laughed, not at all put off by Vanessa's manner. "It is perhaps well that you care so little for this Mr. Talverton," the woman said serenely while fingering a brilliant swath of red silk, "as he is not long to be alive."

"What are you talking about? What do you know of Mr. Talverton?" Vanessa demanded, suddenly very frightened for there was something about the woman's calm manner that instilled belief in her words.

Adeline pulled on her sister's arm. "Come away, Vanessa. Don't talk to this woman."

Vanessa ignored her, her eyes locked with those of the beautiful quadroon.

"My—ah—gentleman has arranged for his demise this very day," she said with a smile, her dark eyes expressive. She ceased her contrived interest in the fabric around them.

"It seems this Mr. Talverton has caused him no end of inconvenience."

"What? Are you Mr. Wilmot's—" Vanessa began then stumbled to a stop, uncertain what to say.

The woman laughed again. "You ladies are all so prim and formal. Yes, I am his mistress, and he belongs to me. You are lucky you did not see fit to marry Russell, for if you had, you would not have lived long. I would have seen to that," she ingeniously added, as if it were no great matter.

"How dare you!" exclaimed Adeline. "Come Vanessa, this woman is obviously a troublemaker."

"No, wait," Vanessa said, grasping her sister's hand when Adeline would have left. She cocked her head to the side as she considered the quadroon. "You have some reason for telling me all this."

The woman's finely plucked brow rose in appreciation for Vanessa's understanding. "Indeed." The woman's eyes darkened, and she seemed to look past Vanessa as she spoke, her voice low and vibrant with conviction. "Though Mr. Talverton has defeated Russell at his game, it is still for me to strike a lesson home. I wish to teach Mr. Russell Wilmot that I am not a trifle he may shuffle aside at his convenience. I take second place to no one." She looked back at Vanessa, her sultry eyes gazing into hers. "So, I tell you of Russell's plans for Mr. Talverton, and leave it to you to effect a rescue—if you're able."

"What does he have planned?" Vanessa asked hoarsely, her grip tightening on Adeline's hand.

"An accident at the docks. Before he boards the steamboat."

"How? When?"

The woman shrugged expressively. "I know not, but you may be certain he shall not escape as easily as he did last week, for I understand a certain river man is also out for his life."

"Trevor said he was to be off at noon, or as soon as the last of the cargo was loaded," Adeline offered.

Vanessa glanced around until she spotted a lovely ornate clock in the corner. "It's after eleven, now!" She dropped Adeline's hand and reached out tentatively to touch the quadroon. "Thank you," she said simply, then grabbed her skirts and turned to run from the store.

"Vanessa, wait," called Adeline, starting after her.

The quadroon woman threw back her head and laughed richly. "Run, mamzelle, run."

"Adeline, what's going on?" called Paulette from where she stood by the door, waiting for her package to be wrapped.

"Mr. Talverton's in trouble," she said as she pulled open the shop door.

"Hold that package, I shall return," Paulette ordered the shopkeeper over her shoulder as she followed in Adeline's wake.

The banquette was crowded and forced Vanessa to walk in places as she threaded her way through the people. Tears of frustration nearly blinding her, she finally lightly jumped off the walkway to the dirt street, moving faster among the carts and dray animals on the thoroughfare. At one point she passed so near a horse that ends of her shawl, fluttering behind her, lightly flickered in the corner of the animal's sight so it reared in its traces causing his driver to ring down curses loudly and fluidly on Vanessa's head. She ignored him, her concentration centered on her achieving the docks.

She turned down the Rue St. Pierre alongside the Place d'Armes, dismayed to find it busier than the street she'd left. Now, however, her determination increased, for straight ahead of her, across the Chemin des Tchoupitoulas, lay the harbor.

Her heart pounded loudly in her head, drowning out the oaths and comments her undignified flight aroused from those she brushed past. She paused on the levee, looking frantically up and down the docks. There were so many ships and boats that for a moment she despaired of going in the right direction until she spotted the tall chimneys of a riverboat. It was the only steamboat in the harbor. She inhaled deeply, her eyes frantically searching for Hugh Talverton. She couldn't see him but she knew that did not mean he wasn't down there. It was just that the harbor was so crowded, and finding one man was difficult. She hoped it was as difficult for Mr. Wilmot's henchmen.

She set off in the direction of the steamboat, her eyes darting about, searching out a location for a possible ambush or accident on the busy dock. Barrels of sugar were being loaded onto the steamboat when she approached. She passed men who stopped and stared rudely at her, some so close she was forced to brush against them as she passed. The impropriety of her presence, alone on the docks, did not escape her. She trembled slightly but bit firmly down on her lower lip and lifted her chin. Her eyes shown bluer than normal, her agitation clear in her expression. There were so many big, rough-looking men on the docks, any or all of whom might be willing to accept blood money. What could she do even if she found Hugh? She should have gone for help, but there just wasn't any time! And where was Hugh?

She leaned against a stack of sugar barrels to rest, only to jump back hastily when one teetered precariously. Then she saw him striding confidently toward the steamboat. "Hugh!" she called, wildly waving her arm. She turned to run toward him, panic seizing her when she also saw a gang of men in dirty leathers skulking nearby. "Hugh!" she cried louder as she tripped over a tangled rope. Her arms traced mad circles as she fought to keep her balance. She staggered backward, bumping into the sugar barrels again. The top barrel, already uneasy in its position, tumbled down the stack, sending another barrel sliding in its wake. Vanessa screamed as the barrel crashed heavily onto the dock and began rolling on its side, headed straight for the tall, broad-shouldered figure of Hugh Talverton.

Hugh had stopped the first time he thought he heard Vanessa's voice calling his name. He looked around, about to dismiss the sound as his wishful imagination, when the call came again. This time there was no mistaking the voice. He turned in time to see Vanessa stumble backward into the sugar barrels. His heart leapt in his throat when he saw the top barrel fall, certain it would crush her slender figure. Miraculously it missed her. He saw it rolling toward him but his mind only vaguely took it in as a threat—he was more concerned for Vanessa. Without conscious thought, he vaulted the barrel as it approached him and ran to her side.

Vanessa cringed and nearly hid her face in her hands when she saw the barrel hurtling toward Hugh. It was only tardiness, and a slim hope that he would escape, that kept her eyes from being totally covered. Nonetheless she was astounded when he jumped the barrel, but her astonishment increased when, looking past Hugh as he ran toward her, she saw his would-be attackers mowed down like tenpin by the runaway barrel! As Hugh reached her and his arms went around her, near hysterical laughter bubbled up within her.

"Vanessa, what are you doing here?" he cried, hugging her tighter as his heart raced at the memory of the falling barrel.

"Yo! Hugh!" called Trevor as he and a band of nine men came running, pounding down the docks.

"Trevor?" Hugh said, looking perplexed.

Vanessa hurriedly straightened and pulled herself out of Hugh's arms. "Get those men!" she yelled, waving her hands in the direction of the keelboat ruffians.

"What?—" Hugh asked, his eyes following the direction of her waving hands. When he turned, his eyes widened, and a broad smile split his face. He began to laugh, for there, picking themselves up off the ground and pulling a large sugar barrel off their leader, were the four would-be attackers of the previous week.

Trevor Danielson also recognized the men, and with clear

presence of mind, he and his companions quickly surrounded them. rapiers and pistols at the ready. The leader of the attackers snarled ferally at them all, but he was helpless to fight his way out or encourage his gang to do so, for the rolling sugar barrel had landed squarely on his leg, breaking that member.

Hugh turned back toward Vanessa, who was now standing as calmly and elegantly as she could in a dirt-streaked frock with a bedraggled, broken hat feather swaying in front of her eyes. The only signs of her remaining agitation were the rapid pulse visibly throbbing in her neck, and her overbright, feverish eyes. "What's going on here? How did you know?"

"I was told Mr. Wilmot was displeased with your meddling in his affairs and intended to—intended to—" she gulped, the words catching in her dry throat

"Kill me?" Hugh asked incredulously. She nodded miserably. "I would not have thought that of him. It seems I greatly underestimated the man. But how did you find out?"

Vanessa looked down at her hands. "I'd rather not say," she said softly. She looked up at him swiftly, entreaty evident in her eyes. "Let's just be thankful I knew."

"But—"

"*Mon Dieu*, we have missed all the excitement!" Paulette's voice was heard to lament to Adeline. Behind them trailed a couple of constables who, taking in the situation, passed them by to join Trevor and his group. "I should have left you to fetch Mr. Danielson and the constables yourself, while I joined Vanessa," she said petulantly as they approached Vanessa and Hugh.

"But then you didn't know what was going on," Adeline protested laughingly, then turned to face her sister, her face suddenly sober. "Are you all right? What happened?"

"I'm fine, I just tripped," Vanessa assured her.

"And inadvertently stopped me from being attacked by knocking over a sugar barrel and sending it rolling into these men, knocking them over like so many wooden pins!"

"It almost knocked you over as well," Vanessa reminded him, shuddering slightly at the thought.

"Ah, but in battle there are many times one must leap over man-made and natural obstacles." He laughed. "I believe I jumped that barrel without even thinking about what I was doing."

Paulette clapped her hands. "Oh, that I could have seen all! Our Vanessa, a heroine!"

"Please," Vanessa protested, "spare me."

"Hugh!" called Trevor, striding toward him.

Hugh bowed briefly to the ladies before joining his friend. "What have you discovered?" he asked softly.

"It is as Adeline relayed to me when she came to get me. Wilmot's behind this, as he was on the attack last week. These men are so concerned that they not take all the blame that they are falling over each other to confess. They've said some other interesting things that have the constables's eyebrows raised, too."

"Hmm— I wonder if we might not turn this entire venture to our advantage," Hugh mused, a mischievous glint in his eyes.

"What do you mean?"

"While the constables take these four into custody, let's you and I pay a little visit to Russell Wilmot," he suggested.

"You have something in mind?" Trevor asked.

"Yes, I believe I do."

Trevor smiled and nodded, his eyes lighting with unholy amusement.

CHAPTER

SEVENTEEN

♥

Vanessa paced the spacious entrance hall. It had been two hours since they parted company with the gentlemen. They said they had some final details to clean up, then they would join the ladies at their home. Vanessa had quickly bathed and changed clothing in anticipation of their arrival, only to be left kicking her heels as the hands of the grandfather clock in the hall ticked off the passing minutes.

Hearing of the impending threat to Hugh had been the catalyst to crack the stubborn high walls of her pride. Her headlong rush toward the dock had sent them crumbling to her feet. She loved Hugh, and it didn't matter where they lived. So long as she could live with him, she would be content. It was ridiculous to imagine he would sever all his ties with England to remain with her. He had just given seven years of his life to his country and could not be expected to abandon his allegiance easily. Besides, what would he do in New Orleans? He was obviously not a man given to playing the gentleman of leisure.

Fool! she thought angrily. She had been a complete fool. She only hoped the embrace she received on the docks was indicative of his true feelings, and that he'd give her the opportunity to make amends.

"Vanessa," called her mother from the parlor door, "come and sit down and have a cup of tea before you wear a hole in your shoes from all that pacing. They'll be here when they can, dear."

Vanessa rubbed her hands together nervously. "I know, I know, but I can't relax. There is so much I would say—so much I would have him understand—"

Her mother smiled at her sympathetically. "I know, dear, and I'm sure you'll have the opportunity. But you're not doing yourself a bit of good by working yourself into a lather."

A faintly hysterical note tinged Vanessa's answering laugh. "I know—" she began ruefully. "What's that?"

From out in the street came the faint sounds of male revelry. Vanessa crossed to the door and opened it. Astonishment colored her visage, for coming down the street on the shoulders of their fellows came Mr. Talverton and Mr. Danielson! She went outside and stood on the edge of the banquette as they approached. There was laughter and snatches of bawdy songs emanated from the group and drew bright pink color to her cheeks.

Hugh looked up and saw her. He tapped the shoulders of the gentlemen who carried him to signal he wanted down. When he did so, the other gentlemen became aware of Vanessa's presence, and the lilting bawdy tunes died in their throats. Vanessa tried hard to hide her amusement and maintain a forbidding glare at the group.

Hugh was not fooled by her expression and sauntered over to her. He grabbed her around the waist and holding her high, twirled her off the banquette.

"Hugh! What are you doing!" Vanessa exclaimed, blushing furiously. "Put me down!"

"Not until I claim the conquering hero's reward," he exclaimed happily.

"What—" she began, only to have her lips suddenly caught in a bruising kiss that robbed her of breath and sent the tingling rippling through her veins. The world spun dizzily on its axis then slowly righted as he gently set her down again.

A smattering of applause and hoots of encouragement brought her sharply back to reality. She ducked her face down to hide the deep red blush that warmed her cheeks. "Come inside and tell us all," she said, pulling on his arm.

He lifted her up to set her back on the banquette, then turned to salute the crown of men behind them whose numbers seemed to have swelled from the size of the original group down on the docks. Trevor crossed to his side and clapped him on the back before he, too, waved to the jovial crowd.

"We'll see you tomorrow, Talverton," someone yelled.

"Yes—and see if you know what you've gotten yourself into!" called out another to accompanying laughter from the group.

"What do they mean?" asked Vanessa.

"Sh-h," hushed Hugh as he waved farewell, smiling broadly.

Vanessa stamped her foot. "Don't you sh-h me. I saved you today. I have a right to know," she declared.

"Yes, my love, you do, and you will, soon," he said consolingly as the three of them turned to enter the house.

She was delighted by the endearment and was moved to make some comment in return when she looked up and noted the entire household seemed to be standing in the doorway, waiting. She clamped her lips firmly together, the twin red flags flying again in her cheeks.

Trevor went eagerly to Adeline's side, placing his arm around her waist as he bent down and whispered in her ear. She glowed with pleasure, and they turned to walk slowly toward the parlor. Everyone followed them, smiles all around.

Hugh held Vanessa back from entering the room. Grasp-

ing both her hands in his, he solemnly looked down at her.
"I have been every kind of fool there is," he began gruffly.

"No, no—" she protested, "it is I—"

He held his finger up to her lips to halt her outpouring of
impassioned words. "Hush, my love," he murmured, then
his hand fell away from her face and slid down her arm in a
gentle caress. "I need your help," he said earnestly. "I am
buying a business here in New Orleans, and I know I'm
going to need assistance in acclimating myself so I don't
offend."

"What?" began Vanessa excitedly.

"Now wait, I must warn you it is likely to be arduous
labor and take all of your energies to turn me into a proper
American."

Her eyes shining, she stared up at him, "Oh, a seven-
days-a-week job, I'm sure, with very long hours will do."

He nodded solemnly, "A great many long, private hours,
I'm certain."

Doubt clouded her eyes briefly and she bit her lip. "Are
you sure, very sure? For I know now I would come with you
wherever you chose to live."

He smiled down at her, raising a gentle finger to trace the
faint frown line in her brow. "Very sure. But actually," he
continued, "I don't have much choice, for I don't believe in
perpetual absentee management."

She pulled away from him slightly. "What are you
talking about?"

"You are now looking at the owner of numerous warehouses down on the battery."

"What!"

"We advised one Mr. Russell Wilmot of the capture of
his confederates and their subsequent volubility in regard to
his actions. We convinced him he might be wise to sell out
and leave town before the constables arrive to instigate his
own arrest."

Vanessa raised her hands to her lips in delighted surprise, straining to keep her laughter in check.

"After a bit of—ah, persuasion, he decided that was his best course of action and speedily signed over his assets to me. I, in turn, wrote a letter to my bank, which I hand delivered in Mr. Wilmot's company, saw him paid, and sped him on his way."

She clapped her hands excitedly. "Oh, 'tis rich, I vow!"

He smiled down at her and shook his head. "Not as rich as I feel right now," he said ardently, sensuous flames leaping in his eyes.

Within Vanessa a strange fluttering sensation tickled her stomach, followed by the tingling this man's nearness always seemed to promote. She looked at him shyly, then a smile curved her lips upward, radiating her face. On tiptoe, she leaned toward him, tilting her face up.

Her name, a soft moan on his lips, was all she heard before his mouth captured hers in a searing kiss.

Behind them, Paulette opened the parlor door, for everyone was anxious to congratulate Hugh and was curious as to his failure to follow them into the room. She blinked, and shut it quickly, leaning against it.

"*Je suis très stupide,*" she remonstrated herself softly while hitting her forehead with the heel of her hand. She looked at the rest of the assembled company expectantly waiting. She dimpled at them and winked. "Me, I think I shall do some embroidery. It may be a long while before we hear the tale from Mr. Talverton. At least now he shall be around to tell it, *non*?"

Regency Romances

___**LETTER OF INTENT** *by Leslie Reid*
(D34-460, $2.95, U.S.A.) (D34-461, $3.95, Canada)
When American businessman Richard Avery asks impish
Jennifer Somers to care for his motherless children, both
get delightfully more than they bargained for.

___**THE MAYFAIR SEASON**
by Nancy Richards-Akers
(D34-537, $2.95, U.S.A.) (D34-538, $3.95, Canada)
An Irish beauty yearns for the heart of the one man in her
life who remains aloof. Now she must cultivate her
feminine wiles and lure that distant heart as close as she
can to her own.

___**TOBLETHORPE MANOR** *by Carola Dunn*
(D34-863, $2.95, U.S.A.) (D34-864, $3.95, Canada)
Richard Carstairs, a handsome aristocrat, finds a lovely
lass who's been thrown from her horse and knocked unconscious. When she awakens she can't remember who
she is, but Richard is instantly captivated by her.

___**THE GALLANT HEIRESS** *by Mary E. Butler*
(D34-571, $2.95, U.S.A.) (D34-572, $3.95, Canada)
Lady Annabelle Gallant collapses on Jesse Norwood's
doorstep while escaping the clutches of murderous
guardians. The mysterious beauty tries to hide her
identity, but Jesse falls in love with her and guesses who
she really is.

**Ⓦ Warner Books P.O. Box 690
New York, NY 10019**

Please send me the books I have checked. I enclose a check or money
order (not cash), plus 75¢ per order and 75¢ per copy to cover postage
and handling.* (Allow 4 weeks for delivery.)

___Please send me your free mail order catalog. (If ordering only the
catalog, include a large self-addressed, stamped envelope.)

Name _____

Address _____

City _____ State _____ Zip _____
*New York and California residents add applicable sales tax.

305